London Borough of Tower Hamlets
91000008110108

D0296847

WITHDRAWN

A Precious Daughter

By Diane Allen

For the Sake of Her Family
For a Mother's Sins
For a Father's Pride
Like Father, Like Son
The Mistress of Windfell Manor
The Windfell Family Secrets
Daughter of the Dales
The Miner's Wife
The Girl from the Tanner's Yard
A Precious Daughter

DIANE ALLEN

A Precious Daughter

MACMILLAN

First published 2021 by Macmillan

This edition published in paperback 2021 by Pan Books
an imprint of Pan Macmillan
The Smithson, 6 Briset Street, London EC1M 5NR
EU representative: Macmillan Publishers Ireland Limited, 1st Floor,
The Liffey Trust Centre, 117–126 Sheriff Street Upper, Dublin 1, D01 YC43
Associated companies throughout the world
www.panmacmillan.com

ISBN 978-1-5290-3716-6

1 3 5 7 9 8 6 4 2

A CIP catalogue record for this book is available from the British Library.

Typeset by Palimpsest Book Production Ltd, Falkirk, Stirlingshire
Printed and bound by CPI Group (UK) Ltd, Croydon, CR0 4YY

To my lovely daughter Lucy and my perfect
granddaughter Amy, with all my love.

1

1896.

Fourteen-year-old Amy Postlethwaite closed her eyes and smiled as the sun warmed her skin. Above her where she lay, the skylarks sang and the soft warm winds of late summer were filled with the scent of wild thyme and heather. She opened her eyes to watch the shadow of the clouds scuttle along the dark hill of Whernside and then turned to look at her lifelong friend, Joshua Middleton. He was lying next to her, with his legs crossed and his blond head resting on his folded arms behind his head, as he sucked a piece of moorland grass in his mouth. Both of them had wandered together that morning, to get out of the way of having to sit in quiet contemplation, as they did most Sundays.

Amy had been worrying about her family's decision to change their lives and had moaned most of the morning to Joshua about it. 'I don't want to leave here, Joshua.

I want to stay here forever. Dentdale is my home. They shouldn't be making me leave the ones I love, just to go searching for gold. It's the other side of the world we are to go to – I'll never see you again.' She sighed and rolled on her side, then looked at her best friend, whom she regarded as her big brother.

'Tha'll have to go, if your father says you have to. You can always come back. Dentdale's not going anywhere, and your grandparents will always be here.' Joshua turned his head and looked lazily at Amy, as she moaned once again about her parents' decision to make a new life for themselves in the goldfields of the Klondike. 'I'll be honest, I'm going to miss you. I know my mates plague me about you always being with me, but they don't understand that we are like sister and brother – and nothing else.' Josh smiled and put his arm round her.

'I'm going to miss you and all. You make up for me being an only one, and I love our time together. I wish my father wasn't full of dreams and rubbish. My mother's content here, and my grandmother and grandfather will be broken-hearted when they find out what my father's been planning. Every night when I'm lying in my bed I hear my parents talking; they've planned their trip and have been saving for months. Who in their right mind would leave the peace and tranquillity of this dale? I just don't want to go.' Amy buried her head in Joshua's shoulder and sobbed.

'Hey, I'll always be here for you to come back to – and we can write. You can tell me about your adventures. Think of all the things you'll see. There'll be bears and buffalo and wolves: you'll love it out there.' Joshua smiled at Amy. She had no choice but to go and leave him, if her father had set his mind on travelling to the goldfields. In truth, he'd miss the lass, who had tagged along with him no matter where he went. His feelings towards her were starting to change and sometimes he had the urge to kiss her, which he worried about; after all, this was Amy, with her tangled wild hair and cast-off clothes – she was just a friend.

'Well, I hope my grandfather stops them from going. My mother said that he'd have plenty to say about what my father had done this week. I want to stay here always with you. They are not thinking of me and what I want,' Amy growled.

'Parents never do, Amy. You'll have to make the best of it. Now whisht and enjoy the time we have together. Try and forget about it for an hour or two – it might never happen.' Joshua lay next to Amy and felt a wave of sadness come over him. This would be one of the last times they would be together, and both of them knew it.

George Oversby sat quietly in the Quaker Meeting House at Lea Yeat at the top end of Dentdale, which was known locally as Cowgill. His mind was troubled, and instead of dedicating his time to the good Lord, he was worried about his family. A stream of light shone in through the small-paned window, and George looked at it and hoped the spirit of his God would enter him and quell his anxieties, giving him the faith he needed at this time in his life when his world was being turned upside-down. It had been a silent meet so far; nobody had stirred to say anything, so the meeting was taking its time. All the Friends had troubles; life was getting harder for the hill farmers who etched their meagre living on the steep hillsides of the Dales. His family was no different, especially as the smallholding was the main source of income for him, his wife Ivy, his daughter Grace, her husband Ethan and their daughter Amy.

Ethan, his son-in-law, had appeared on the scene back in 1874 with the completion of the Settle–Carlisle railway line and was now working as a porter down at the station, on the days when he could be bothered to get out of bed. He was a town lad, from Burnley, not cut out for country ways. Whether it was Christian or not, George often wished he'd go back to where he belonged. Ethan had appeared when the dale was filled with navvies building the railway that was cutting its way high up through the fellside. They had been encamped high up the dale at Arten Gill, Stone House and Scow House, and with some of the families of the dale. They were there to build the huge viaducts, blasting their way through tunnels and laying iron rails to take the steam trains that were to connect London with Scotland. The navvies were not in any way like the peace-loving Friends who sat together in silence; but as they valued all men as equals, the Quakers had tried their hardest to accept the newcomers to the dale.

George breathed in now and tried to focus his thoughts, attempting not to think of the day his daughter had brought back the tall, handsome dark-haired man who had helped her carry her shopping up past the railway's workings to their home, called Gill Head, high above the railway's path, on what locals called the Coal Road. It was so named because, until recently, the locals had dug coalpits there, extracting poor-quality coal for domestic use and for their lime kilns. The pits were high on the top of the fell, between Cowgill and Garsdale, but there were only slag piles to show any signs of activity, the pits now failing to yield any of their black gold of warmth.

It had been a dark day when Grace had brought Ethan Postlethwaite into their home – a day he wished had never happened. And now the man was bringing more disruption and heartache, with this latest news. George kept his head bowed and tried again to take his mind off his own domestic troubles, but without success. It was eating away at him every day and night: Ethan's words when he had told George that he was going to leave the family home and take his beloved daughter and granddaughter with him. If he had said he was leaving to take a smallholding or to find work in Kendal, George would not have minded. However, this was Ethan and he had big ideas; big ideas to make his fortune quickly, without much work. So George shouldn't have been surprised when Ethan announced his latest venture. He was taking George and Ivy's family to Canada, after reading that there were fortunes to be made in the newly found goldfields, and nothing was going to stop him. The newspapers were full of the Klondike gold rush; of men finding nuggets of gold as big as their fists, and of fortunes being made in minutes. But George knew there were two sides to every story, and that Ethan would not have the willpower to work and to endure the hard conditions that the gold rush would ask of him.

'Friend, our meeting is at an end.' Marmaduke Baines touched his neighbour's shoulder and smiled at the man sitting next to him, deep in thought.

'Thank you, Duke. I'd a lot to discuss with the Lord today,' George said and felt bad about not telling the truth. 'How are you and Mary?' he asked as he followed his best friend out of the sparsely furnished meeting house.

'We are both well, thank you. Is thou alright? I hear thy lad wants to leave and find his fortune in another country.' Duke looked at George and could see the hurt in his friend's eyes as they stood together in the summer sunshine.

'He's not a worker, Duke. I wouldn't mind, but he's glass-backed. Ethan finds being a porter on that station hard work, and he never helps around the farm. He'll not last a minute out there, where men are men and they fight for their living. I've pleaded with him to leave our lass and her bairn with us, but he won't listen. How have you heard? We have kept it to ourselves, hoping Ethan would change his mind. But he's booked a passage for all of them on board a ship from Liverpool and they sail in September – the worst time of the year they could be going.'

'I heard at the monthly meeting of the Dales elders last night. Ethan was there asking for assistance for his passage, and for the things he needed to be able to apply to Canada to be allowed in. Though he said nowt about taking your Grace and Amy. If he had, I doubt the elders would have given him the time of day. He made us all think he was going on his own, and that any money he made he was going to send to you for their keep.' Marmaduke stood feeling awkward, on hearing that he had given his blessing to Ethan Postlethwaite, without knowing all the facts. He'd thought he had done right when he agreed with the others to give ten pounds out of the Dales charity fund to help Ethan seek a better life for himself – and that of his family, if he was going to send money home. 'I'm sorry, George, I'd no idea Ethan was planning to take his family with him, or I'd have said something against it. I thought it would help you out in these hard times – all the elders did, too. Ivy will be worried sick.'

'Aye, she is. How dare Ethan go cap in hand to the elders! Our family has never sought charity, nor do we need it now, if he'd just get off his backside and work, like the rest of us. Instead he's breaking my Ivy's heart, and taking our family halfway around the world to a godforsaken place where he won't last more than five minutes.' George bowed his head and looked at his fellow Friends, standing in groups talking before they made their way home. 'I'll talk to Len Sedgwick – tell him not to give Ethan the money and thank the elders for their generosity. There's others more in need in this dale than us.' George stepped away from Marmaduke, looking at the head of the Dales elders, Len Sedgwick, hoping to catch him before he made for home up the lane to New Closes, his farm.

Marmaduke caught his arm. 'He was given the money last night, George. It's already written down in the book. Ethan asked if he could have it there and then. Len gave him his blessing, thinking the same as I did. He'll not want to go back on his word now. Hold thy noise – perhaps the lad will do good.'

George sat down on the low bridge that spanned the small Money Beck stream and sighed. 'I don't usually say this of any man, Duke, as I try and see the good in everyone, but I know this is going to end in tragedy for my family, especially our lass. Then there's our Amy; she's the apple of her grandmother's eye and we'll never see her again. I curse the day Ethan entered our home.'

'Now then, George, it might not be that bad. He might make his fortune – it might be the making of him. Get yourself home to Ivy, and just take Ethan to one side and let him know that you know he's been a-begging. Suggest he pays the money back, and more besides, when he's a rich man. I'm down at The Hill if you need me, but for now get yourself home and enjoy what time you have with your family, once you've had words with Ethan. He'll not be the first to take his family out of the dale, and he won't be the last. There's nowt here, friend, for the likes of him. It's a pity he stayed after the railway was built.'

'It's a pity he ever set eyes upon our Grace,' George said as they both started to walk up the steep Coal Road that led to the station and both of their homes.

'But he did, and thou has a bonny granddaughter out of their union. Be there for her when she needs you, George. Your Grace has made her own bed and is loyal to her husband, which is to be applauded. It'll all turn out right in the end, the good Lord will see to that – have faith, Friend.' Marmaduke patted George on the back as he opened the field gate that led to his farm, The Hill, which sat a few hundred yards up from the main road to the village of Dent and the wilds of Dent Head.

'Aye, I'll have to, because nobody else out there can do owt about it. It's going to test my faith in the Lord – there are no two ways about that. Go and enjoy your Sunday dinner, and give Mary my blessings,' George said, before he set off on the walk up the hill to the station and his farm above it.

The road twisted and bent high up the fellside, every step getting steeper and steeper, making George sweat in his Sunday best as the sun shone down on the deep valley and steep fellsides. He stopped halfway up and gazed down at the valley as he took off his jacket and mopped his brow with his handkerchief. This dale had been his family home for centuries, and it should have been his Grace and Amy's home all their lifetimes, too. He'd looked down upon the sparkling River Dee running gently over the limestone, and had listened to the wind through the rushes, for as long as he could remember. He turned his face up to the blue sky and smiled as a skylark sang its sweet tune for all the world to hear.

Breathing in the clear air, he stopped for a further minute or two, looking around him at all the farms and the green meadow fields leading up to the rougher fell-sides. He knew every family in the dale: some were kin, and others close friends. To think that one of his own had gone to some of them, cap in hand, asking for money went down badly with him. The elders had steered the dale through rough and smooth years, but never once had his family asked them for anything. It was no good; when he got home he would have to say something to Ethan, whether it made for an argument or not.

'Now then, Father, sit yourself down and have a drink of water. The day's warm and that climb up the hill doesn't improve with age.' Ivy Oversby looked at her husband and knew instantly that something had happened at the service down at the meeting house. Nothing would have been said within its walls, but plenty was always discussed outside afterwards, when everyone was making their way home.

'Where's everybody at?' George stayed standing and looked around him. The small, homely room that served as a kitchen and living room was empty, except for his wife, although the table was set for all five of them and a pot of stew was simmering on the fire.

'Amy's gone wandering. You can't keep her from trailing these fellsides on a day like today. She'll be with young Joshua Middleton; they are as thick as thieves, and it's nice to know she's got a good friend. She knows she's to be back for her dinner, so she'll not be long. Grace and Ethan are in their bedroom. He said he needed to talk to Grace in private, as soon as you went out of the house.'

'Aye, I can believe that, because before getting Grace on his side, he couldn't say what he's been up to, and he knew I'd come back in a bad mood, realizing what he's done.' George shook his head and sat down in his usual chair, then looked up at Ivy, his wife of thirty-two years.

'What have they been gossiping and saying now? It's why I don't go with you any more. Besides, Quakerism is on the decline. I'm thinking of going to the Methodist services once Grace has left us,' Ivy said, then quickly regretted her words as George gave her a hard stare.

'It seems everything I stand for – folk and the lot – are going against me, even my own wife.' George rose from his chair, after taking a swig of the cold, fresh spring water that Ivy had given him. 'I'll say what I've got to say to the two of them upstairs. I'll not have the meal on the Lord's Day spoilt by their foolishness. It's best the air is cleared before Amy returns, as she's the innocent one in this shambles.'

George stomped his way up the stone stairs. 'Are you two decent, because I'm coming in to talk to both of you?' he shouted as he opened the door and walked into the low-beamed bedroom shared by Ethan, Grace and Amy.

'Father, what on earth is the matter?' Grace said, seeing the colour in her father's cheeks and the thunderous look on his face.

'Tha knows what's the matter, and so does he, so you needn't both look so innocent.' George stood in the doorway and looked around the bedroom, and scowled at the articles scattered upon the quilt and on the floor. His eyes rested on a box with money piled up in it, and on the map of Canada and Alaska that the pair of them had obviously been studying. 'I suppose that's the brass Duke Baines has told me about – the money that should be in the elders' coffers, instead of yours. You'd no right to go and ask them for assistance: you've brought shame to the family.' George moved to the small window and blocked out the bright sunshine as he looked at Grace, who bowed her head.

'I didn't ask for much, just enough to pay for our passage. I was told the other month that I had to have everything on this list before they'd let us all into the country. I've been saving, so that I can buy what I need and be able to prove that I can support us all.' Ethan passed George a piece of paper, which showed a run-down of what the Canadian government expected him to have before going prospecting deep in the Yukon, where gold had been found – reportedly by the wagon-load.

George glanced at the paper and shook his head. 'You'd have been better putting your money into this land, and putting your back into working here for your family, than taking them halfway around the world to a frozen hole that's not even civilized, from what I hear. You want to stop reading rubbish like that.' He pointed to a pamphlet laid open on the bed, entitled *Klondike: What everyone needs to know before they go seek their fortune*. 'And look after my lass and granddaughter here, where they belong.'

Ethan stood up straight, his face dark with anger, but inside he was trying to curb his words, as he paced back and forth across the small bedroom. He didn't want to fall out with George Oversby, but he would if he had to. 'No, I know you think little of me; and that you've never thought me good enough to marry your daughter. I was a railway navvy, rough and ready, and not like you Dales folk. But I've ambition. I don't want to spend my life living from one season to the next on a few acres of land, or doffing my cap while carrying folk's luggage onto the train. I want better for Grace, Amy and myself. I want Grace to have nice clothes and not to worry about going hungry. You'll not stop us, sir. Grace is in agreement with my decision – there's nothing here for her any more.' Ethan looked in earnest at his wife, wanting her to back him against her dictatorial father.

'Is that what you think, our lass? That there's nowt here for you? We've always done our best for you, and you know it. I realize we've not a lot, but nobody that farms in this dale has.' George looked at his one-and-only daughter, deeply hurt by Ethan's words.

Grace, who had never argued with her father before, looked worried as she thought how to reply so as not to hurt her parents' feelings. She fidgeted with a piece of paper as she raised her gaze and looked pleadingly at her father with her sky-blue eyes. 'Father, I love you and Mother, and this dale, but I don't want to spend every day of my life here. And I've to think of Amy. I want the best for her. I don't want her to know an empty belly, and having to make do with mended shoes, as I did. This farm hasn't enough acreage to feed us all; even if Ethan gave you every penny he earns at the station, it wouldn't be enough.' Grace held back her tears and composed herself as she made her wishes known. 'We should go and make our own way in the world. Please give us your blessing, else you'll break my heart if we have to leave on bad terms.' She went over and hugged her father. 'I love you, Father, you know I do. But Ethan is my husband, and where he goes, I go. And I have faith in him to look after both me and Amy, no matter what your doubts about him are.'

George looked at Grace. She was his future, and he'd wanted her to follow in his footsteps and farm at Gill Head. She was his kin, and she and her daughter were now going to be taken away by a man who, unlike Grace, he had little faith in. 'You've never gone without anything. Your upbringing might not have been one full of brass, but it was the best me and your mother could do.'

'Please, Father, give us all your blessing. It is a chance to change our lives. Even you must admire that we want to search for better lives. Is that not what you are told at the frequent meetings of the Friends that you attend?' Grace felt tears running down her cheeks; she loved her father, and the last thing she wanted to do was break his heart and her mother's. 'I'll write every day, and so will Amy. And once we have made our money, we will return to visit, or perhaps buy a property in the dale.'

'Hold your noise and stop your blubbering. If you've got to go, I suppose I can't hold you back. You are Ethan's responsibility now – for what it's worth.' George glared at Ethan. 'You'll have mine and your mother's blessing, on the understanding that you send Amy back to us if anything goes wrong; or you leave her here with me and your mother. I'll not lose my granddaughter as well as my daughter. Amy's had no say in this foolhardy venture, and I'll not have her dragged off and trailed halfway around the world when she's got a stable home here with us.'

'She's coming with us, sir – she's my daughter.' Ethan stood his ground. 'But if we can't make a life for ourselves, we will send her back to you, if that's what you wish. I may be worth nothing in your eyes, but I love Amy and will always protect Grace and her. I have not done this lightly, sir. I aim to go out to Canada and make my fortune. Please don't think badly of us.'

'No doubt like you thought you'd make your fortune building the railway that's cut through our peaceful dale. I thought you'd have learned your lesson from that,' George growled.

'But I did find riches, sir. I found your daughter, who I love with every breath in my body. Amy will be returned to you if she is unhappy, we promise. And I promise to take care of, and lay down my life for, your daughter and granddaughter if I have to.' Ethan held his hand out to be shaken.

George ignored the outstretched hand. 'I'll be honest: I regret the day you entered our lives. But you make my Grace happy and she's your wife, so I can't stand in your way. You have my blessing, but you take care of my girls, else it will be the worse for you. They are all Ivy and I live for.' George looked at his daughter as she went back into her husband's arms. 'Now your mother will be cursing me; her dinner will be burning, and I can hear Amy chittering to her down in the kitchen. Let's sit down and thank the Lord for what we have, no matter how small or how bad the quality. It's still Him we have to put our trust in, and don't you ever forget it.'

2

The sea crossing to America had been bad enough, but nothing had prepared them for Skagway itself. The streets were muddy and full of ruts, while the wooden buildings were full of gamblers, thieves and drunks, all making a killing from the vulnerable people who were trying to reach the fabled goldfields. Traders were charging prices so high that Ethan's pockets were emptying far too fast, leaving the family vulnerable and at a loss in their hostile new surroundings. Grace and Amy longed for the security of the Dales back home and the comfort of their poor but humble life, which now seemed like a lifetime away as they struggled, hungry and tired, with the next leg of their journey out to the Klondike.

'We can't go no further, Ethan. Amy is on her last legs and I'm exhausted.' Grace looked around her at the bleak scene of the White Horse Pass, which they had to get through before crossing the mighty Yukon River to reach Dawson City to stake their claims. The sky was threatening more snow and the packhorses were laden down. The Canadian government had made everyone chasing the gold, whom they called 'stampeders', buy adequate supplies before crossing the Canadian border to Yukon territory, where the gold lay.

'We are winning now: we are halfway up the pass.' Ethan looked back at his wife and daughter; they were both cold, and their skirts were heavy with the mud that coated everything and everybody on the frantically busy narrow pass between the high ranges of mountains that cut them off from the Yukon River. They'd walked and ridden for miles, passing folk returning from the gold rush and joining those who were sure they were going to make their fortune in the inhospitable land ahead. 'Put Amy on one of the packhorses – it will manage her weight,' Ethan shouted as he ploughed his way past other prospectors and a dead horse lying in the thick, unforgiving mud. It was a living hell they were enduring, passing people ill-prepared for the oncoming winter's weather and not having sufficient food to feed themselves, after failing to heed the Canadian government's rules.

'No, the poor creature is nearly on its last legs anyway. We should never have come – you should have listened to my father. This is a hostile land. You thought Dentdale was wild, but it is truly heaven compared to this.' Grace looked around her at the grisly men with layers of clothing and boots caked with mud, pulling the same amount of supplies as they had, but with no women or children with them. She and Amy were two of the few women who had been brave enough, or stupid enough, to follow their man into the wilds. How she wished she was back in the comfort of her old home as she turned to Amy. 'Put your arms around my neck and climb on my back. I'll carry you to the top – we are nearly there now.' Grace caught her breath and looked at her daughter, who was being put through hell.

'No, Mam, I'm alright. My legs ache, but I'll manage.' Amy pulled her cold feet out of the knee-high mud and looked in hope towards the summit. She'd never seen anything like this place, and she had to hold back her tears at the dead horses that littered the pass, which had been weighed down with their load. 'I'm hungry and cold but, like Father says, we are nearly there.' In truth, Amy could have given up there and then, but she knew that would not help her family's situation.

'Another few yards and we are there.' Ethan looked back at his exhausted family and pulled on his pack-horse's reins. He switched it with his stick, to urge it on and not give in to death on the unforgiving narrow pass. Progress was slow, but he was determined they would be down in the valley before the snow started to fall even harder. And then tomorrow they would tackle the river. He pulled on the reins, swearing. The book he'd read, promising more gold than anyone could wish for, had never mentioned this. Already they had crossed the Atlantic in a ship that treated them no better than animals and then, laden down with supplies, they had made their way to the Alaskan town of Skagway. There they had rested for a day in a hotel that had been crawling with lice, before riding and walking the endless miles to Dawson City. There all his dreams would hopefully come true, although seeing the state of some of the souls travelling in the opposite direction, Ethan was beginning to have his doubts. He too was starting to wish he had heeded the words of his father-in-law, George.

The bitter wind tore through their clothes and the snow whipped at their faces as all three stood at the summit of the White Horse Pass Trail, looking down into the valley below and at the lakes and mountains behind them. Through the tall fir trees and falling snow, they stared down at the powerful Yukon River, which they had to sail down, if they were to reach their destination of Dawson City. It had taken them a full day to travel five miles because of the mud, snow and other stampeders in their way. But the worst part was yet to come, and they glanced down at the distant white waves of the rapids that had to be negotiated, and cringed.

Grace stood next to Ethan, her arm around Amy, and could feel icy tears rolling down her cheeks. 'We have to master those waters, Amy, and I can't swim, and we'll be drowned for sure.'

'Hush now, it looks worse from up here,' Ethan said. 'We'll make camp down in the bottom – look, where those campfires are burning. And after we've eaten and slept, it will not look so bad. I'll rent a man and his boat to take us; they'll know the river, and they'll make sure we are safe. That's what I was advised, back in Skagway.' Ethan started walking, not daring to look at the scene in the distance, where he could see men and women camped along the river bank, desperate to master the river that was keeping them from making their fortune.

'We've little enough money, without wasting it on a man to get us down a river that looks impassable. Let us turn back now and keep what money we have, to secure a passage back home.' Grace pulled on her husband's arm. 'I don't want to die out here and be buried like a dog in an unmarked grave. Ethan, think of Amy!'

Ethan looked at his daughter, who was in tears and shivering in the biting cold wind, and had a minute of uncertainty. 'It's because of her that we are doing this. I want her to grow up wealthy. We will survive the rapids of the river, trust me. Now best foot forward, and let's get down from this mountainside and out of the snow. I'll put the tent up, tether and unpack the horses, while you light a fire and make something warm to eat. There looks to be a few buildings down in the bottom. Folk will tell us what's the best way across, and you might be able to buy a few extra supplies to get us to Dawson.' Ethan stepped out; he hadn't come this far and risked everything to turn back now. Besides, he was not going to go back with his tail between his legs to his father-in-law, who would relish that he had failed in his quest.

At long last, after a treacherous journey down the mountainside, they reached the valley bottom. It was thronged with stampeders, who had camped and were trying to gain a boat to navigate the winding Yukon. It was a trip of yet more miles, over rapids and fast-flowing water, until they reached their destination of Dawson City to stake their claim.

Amy sat with her arms around her legs next to the campfire, for which her mother and she had scavenged dry wood from the mountainside. She'd been scared to within an inch of her life when one of the prospectors had grabbed her by her collar and yelled, 'Be careful of the bears – they'd not think twice of giving you a swipe with their huge paws.' And then he'd growled like a bear, pulling a face at her, before laughing and going on his way.

She hated this place; she was fed up with being wet, cold and hungry, and no matter what Dawson was like, it would not compare with her grandmother and grandfather's home. She looked across at her mother and father as they argued over money, and how to traverse the river that was their next obstacle in the search for wealth. The air was filled with the smell of pine and wood-smoke, and Amy looked up to the clear sky filled with a million stars and watched as the sparks from the fire flew up to join them. At least her belly was full now and she was beginning to get warm, but tomorrow it would start again: the trudge to make easy money by finding gold, and to succeed in life. She yawned and stretched; her body and mind were tired as she got to her feet and tapped on her mother's shoulder.

'Mam, I'm going to my bed now,' she said and looked at her mother, who brushed away the tears that her daughter was not supposed to see.

'Alright, my love. You know where you are to sleep.

Keep your clothes on, as it's too cold to undress, and don't go too far away from the tent to do your business.' Grace got up and hugged her daughter, then watched Amy disappear into the small tent that they had bought once they had set foot in Canada, and which had cost them dearly, with traders taking advantage of their situation.

Amy curled up under the coarse blankets that made her bed and closed her eyes. Outside she could hear her mother and father still arguing, but also travelling on the air was the noise of somebody playing the harmonica, and somebody singing mournful tunes about the home they had left far behind. She was not the only one who wished she was safe and sound in a warm bed, with loved ones wishing her goodnight. Why had her father been so foolish as to risk their lives for something that might not even exist?

She closed her eyes and thought about her grandmother's warm arms, and the smell of her grandfather's favourite tobacco as he sat next to the homely fire. Sleep and exhaustion overcame her quickly, and soon she was protected from both her worries and the cold.

Harry Bloomfield was in his late twenties, rugged in looks, with long blond hair and a chiselled jaw, and was dressed in buckskins from head to foot. He'd been brought up in the backwoods, and now he was making a living getting what he could from the ignorance of those who would seek their fortune.

'So you managed to cross the Dead Horse Trail? A lot

don't even do that – you must be made of stern stuff, or you are stupid.'

Harry looked at the family that stood in front of him. He'd been boating people down the Yukon for the last two years. He'd seen folk come and go, full of dreams when they were setting out to the fields of gold, but full of despair when they returned, their pockets empty and their hearts heavy – apart from the very few who had struck it lucky, like George Carmack and Dawson Charlie, who had started the gold fever by finding gold in Rabbit Creek, a Klondike River tributary that ran through both Alaskan and Yukon territory.

'I'm telling you now, the main rush is over, there's nothing out there. Turn around now and take your family back to civilization, because Dawson is no place for a woman and daughter like yours. Or at least wait here for the horse-driven tramway that Norman Macaulay is near to finishing, which will take you past the rapids.' Harry pointed to work taking place on the edge of Bennett Lake, then looked at the man who stood in front of him and knew he might just as well be peeing in the wind – in his mind, the man was set to make a fortune and would listen to nobody.

'No, I've come this far, I'm not about to turn us all back now, and I haven't time to wait.' Ethan looked around him: prospectors were building their own boats and rafts along the shore of the Yukon, out of logs and wood, strung together with rope and covered in pitch. They would be alright for one man who had nothing to lose but his own life, but Ethan had his family and all his worldly possessions to protect and make safe. 'Now, how much, and when can you take us? I can't wait for the tramway to get us past the worst of the rapids. I need to go now and stake my claim, but I need someone to take my family safely.'

'Listen to my advice and go back. The Yukon takes lives, she's not a caring bitch.' Harry Bloomfield started to walk away.

'You'll take us. Here, this is what I'll give you: that'll be more than some folk would offer you.' Ethan thrust a bag of money into Harry's hand and grabbed hold of his buckskin jacket. 'We need you, else I'll do like some of these other folk are doing and I'll build my own boat. Then we will be at the river's mercy.'

Grace glared at her husband and prayed that the wild-looking man, who had the only decent boat and experience of the fast-flowing river, would agree. She knew that Ethan would get there, with his help or without, even at the risk of their lives. Amy stood next to her mother and put her arms around her waist. She was fearful that there was to be an argument between the two men.

Harry felt the weight of the small bag and opened it to see the money within. 'Is this all you've got?' he said, looking at Amy.

'It is. Our lives are in your hands,' Ethan said quietly.

'Then you'd better have some of it back. Here, take this, and be ready to board my boat in the morning. I'll have to hide you all. You need to know that I'm not licensed; the robbing mounted police need twenty-five dollars from me to do that, and even then I couldn't take women and children.' Harry took some of the money out of the bag and placed it back in Ethan's hand. 'I'm only doing this because I don't want to see that bonny lass of yours washed up and battered on the rocks; and if you go with somebody else, that's how she will end up. You'll have to leave your horses, so sell them or turn them loose. It'll take us a few days to reach Dawson. We'll be camping along its banks for a night or two. You'll need your supplies, Missus.' Harry looked at Grace and shook his head. 'There's talk of a railway line to be built, and there will be a bridge across this bitch of a river, and folk will not have to risk their lives to get to the shithole of Dawson for much longer. I'll see you at first light, here. Just bring what you need.'

'Thank you, sir,' Grace whispered.

'Thank me when you and your family get safely to Dawson. Lord knows why you are going at this time of the year. The ground will be frozen before long, and you'll have to wait for the ground to thaw and the rivers to clear of ice. You'll be wishing you'd never seen my face, by the time spring comes.' Harry spat out his chewing tobacco and left Ethan and his family watching him go into the log cabin that had been made into a small trading station for those in desperate need of supplies.

The following morning Ethan and his family were packed and ready by daybreak. They walked hesitantly with their horses to the rough-looking smithy where they hoped to sell their horses. Ethan was doubtful; without them in Dawson, how was he supposed to do any mining? However, at the same time he knew he couldn't take the horses on the boat, as Harry was breaking the law on his behalf, and he had no other choice.

Grace and Amy sat outside the smithy, which was already busy with folk coming and going in the darkness before dawn, with their worldly belongings at their feet. The two packhorses, which were not in the best health, walked past them, their heads low and their bellies empty. They would not make the family much money and, with their sale, there was no going back over the pass to Skagway.

'I can't grumble at that. He gave me seven dollars each – seemingly, live horses are worth a bob or two, no matter how knackered they are,' Ethan said as he walked out of the smithy and looked at the load they had to carry to the boat, which was waiting for them a few yards away on the shore of the lake. 'I'll come back and forth for some of this; you carry what you can. And let Harry hide you both and make you safe, while we pack this on board.' The three of them, laden down with supplies, pickaxes, shovels, tent and everything else they had been told they would need in Dawson, walked in silence to Harry Bloomfield's boat.

Harry sat upon the deck of the boat, which had survived many trips back and forth down the hundreds of miles of the mighty Yukon. 'You've not changed your minds – you've not seen sense overnight then?' He jumped down onto the lakeside and hauled the first package of goods on board. 'You, young lady, need to be in the centre of the boat next to the mast, then we can tie you and your mother to it before we get to the rapids, for safety.' He bent down and helped up the silent Amy and smiled at her. 'My most precious piece of cargo, I'll see you safe, so hold those tears,' he said as he heard her snivels. 'Now you, Missus. And then your husband and I will go and get the rest of your stuff, when I've pulled the tarpaulin over you. There's always some damned nosy Mounties sniffing about at this time of the morning.'

Grace climbed into the boat next to Amy and held her tightly, and they both quivered in the darkness as the fishy-smelling tarpaulin was pulled over them and they were left, until both men came back with the rest of their belongings.

'Mam, I'm frightened. I want to go home. I want to go home to my gran and grandad. I don't want to go to Dawson City – I am not bothered about money. I just want to go home,' Amy sobbed.

'Shh, my love. Mr Bloomfield will get us there safely and, once we are at Dawson, life will be good. You'll be able to go back to school, and we will have a home again,' Grace whispered, wondering if she was trying to pacify herself as well as her daughter. She had no idea what lay in front of them at Dawson. That was, if they ever got there.

The rapids roared in front of them, the currents sweeping round and round the jagged rocks that littered the deep-sided canyon.

'Hold on – make sure the ropes are tight around your

waists and the mast,' Harry yelled as he battled with the tiller and hoped he would be able to deliver his precious cargo of fearful people to the other side of the White Horse Rapids. The boat thrust and fought its way between the rapids, water washing over the decks, drenching Ethan, Grace and Amy. The white waves curled up and invited the bodies on the boat to join them in the depths, like so many souls that the wild waters had taken to their deaths. Grace and Amy screamed, fearful for their lives, as an extra-strong current swept the boat the wrong way round, while Harry fought to regain control with the help of Ethan. 'Once we are through Mile Canyon, the river calms down,' Harry shouted, drenched to the skin and exhausted from his fight.

'Lord, if you can hear us, help us this day. Save us from drowning,' Grace muttered under her breath as she watched one of their much-needed packages cut loose from the rest and nearly go over the side, until Ethan reached for it and shakily put it back in its place.

Amy cried and shook, her tears and yells unheard over the pounding of the river's boulders and the force of the water.

'Are you alright? It's not like this all the way. We'll be out of it by night.' Ethan touched Grace's arm and smiled at Amy. 'See, it's quietening now. The river is broadening – we've made it through the worst.' Just as suddenly as the rapids had come upon them, the river lost its anger.

'We might have made it through the worst, but there are other rapids along the way, and we still have a long way to go,' Harry said and looked down at the family, huddled together at the bottom of his boat. 'We'll make camp for the evening down around that bend. There's a pier a little further down – the Macdonalds live not far from there. They are a family of brothers who have made their home along the bank, but they are not that friendly, so we'll not be visiting them in their log cabin in the woods. Once we've got a fire going, you can dry your clothes and fill your bellies, and then we'll head to our beds. It'll be another early start in the morning. We've done the worst and survived and you'll soon be at Dawson, and you are lucky we lost nothing on our voyage so far.'

Harry stood, tall and proud, and steered the small boat with its wards through the calmer waters. Another two days and they would be in Dawson City – not before time, he thought, as he noted the weather that was quickly closing in. These prospectors had no idea of the life they were heading for. Life might have been hard back home, but it was nothing compared to what they were going to have to endure in order to survive here.

3

It was a complete white-out when they navigated the last bend on their journey down the Yukon. Dawson City was just visible as Harry and Ethan, clad heavily with snow, steered the boat onto the shore.

'Well, this is it – you are here. Lord knows why you've come at this time of the year. There'll be little food and nowhere for you to sleep, and the ground will be so hard with permafrost that you'll not be able to do any prospecting until spring, and then the mosquitoes will drive you crazy.' Harry pulled on his boat, securing it on the frozen mud, and shook his head at the disheartened family as they gazed at the city, which they had expected to look wealthy and well built. Instead, wooden buildings and tents were erected everywhere, looking from the river bank more like a dilapidated farmyard than an important town.

'Where do I go and make my claim?' Ethan asked, thinking that no matter what Harry Bloomfield thought, he'd get a stake and would soon be rich in gold.

'You'll not be doing that yet. Nobody can do anything at this time of year. Besides, there are no stakes left, unless someone who's seen sense has returned to their home, and then you can claim it after three days. But you'll need fifteen dollars and, if you can get another, you can register that in your wife's name. You could be lucky, because I've watched a lot returning from Dawson; there's not much food here, from what I've heard. That's why we will have to unload your packages, before someone helps themselves tonight under cover of darkness. The best stakes are up the Klondike and Bonanza Creeks, if you've not had a bellyful of Dawson by spring.'

Harry picked up his shotgun and slung it across his shoulder.

'Come on: first stop the saloon. Rosie will get your women warm and, hopefully, fed. And she will know if there are any empty shacks, instead of you sleeping in that so-called tent, which is worth nothing against the cold up here. The traders at Skagway are just out to make a fast buck from greenhorns like you.' Harry looked down at Amy, who was shivering. 'Best that we keep you and your ma warm. Your father is big enough to look after himself.'

'Thank you and God bless, Mr Bloomfield. We owe you a great deal,' Grace said while taking Amy's hand. 'Somewhere we could light a fire and keep warm would be so much better than the canvas tent.'

'Like I say, ma'am, this man of yours shouldn't have brought you here.' Harry glared at Ethan.

'I'll do what I want with my family, so be careful what

you say,' Ethan retorted, but he also knew he was half the size of the hard-living Canadian and no way could he ever confront him.

'It's your lives . . . Now, instead of freezing here, let's step out and we'll get this boat unloaded and you settled before nightfall. You can perhaps sleep warm and easy tonight, if Rosie can help us.' Harry held his hand out for Amy. 'Welcome to Dawson, Missy. I hope you'll be happy here.'

'Thank you, Mr Bloomfield. It's quite an adventure. But just now I want to get warm.' Amy looked up at the man she had grown to admire; in fact she secretly thought in her young heart that if she was a little older, Harry would be the sort of man she would like on her arm. He was everything that her own father wasn't, and she knew she would always be safe in his company.

The streets of Dawson City were busy, despite the falling snow. Prospectors dressed in thick coats and animal skins filled the streets around them, and those in business looked out of their various windows, noting that another new family had come into town with Harry Bloomfield. The houses were nothing like the Postlethwaite family had imagined. They weren't built from the sturdy stone of back home; instead they were all built of wood. Wooden cabins would stand next to a three- or four-storey building, and next to that there would be a tent filling the space between buildings. Along both sides of the main street most houses were built on what Harry called a boardwalk: a wooden walkway two feet above street level, keeping people clear of the dirty, muddy and snow-covered road. Oil lamps were lit in most windows, even though it was only just past noon, and there was the sound of music and folk laughing and talking, as Harry took them through the swing doors of the tallest building on the street, which he called the saloon.

'Are you alright, Amy? We'll soon be warm. Now don't stare when you walk in here. These folk live different from our way of life back home. They like to drink and they'll swear, so close your ears,' Grace whispered to her daughter, as she looked around her, fascinated by her new surroundings.

'She'll have to get used to it, if we are to survive,' Ethan said, then went after Harry into the warmth of the saloon and the smoke-filled noisy bar, followed by Grace and an awe-inspired Amy.

Amy looked around her: she'd never seen anything like it in her life. She had, unbeknownst to her grandfather, on occasion looked through the windows of the Cow Dub Inn back in Dentdale, but the inside of the Dawson City Saloon was nothing like the sleepy inn. It was full of larger-than-life characters: miners, card players, women who showed parts of their bodies that Amy dared not mention, in their brightly coloured clothes; and behind the bar was the largest mirror she had ever seen, with drinks on shelves on either side of it. The bartender was lining up drinks of amber liquid, which the men were drinking as fast as he poured it.

Amy watched as one of the bonniest women made her way to Harry, smiling and looking at her and her family. She had long black hair and was dressed in the gaudiest dress, which was so low-cut that her breasts nearly fell out of it.

'Harry, back again! I thought you said you'd had enough of this den of iniquity when you left me the other morning.' She smiled and kissed him on the cheek.

Amy watched her mother blush, and her father look at the woman and Harry, perhaps with a sense of envy on his face.

'Rosie, I've brought this family down the river. I felt I had to, else they would have risked their necks to get here. This is Ethan Postlethwaite, his wife Grace, and Amy here is their daughter.' Harry scowled at Rosie as she ran her hand down his face and pouted her lips, before turning to talk to the new family.

'Well, glad to make your acquaintance. Harry is always bringing new folk to our city. He's a regular hero. He must have saved many a life, bringing them safely over the rapids.' Rosie smiled at Amy, but Amy was battling with the pang of jealousy that she felt towards the woman, who was obviously more than mere friends with Harry.

'It's good to make your acquaintance, Miss, er . . .' Ethan stopped in his tracks.

'It's just Rosie – everyone knows me as Rosie,' she replied and smiled at Ethan.

'Harry says you might know of somewhere for us to stay, rather than living in the tent,' Grace said quickly. She'd heard of women such as the one who stood in front of her, and the sooner she was away from the likes of her, the better. Especially as Rosie was eyeing her

Ethan up and down, and no doubt wondering if he was worth getting her claws into.

'Did he now? Well, I'll think, while you warm yourself next to one of these stoves. Are you hungry? Can I get you some of cook's moose stew? It'll warm you through, if nothing else. He's not the best of cooks, but he makes the most of what we have here at Dawson.' Rosie turned round to a group of men seated at a table next to one of the many iron stoves that filled the large bar room. 'Shift yourselves – go and sit with old Tommy over there and let this family warm themselves. Show them we have some manners, even though we are miles away from civilization.' Rosie put her foot on a chair and tipped it backwards, making the man sitting upon it swear at her, but at the same time the lot of them moved without arguing.

'Thank you. The stew would be most welcome. How much is it?' Ethan and his family sat down at the table and looked at one another.

'Have it on the house this time. If you are like the rest that come here, you are going to be in for a shock. The Klondike and its gold have been romanticized, and you'll either make it or will be returning with your tail between your legs within six months. They that found it first have made it big, but the gold's mined to within an inch of its life now. Gone are the days when you could sweep the floor here in a morning and there would be enough gold dust in the sweepings to make you a living.' Rosie took Harry's arm. 'I need a word with you, Harry, come with me to the bar.'

'Mam, did you see her dress? And have you seen those women sitting on those men's knees?' Amy's eyes widened as she noted all that was going on around her.

'Don't look, Amy. They aren't the sort of women a God-fearing family associates with. Neither is this place. Your grandfather would have plenty to say about all this,' Grace replied softly.

'It's just as well he's back in Dent then. Say what you want, but this place has given you warmth and is about to feed you. Now I might have got it wrong, but doesn't that sound Christian to you?' Ethan said sarcastically. He smiled as he watched one of the women pull on a man's hand and lead him up the winding stairs to her room. So that's how they passed the long winter months in Dawson.

'Why don't you persuade them to turn back and return to where they came from, Harry? We've typhoid running rife, and there's no fresh fruit or vegetables – it's a living hell. There has been plenty of gold in the past, but not now. And nothing else. Another week and the river will be frozen over, and then they are here until spring,' Rosie said in a low voice, while looking at the family who risked everything if they stayed. She'd been in Dawson the best part of her thirty years on God's Earth and if she had anywhere else to go, then she would gladly have left. Dawson owned her. She ran the saloon that Jimmy McMahon owned, which meant that he also owned her, controlling any money she earned, like he did with most of the folk in Dawson City.

'You try and tell that bastard of a husband that he's got it wrong! He thinks he'll be rolling in it within a week or two. It's his wife and daughter I feel sorry for. They've followed him here without question, and she's a Quaker, from what I've heard her saying on the trip down here. She and her daughter are as innocent as they come: stubborn but innocent! Do you know of anywhere for them? They'll not last long in the tent they've brought with them.'

'Have they provisions? There's not much food in Dawson, as you know. They will starve, one way or another, if they haven't,' Rosie said.

'Yes, he's made sure of that, but it won't last long if I don't get it off my boat and into safety, as folk will help themselves. They need a cabin, Rosie.' Harry looked across at his wards. He had no time for the husband and thought him a clever bugger, but Grace and Amy he had to do right by, else their lives would be on his conscience.

'Old Jake Feathers was found dead on his stake yesterday. Stupid old idiot, wouldn't leave it, even though he could hardly draw breath, last time I saw him. His stake will be available. But more importantly, his cabin down by the creek will be empty, and who's to say they can't have first say in renting that? It belongs to Jimmy McMahon, so move them into it as soon as they've eaten and I'll make it right with him tonight.' Rosie sighed.

'You are a good soul, Rosie. You come over as hard as nails, but you have a heart of gold. I just want the young one to be safe, if nobody else. And if they can survive this winter, then I know they'll be alright.' Harry looked at Rosie, whom he secretly loved, although he knew she was attracted more to prospectors with money. 'So you are still entertaining Jimmy – he's more money than sense. Is it right that he spent twenty-eight thousand dollars on one night alone, bringing a fancy singer from Paris down the river this summer and buying everyone drinks? Flash devil – he had nothing at one time.'

'You know me, Harry. A girl likes the better things in life, and if I can get them off Jimmy with a smile and an hour of my time, I will.' Rosie looked down at her feet. 'It was a bit of a night, that one, but that's Dawson: plenty of money but nothing else. You'd better move your chickens. They've finished the stew I ordered, and the sooner they have shifted their supplies into that cabin, the better. The sun will soon be down and they need to be settled. Do you know where Jake lived? Three streets behind Front Street, look right ahead of you and it's the cabin on its own by the creekside. It'll be in a state, but it's a roof over their heads.' Rosie looked at the family she'd made safe. They were all enthralled watching the gaming table, where the flamboyant Bud Yates was betting, with a girl on both of his knees. 'They'd better get used to this life quickly and hold back on their high morals. It's sink or swim, as both you and I know.'

'I know it looks nothing, but believe me, this is a palace compared to the tent you were going to have to live in.' Harry caught his breath as he placed down the first of the large packages that were the Postlethwaite family's only possessions.

'We find ourselves having to thank you once again, Harry. And please make sure you give our thanks to Rosie. We know that if it wasn't for her we would, as you say, be living in our tent, and perhaps not surviving the winter,' Grace said as she breathed in and looked at the ramshackle cabin that was to be their home.

'I'd have found something in the morning, but you were adamant you wanted to get us settled. I suppose it will do for now,' Ethan commented, placing another package of goods down on the dusty floorboards.

'Whatever you say. But I'd count yourself lucky no one has thought of moving their selves in here yet, and that Rosie has a special arrangement with Jimmy McMahon. He'll be around here first thing, if I know him, and he'll want a quick understanding about payment for rent.' Harry looked in disdain at Ethan, who thought he knew everything, and yet he knew nothing about the life he was about to lead.

'Who's Jimmy McMahon?' Amy asked, listening into the conversation as she gazed around the one room that was to be their home, with its wooden bed covered in fur skins, while thinking that back home her grandfather's shed was bigger and cleaner.

'Jimmy McMahon is one of the wealthiest prospectors in Dawson, young Miss. He owns a lot of Dawson City and found one of the biggest nuggets yet to be discovered in the Klondike. He's the man to keep as a friend rather than an enemy.' Harry gave a warning glance to Ethan, hoping he'd take note of his words.

'I'll go and get our stove, and then that's the last thing

out of your boat. The stove the previous owner had looks past its best.' Ethan nodded his head to the corner of the cabin, where an iron pot-bellied stove stood, with a chimney made out of tin leading to the outside to let out the smoke.

'The one that's fitted will do its job better. I'd give it a good clean in the morning before you light it. It's a lot better-built and already fitted, so why break what is not broken?' Harry heard Ethan grunt as he turned his back on him to go and collect the stove from his boat. 'Here, let's get it lit for tonight. There are logs stored on the boardwalk at the side of the cabin, and there are kindling sticks still beside the stove. A fire in the old place will soon make it feel like home.' Harry bent down and riddled the remains of a fire in the little stove, then added some kindling sticks and a page of newspaper that lay on the wooden floor. He struck his Vesta and a spark soon turned to a flame as the kindling sticks took hold. 'Amy, run around to the side of the house and bring a log or two of the wood that we saw there. Mind how you go, though.'

Amy ran out of the log cabin to the pile of logs they had all seen when they entered the cabin. If Harry had asked her to run to the ends of the Earth, she would have done so. She found herself blushing as she passed him the few logs she could hold in her arms. Harry was everything her father wasn't, but she was also experiencing her first crush; her hormones were already seeking the man who could protect her in life.

By the time Ethan returned, there was a good blaze

from the old stove, and Grace had thrown onto the boardwalk the flea-ridden fur coverings that had belonged to the previous occupant, which could not be used by the family, and Amy was sweeping the bare wooden floor in preparation for a good scrubbing in the morning.

'You've plenty of water in the four water butts at the corners of the cabin and enough firewood for a month. By the time the wood runs out, you should know how everything around here works, and who's best to get some more from; or just help yourself – it's not like there's no trees up here!' Harry looked at the red-faced Ethan and reckoned it was time to get out of the Postlethwaites' lives. They would either sink or swim, but he'd done his best by them.

'Thank you, Harry, you've done much more than we paid you for. We are most grateful,' Grace said and looked at her husband. He said nothing, but turned his back on the man who seemed to know everything, and with whom his family was smitten.

'Will we be seeing you again?' Amy asked as Harry picked up his broad-brimmed hat from the rocking chair he'd left it on.

'I'll no doubt be about, come spring. But I'll be away first thing in the morning. I need to get back to my own cabin before the river freezes over. Until then, you take care, young Missy.' Harry looked around him and then closed the door on the family. The pig-headed father would have to better his ways, if they were to rely on him for their survival.

'We all know where he's going: to the tart in the saloon. But I saw how he looked at you,' Ethan growled at Grace.

'Don't be daft, he's been the perfect gentleman. Without him we would not have got here, nor would we have this cabin, if that tart – as you call her – had not helped us.' Grace started unpacking their goods, grateful they still had food supplies left from their original Klondikers' supply list, because Ethan had probably not noticed that there was little to look at in the way of food shops on Front Street. Plenty of banks, saloons, drinking places and dentists, but when she had glanced at the grocery stores she had noticed how little stock they were displaying. It was going to be hard to survive in Dawson, especially for her and Amy.

Ethan opened the door to the big man dressed in a white fox-fur coat and buckskin boots, and couldn't help but stare at the gold tooth that shone and glistened in the early morning light when the man bellowed his hello as he hammered on the cabin door.

'Rosie told me I'd find you in Jake's fleapit. Now we need to come to an understanding, if you are to live here.' Jimmy McMahon walked past Ethan, straight into the cabin he owned, and sat down at the now-spotless table on one of the rickety chairs that old Jake had made out of local wood. 'He'd have a fit if he came back, to see you all here, the old rogue.'

'Mr McMahon, would you like a drink of tea? We've no milk, I'm afraid.' Grace looked at the giant of a man and then at Amy, who couldn't stop staring at him.

'You'll have to get used to no milk in your tea. There's only one cow in the whole of Dawson and it might be gone soon, if things get bad and we need a bit of meat. We have one cow and six horses. We can live without the likes of that here in Dawson, but not without whisky or gold – it's that which makes this city. Now, down to business. You need this cabin and Harry says you need a stake. Well, I'm your man for both, but it'll cost you!' Jimmy slammed his hand down on the table and looked at Ethan.

'That we do, Mr McMahon. I thought I'd be able to go out onto one of the rivers and find my own piece of land to make a stake, but from what I understand, I've got that wrong. As for the cabin, aye, it would make a home for us, if you are willing to rent it to us?' Ethan sat across from the big man and looked at him.

'That's what everybody thinks when they first come here, and at one time that was what we could all do, but not any more.' Jimmy nodded his head as Grace gave him a drink in one of the tin cups that had come with them from Skagway. 'I can rent you the cabin for fifty dollars a month: that's the going rent at the moment for such a prime location as here.' Jimmy grinned as he looked at the dismay on the family's faces. 'I can tell, by your faces, that you are not impressed, but that is fair, as cabins on Front Street are renting for that.' He waited for an answer.

'I'm sorry, we are wasting your time. We'll pack up and leave – we can't afford those prices. They are bloody scandalous. No wonder you are the richest man in

Dawson.' Ethan scowled at the man who put money before anything else.

Amy went and sat in a corner and could nearly have cried, as her mother put her arm around her. She was tired of being cold and on the move, and her legs ached from walking.

'Now hold your hosses! I know you can't afford that, and Harry said that I'd to treat you right. I could do with a seamstress for my girls in the saloon. They might look like strutting peacocks, but their clothes always need mending. Is your missis any good with a needle? If she is, she's got a job and I'll just charge you twenty dollars to live here.' Jimmy sat back in his chair and it creaked with his weight. Amy couldn't help but think it would collapse under him, if he wasn't careful.

'I'll not have my wife working in a saloon for a load of hussies!' Ethan stared at Jimmy.

'Ethan, don't be so rash. I wouldn't have to go near the saloon every day. Besides, it's me that should have the problem with the drinking that goes on there. You, no doubt, will enjoy a tot or two once you've made some money.' Grace stepped forward and looked at Jimmy McMahon. She knew her life would have to change if they were to stay in Dawson. 'It's a deal, Mr McMahon, I'll mend the dresses. The girls can bring them to me or I'll collect them once a week, as long as we can rent here for ten dollars?' Grace smiled at the businessman; she'd learned how to barter from her father, and now she was going to put it to good use.

'You've got a woman with some spirit here, lad. She

follows you to this godforsaken place and then tries to get the better of me. I like her. And providing it's not going to cause any upset between you all, you have a deal.' Jimmy laughed.

'It seems we'll be staying here then,' Ethan replied and then glared at his wife. 'Now, you old rogue, how much is the stake that used to be Jake's, which I understand you now own?' Ethan asked and watched Jimmy's face cloud over.

'I'm no rogue. I've worked hard for my money, so you watch what you say. I bought the claim the other day from the Canadian government, after they found Jake dead on it. He'd minded it for near eighteen months, so I claimed it for fifteen dollars. After a year I've to pay the government a hundred dollars for the right to mine there, but if I find any gold on it, I pay the government a royalty of ten or twenty per cent, depending on the quality. I have a man panning on the stake now – he'll be near frozen, but he'll have the fires going, thawing out the permafrost to get to the gold. Now how about I employ you to dig that mine, then you've no outlay, but you'll benefit from a cut of the gold found at that mine? Say, another royalty of ten per cent and a wage of twelve dollars a week?' Jimmy sat back and waited for an answer, smiling at Amy while he let Ethan think.

'I wanted my own claim – that's what we came for. I want to make money and find gold. I didn't come all this way just to work for another man.' Ethan looked at the cunning fella who sat in front of him and then glanced at Grace, who was urging him to say yes to the deal.

'Well then, you must return to where you come from, or move on to another field. Perhaps Atlin Lake, a good few hundred miles on. I hear folk have gone there.' Jimmy sat back and waited yet again.

Ethan looked at Amy, who was about to cry. 'Where's the stake at, and how big? And has there been gold found on it?'

'It's up the bed of the Klondike, a twenty-five-yard strip, and Jake found gold on it. He sent his finds back home to his daughter in Kansas fairly regularly. As long as it's not worked out, you'll make the money you are after.'

Ethan ran his fingers through his hair and looked at his family. He could see they were begging him to say yes to the deal. He hated to have to admit it, but there was not a better way of making a fortune in the place he had dragged them all to. 'Alright, you've got a deal.' He held his hand out. 'But if I make a find and I can afford my own claim, then that's what I'll be doing,' he said as the big man shook his hand.

'That's what I'd expect, but worthwhile claims are few and far between. You've arrived too late; the best days of the Klondike are beginning to be behind us now.' Jimmy smiled and looked at Amy. 'Now, young lady, what about you? You look too old for school, but too young perhaps to work with some of the ruffians of this city. We've not many children in Dawson – it's not the place for them – but we do have a school. I'm sure Miss Eleanor could do with your help with the young ones we do have here. I'd suggest you go and see her, unless your mother wants you to stay at home?'

'That might be an idea, Mr McMahon, thank you.' Grace smiled and was relieved that things had been settled for them all.

'My man will come for you in the morning and will show you the stake. Don't let him be leading you up to Klondike City or on the back streets of Dawson. There are women there who would eat you alive and leave you penniless. A cigar shop is not a cigar shop, if you know what I mean.' Jimmy winked at Ethan. 'If you want to write home, leave your letter at the saloon and they will see that it gets posted somehow, although they usually wait until there's a batch to be sent on their way. There's talk of a postal service being started, come spring. We have plenty of stores and the like, but at this time of year they are not as full as they should be. If you survive the winter, you'll be alright.'

Jimmy looked around him; at least the family had come prepared and some of their supplies were still intact.

'Now, unpack the rest of your stuff and take the day easy because, believe me, you'll need all your wits and strength to survive in this place.' He stood up and smiled. 'You've already shown that you are damned stubborn and have your head set on settling here. And you can make a good life, if you are prepared to rough it and work hard. Now keep that stove lit and your bellies full, and I wish you well.' He looked at Amy. 'Here, young Miss, go and visit the store on Front Street. They might have some spice left in one of their jars on the counter.' Jimmy flicked a quarter at her and Amy caught it with a smile on her face. 'Daybreak, my man will be here for you. And I'll speak to one of my girls to bring their dresses around to mend.'

Ethan stood up and opened the door of the cabin for Jimmy to leave. 'We all thank you, Mr McMahon – we'll not let you down.'

'Thank me if you are still here and have gold in your pocket this time next year. It takes a certain sort to stomach the Klondike and what she can throw at you.' Jimmy put his hands in his pockets and walked out, heading back to the saloon. The wind outside was biting and a blizzard was about to start. The earth beneath his feet was a mixture of mud and slush, but was not yet frozen, although the mighty Yukon was starting to freeze over. Winter was coming, the mountains around Dawson were already heavily clad with snow, and the fir trees had changed from their usual colours to white. He breathed in. Of all the times for a new family to arrive, they had chosen now and it would be a battle for them to survive.

4

Daylight was just breaking when there was a knock at the cabin's door. Ethan was ready for his first day at the claim, which he had dreamed about for months. By the end of the day, if he was lucky, he might be a millionaire, he thought as he put his gold pan on his back and tucked the shovel and pickaxe under his arm.

'Thank the Lord, it's stopped snowing. I've never known so much snow.' Grace looked out of the door at the man who waited for her husband.

Ben Lawson stood with snow-covered shoulders, wrapped from head to foot in furs. He was used to the winters that Dawson endured, and grinned at the newcomers as the door opened. 'This is nothing, Missus. Another week or two and you may not be able to open the door. You got everything you need – matches and food – else you'll starve up there at the claim?' he shouted to Ethan, then made off into the glimmer of dawn, with Ethan at his heels.

'Take care.' Grace kissed her husband on his cheek and watched as he followed in Ben's deep footsteps, before she closed the door behind him. 'Well, that's your father off for the day. I pray that he'll be safe. We will unpack our belongings and try and make this place look more like a home, although I must confess I fear that is going to be hard to do.' She smiled at Amy, who was clearing the table after their breakfast of bread and cheese. 'I've no oven, the water butts will be frozen, and we need wood bringing in to keep that stove going. Thank the Lord there is a supply of logs packed to the rafters outside – at least we can keep warm, unlike your father.' Grace sat down and placed her head in her hands.

'I'll clear the path outside, and the steps, and bring more wood in. Don't worry, Mam, we are better here than still trying to reach the goldfields. Father will be alright, he's doing what he wanted. And I think this place is like nothing I've ever seen in my life. The people are so different and, although it's a city, Dawson's not like any other city I've ever come across. I can't wait to be able to explore.' Amy looked around her excitedly and pulled her thick woollen coat on over the top of her knitted jumper and skirt, before picking up the spare shovel that her father had left behind in a corner of the cabin.

'You'll do no such thing, not without me by your side – just until we know the lie of the land. You are not up Cowgill now! No wandering off, as you don't know what or who is out there. Did you not hear those wolves howling out in the woods last night? They make me cringe.' Grace looked at her wilful daughter.

'They are only dogs, Mam,' Amy said as she warmed her hands at the stove, before putting on her gloves, which her grandma had lovingly knitted and given her, as she had cried at Amy leaving the family home.

'They are dogs that would eat you in the blink of an eye – don't you forget that,' Grace chastised her. 'Now don't get too cold. Keep coming in for a warm-up.'

'Shovelling all that snow will keep me warm.' Amy had a smile on her face. Now that she had a home and her parents both had employment, perhaps life would settle down, no matter how ramshackle their new place was. She grabbed hold of the shovel and stepped out onto the boardwalk, thinking that they might have cleared a pathway through the snow back home at Cowgill, but here it was a bit pointless. By the look of the sky, another blizzard was on its way. She set to and swept the three steps that led to the boardwalk, then cleared what lay around the side of the house. The water butts at each corner of the cabin that caught water for their daily use were frozen over, and she smashed the ice on each one to make it easier when her mother needed water. Then she picked up as many logs as she could from the pile at the end of the cabin and carried them inside. 'It's freezing out there, Mam, I can't feel my fingers,' she said, then went back outside again after placing the logs down on the wooden floorboards, before returning with another armful and another after that. Then she sat and let her fingers come back to life, the tingling in them nearly making her cry with pain as the circulation returned.

'If you are frozen to the bone in under an hour out

there, think what your father's feeling like, digging in the frozen earth with hardly any shelter. I think he'll regret ever hearing the word "Klondike" before this winter is out. He didn't bargain for such harsh conditions – none of us did. I wish we were back with my mother and father. We should never have left.' Grace sat down at the table and only just held her tears back.

'Now, come on, Mam. We are all tired, as the journey was harder than we thought, but we are here now. The cabin will soon be clean and will become our home. Father is determined to find himself some gold, and he's used to hard conditions; after all, he helped build the railway back home. We'll be fine. Give me the kettle and we will make a warm drink of tea, although it will be without milk. We'll have a walk together to the stores on Front Street this afternoon and see exactly what sort of place we have come to. And then I'm going to write a letter to Grandma and Grandad to say that we have arrived. I miss Grandma so much.' Amy sighed. She didn't want her mother to know that she was missing home, too.

'I'll write as well, and we can put them in the same envelope. Now I'll tidy this place up. That Jake must have been living like a tramp. Nothing that he's left behind him has any value, and everything is filthy, although his deer skins on the wall are worth saving. It is no place to call home, but it will keep us warm. And at least we all have a bed to sleep in at night, and the kerosene lamps light the gloom of an evening. It's going to be a long winter and although it is only just upon us, I am praying for spring already. Why your father didn't wait until spring, I don't know. It would be better if he had.'

'He thought he was doing right for us, Mam. He wasn't to know. I'll go and get another two or three armfuls of wood, and then I'll help you unpack everything. At least we can survive for a while on what the government insisted we buy before we made our way here. I'm sure we will be fine until spring.' Amy walked to her mother and kissed her on the cheek. 'I love you, Mam. We will be alright.'

Ethan followed Jimmy McMahon's man, struggling to keep up in the deep snow. He looked back at the sprawling city of Dawson. It was a ramshackle place, but at the same time there was wealth there. It had grown from next to nothing, but was now home to more than thirty thousand miners, gamblers, saloon owners and those who were out to make a quick profit, like him. Ahead of him, Ethan could see the new sprawl of Klondike City and hoped that he would not have to walk much further. He knew he'd pushed Grace and Amy to the absolute limit, and now they were left almost without any money and living in nothing better than a wooden hut.

His one hope was that he would strike it rich quick, and it was that hope that kept him going as he followed the well-trodden path from the mudflats of the mighty Yukon up the tributary called Klondike, to the mine that he and his fellow worker were to work at in the coming days. All along the path, the banks and hillsides had been cleared of any trees and overgrowth. The wood from them had been made into wooden sluices to wash the soil and dirt free from any of the heavier golden nuggets that lay hidden in the mined soil. Ethan looked at all the weary miners, with their fires lit for warmth and to melt the frozen permafrost to enable them to get to the earth below along the Klondike's bank. There were holes dug everywhere, in search of what they all coveted: gold that could change an ordinary man's life in seconds.

'This is our stake.' Ben, McMahon's man, stopped and took his backpack off. 'At least the fire's still lit – that's half the battle in the morning, getting the fire going again.' He bent down and put his boot into a pile of ashes to uncover some still-glowing logs, going quickly inside one of the dark, deeply dug holes that ran away from the banks of the nearly frozen Klondike to retrieve some dry sticks and wood that were kept there for that purpose. 'You'll soon get warm when you start digging – you'll have no time to feel the cold.'

'I thought we'd be panning in the river, not digging?' Ethan looked at the round, dark pit with a ladder and supports around it, which was buried into the earth and was just wide enough for two men to dig at it.

'That's how the first gold was found, but now we dig down to find a pay-streak. And if it looks like we are in luck, we dig more deeply to the bedrock, where the true gold will be found,' Ben said and looked at the man, who obviously hadn't realized what he was in for. 'Whatever soil we dig out will freeze as fast as we bring it out, so you'll not be using the sluices until spring. You'll not be making much money until then, unless we are lucky.' Ben stoked the fire and soon got it blazing, then split the fire and took some of the burning logs down into the darkness of the hole that, hopefully, was going to be fruitful for them.

Ethan gazed around him at all the sluices and mines that lined the banks of the Klondike, and at the mines on the hillsides. The book that he had read in the comfort of his parents-in-law's home had not told him about any of this; it had spoken of wealth beyond belief, made easily, and he had risked everything, believing every word of it. How on earth were he and his family going to survive until spring when, hopefully, gold would be found?

'Come on, get your arse in motion! Bring your shovel and pick. The sooner we fill this bogey, the sooner we get to that bedrock,' Ben yelled at him. 'I hope you aren't a damned glass-back – I've no time for them.' He scowled as he put his head out of the pit hole and pulled a small wooden cart on wheels, the bogey, behind him. And then he stopped. 'You weren't expecting this, were you? Gullible folk never are. You might get lucky and find a nugget or two while you dig. I'll say nothing to the boss if you do, as long as you do the same for me.' Ben grinned.

'You are right, I wasn't expecting this. I wanted my own claim and had visions of panning in the river in the warmth of the sun, with more nuggets in the bottom of the pan than you can ever imagine.' Ethan shook his head.

'Them days have been and gone, friend, and you are thinking of the wrong time of year. In another few weeks it will be so cold up here your balls will freeze, and all that will keep you going is the thought of that bedrock and the warm cabin that will greet you at the end of the day. Now come on, let's get going. Jimmy McMahon will expect his money's worth out of the pair of us, but what his eyes don't see, his heart won't grieve over. We'll pocket a few bits that we find, so don't fret. And if it's a big find, then bloody hell, we'll all celebrate good and proper.'

Ethan picked up his shovel and entered the dark, shallow pit that was now filled with smoke, thawing the frozen ground for them to dig out. He had done hard work when he helped build the railway, but never had he felt so cold and disheartened. He was going to be digging for days on end – perhaps for nothing. To make matters worse, there was no way he could go home with his tail between his legs, because he had no money and they had been one of the last families to travel down the Yukon before it became impassable with ice and snow. He'd have to make the best of it, and pray for that seam of bedrock to glitter and shine with a wealth of gold.

'There, that looks better. It's still no palace, but at least it's clean.' Grace stood with her hands on her hips and looked around the cabin. 'I'm sure that bed had fleas in it. I've itched all night, from being on it. I've not thrown it out. Let's put it outside on the boardwalk to get some fresh air through it and, if there's any unwanted life on it, they'll soon die out in the cold.'

'I was alright in my bed in the corner. I used my own covers besides, and I had the heat of the stove next to me. Thank you, Mam, for making this curtain out of the tent flap to give me my privacy.' Amy looked at the corner of the cabin that she had been designated. She was thankful that she could lie in her wooden bed and not let her parents see her worrying. Although she had vowed she would make the best of her new life, she yearned to be back at home on the farm high in the fells. She missed her best friend, Joshua Middleton, and her grandfather and grandmother. All she had seen for the last three months was hardship, hunger and, sometimes, death.

'It will do, for now. If your father strikes it lucky we can always move. Surely there must be better living than this? Now that we have unpacked, have we to brave a walk out? See if there are any stores that we can make use of, and perhaps try to find the school for you to help teach in. It doesn't sound as if there are many children here in Dawson, and Jimmy McMahon obviously took it into his head that you were better-educated than most of them, to suggest that you went and taught there.'

'Mam, I don't want to teach. You know that I hated school when I was back home. Please, Mam, don't make me go and help out there. Anything but that.' Amy had been worrying all night about looking after children younger than herself, as she hated the classroom.

'Oh, Amy, we all have to do something we don't like sometimes. You are not a daft child, you are as sharp as a needle, and if we can help the children here, perhaps we should.' Grace put her arm around her headstrong daughter and kissed her brow. 'We'll find the school and see what we both think.'

Amy hung her head and tried to look as if she had accepted her fate, but inside she still hated the idea.

*

'It's going to be an impossible task to keep our skirts clean,' Grace said as she looked at the mud along Front Street. Even though there was a good covering of snow, the main street was churned black with mud from folk's movements. 'No wonder boardwalks are running along whatever buildings there are – at least it lifts you out of the main street.' Gracie picked up her skirts and pulled her shawl around her woollen jacket, with the wind biting into her.

'There's hardly anything here, Mam. Plenty of saloons, a bank or two, the sheriff's office and jail, but there are hardly any shops. Where are we supposed to do our shopping?' Amy gazed around her, noticing all the men coming and going, and listened to the noise of people singing and drinking from the various saloons along the rough-and-ready street.

'I don't know, my love, but we will make do,' Grace said, trying to keep her daughter's spirits up. 'Look, there's a general store here. Let's go in and see what they have in stock.' She opened the door beneath a sign proclaiming *Dawson's Supplies* and stepped into a different world from the one she was used to, back home. The shop sold picks, shovels, rope, knives, gold pans, animal skins, blankets, candles and other essential items for gold mining. And then in the back corner there was a small space given over to food: sacks of flour and oats, sugar and haricot beans, with shelves of tinned treacle, mustard and evaporated milk. There was no sign of any fresh meat, vegetables or fruit. Grace looked at her daughter and saw her face. She didn't have to say anything, as she knew that Amy was disappointed.

'Afternoon, ladies. I don't think I've seen you two before.' A stern-faced woman came out from behind the counter. 'I'm Martha – Martha Black. I own this store along with my brother.' She stood in front of Grace and Amy and looked her two customers up and down. She was wrapped up good and warm, with a shawl around her shoulders and a skirt and bodice that added extra girth to her already-broad frame. She was a formidable sight.

'I'm Grace Postlethwaite and this is my daughter, Amy. My husband has come to the goldfields to make his fortune, and we have followed him.' Grace took in the rough-looking woman and knew that she was a force to be reckoned with.

'Another *cheechako* with ideas of making it big in this hellhole! Good luck to him, and the both of you, but you'd have been better staying at home. Not that I can complain, as I've made a pretty penny, but I was one of the first here when my rat of a husband decided to leave me. You'll either make a life here or be thankful when spring comes and you can get away.' Martha looked at the two women, who must have something about them to have already got to Dawson.

'A *cheechako*? What's that?' Amy asked curiously, staring around her.

'It means, young Miss, a newly arrived miner, a tenderfoot. When your father's been here a while and is an old hand, he'll be a sourdough. It's just names that have been given over the years. Now, what can I do for you? I'd say stock up now, because in another week I'll have hardly anything left. We never get much sent from Skagway or the army post at Fort Yukon through the winter. Don't ask for eggs, as they are worth their weight in gold – valued at more than a good nugget, if you can get them.' Martha shook her head and went behind her counter.

Amy breathed in and remembered collecting eggs at home on her grandfather's farm. Sometimes there had been a glut, and her grandmother had made bacon-and-egg pie, scrambled eggs and poached eggs nearly every day, simply to get rid of them. So much so that Amy had hated eggs back then, but now she would do anything for one.

'I've some tinned butter that I can let you have, and at the moment condensed milk, otherwise what you see is what I've got. It will be a blessing once the train line they are talking about is built. It will open up this part of the world.'

'Have they started it yet?' Grace asked, with interest.

'Yes, they have. According to the news in *The Golden Nugget*, work has started at Skagway, and it's going to make all the difference to everyone here.' Martha nodded to a pile of paper, which looked more like butcher's wrapping paper with print upon it than a newspaper. 'By next year Dawson and Klondike will be a different place. We'll no longer be dependent upon the river boats that bring goods up to us. Now, are you going to buy anything or not?'

'Er, how much is your butter?' Grace counted the bit of change she had in her bag and hoped that she had enough, as Martha reached for a can from under the counter.

'Pay me when your fella has found a strike. You'll have

been through enough these last few months. It's an understanding that I have with new families – but only families, mind. The fellas that come on their own can look after themselves. And it will only be the one thing. But I remember when I first came and it was damned hard for a woman in this godforsaken town. If you get desperate for meat or fish, the natives here will trade with you. They know this part of the world like the back of their hands, and probably laugh at us behind our backs.' Martha passed over the tin of butter. 'Make it last.'

'Thank you, I'm grateful. We don't have much money left after making our way out here. Can I pay for a tin of condensed milk, please? I'm looking forward to having milk in my coffee, although I'd rather have a cup of tea any day.' Grace watched as Martha reached for a tin of condensed milk.

'I'm afraid it's a dollar – I can't sell it for any less. Money is cheap here, but necessities are worth more than the gold they are all digging for. The world's upside-down in Dawson, as you'll soon find out.' Martha took Grace's money and then looked at Amy. 'You look old enough to work for a living. Do you fancy being my shop girl? It would make a bit more income for your family, and there would be a few perks in it for you.'

'She's supposed to be going to see if she's needed at the school here,' Grace said quickly. 'Jimmy McMahon suggested it to her.'

'Oh, Mam, you know I don't want to work there. Please, I'd rather work here,' Amy looked pleadingly at her mother.

'They've all got ringworm or impetigo at the school at the moment. Most of their heads are shaven and they've blue iodine painted on them. You don't want to go there, with that bonny head of hair.' Martha winked slyly at Amy.

'Oh, we don't want either of those. Perhaps you would be better off here. What would you pay her – she's a good worker?' Grace asked, wanting only the best for her daughter in her first job.

'I'll see how she does in the first week and then we'll see. It's just that there are not many lasses of her age about town to help, and she looks decent enough.' Martha winked at Amy.

'I'll not let you down. I'll work well and I'll run errands, once I've got to know the place. Please, Mam, please agree,' Amy pleaded.

'Alright – anything you make will be welcome at the moment. Thank you, Martha, when do you want Amy to start?' Grace breathed in. Her daughter working in such a place was something she had not bargained for.

'Tomorrow, seven o'clock: that's as good a time as ever.' Martha looked at Amy and at the beam upon her face.

'Very well, she will be with you in the morning,' Grace said and then considered her daughter, who had grown up so much in the last few months. She was nearly a woman now. Soon she'd no longer need her mother and would be able to stand on her own two feet. She'd have to, if she was to survive Dawson City, but she'd be looked after by the feisty Martha Black.

*

Ethan sat slumped over his bowl of bacon-and-bean stew. He felt disheartened and exhausted. A day of digging in the frozen earth of the Klondike had revealed nothing, and his partner in work had warned him to expect many more days of the same until the warmer spring months came, when they could riddle the pans of the dirt they had excavated.

'Never mind, you couldn't have expected to find gold on your first day. Amy's got some good news to tell you, and this will make you smile.' Grace ran her hand across her husband's shoulders and looked at Amy.

'I've got a job, Father. I'm going to work in Martha Black's shop. I start tomorrow. It's full of everything, and it's a lot better than going to teach at the school,' she said chirpily.

'It's a good job one of us is happy. I should never have brought us to this bloody place – nothing is as I expected it to be.' Ethan reached for Grace's hand. 'Forgive me. I should never have asked you to follow me here. You should have stayed with your parents.'

'Give over, Ethan. It's your first day in a new job, a hard job. A good night's sleep and all will look different. Amy and I are both content. She's over the moon with her new job, and I'm expecting the saloon girls tomorrow with their dresses to repair. Rosie yelled at me across the street to tell me they were on their way, with plenty for me to do.' Grace took Ethan's empty bowl away from him and sighed. His spirits were broken; he'd planned and dreamed about digging in the Klondike for months, and now that he had arrived, he had arrived too late. The rush was nearly over.

5

Grace sat down at the table and looked around her. It was the first time she had been on her own for a long time, and now a wave of despair washed over her. Ethan had gone early that morning to the stake, which showed no promise of making them wealthy. And Amy had not been far behind him, excited about her first day at work in Martha Black's shop. She'd hoped better for her daughter, but it would suffice for the time being. She put her head in her hands and sobbed. Ethan had promised so much and she had believed every word. If only they had come earlier, Dawson might have lived up to his dreams, but now she knew that if he didn't find gold quickly, he would not be satisfied with his lot. He was never satisfied, and he hated being found to be wrong in his ideas.

She wiped her eyes and blew her nose, then reached for the precious pen and paper that she had managed to bring with her on their journey through hell. She'd write that letter back home to her parents and tell them they had arrived safely, and that Ethan had secured a strike, and Amy a job. But she would not tell them the whole truth: that they had been misguided, and that their lives had changed for the worse. In fact the only person in the family who seemed to be embracing the situation was Amy, and she was enjoying her lot, now that she had a home, and a job of sorts.

Grace put pen to paper and, between her tears, told her mother and father about their journey and their new life. She missed her mother's soft face and the smell of her father's pipe tobacco, and the steady ticking of the grandfather clock in the small but warm home that she had known all her life. She sighed as she signed off with her love, then placed the letter in an envelope, kissing the back of it, before putting it down on the table to be taken to the saloon to join the post, which would hopefully be sent at some date. No sooner had she done that than there was a knock on the door, and Grace could hear talking from the other side.

'Ah, I'm glad you got Jake's old place.' Rosie smiled and pushed her way past Grace, her arms full of dresses and clothes to be mended. 'These will keep you out of mischief. Us girls have needed a seamstress for a month or two, haven't we, Tilly?' Rosie watched as her fellow saloon girl placed her own armful of dresses on top of the pile.

'We sure have. All the girls have something that needs repairing. Some of the men that we entertain can be a bit rough with their hands, especially when they're in a hurry to be satisfied.' Tilly, who was at least six foot tall, with blonde hair piled on her head, stood back and noted Rosie scowling at her. She'd been told to watch what she said, as the two of them had made their way over from the saloon, because the woman who was to mend their clothes seemed a bit demure.

'Have you settled in? It looks like it. Quite a cosy place – better than the weather out there. It looks like we are in for another snowstorm; when the clouds come down over that ridge above Dawson, you know it's going to lay some snow down. Is your fella at the strike? He'll be frozen. Most of the men have shown their faces for the day and come back into Dawson. There's talk amongst them that there's been gold found further up in Alaska, at a place called Nome. Do you think your man will want to go there?' Rosie talked fast as she looked around her, taking in what little the Postlethwaite family had in their cabin.

'I hope not. I've had enough of wandering this Earth. Dawson is where we mean to stay and, with luck, he will find enough gold to make us a decent life.' Grace looked at the pile of clothes; the smell of cheap perfume was on them all, as she picked up the first dress, covered with flounces and frills, and a low-cut bodice that was in need of attention. 'When do you need all these back? I'll do my best, but there are a lot more than I had envisaged.'

'Whenever you've done. Here, I've bought needles and thread. I thought you might not have them, although it's only white cotton, but nobody is going to look that closely at the stitching.' Rosie reached down the front of her bodice and pulled out an unopened packet of needles and two cotton reels from between her breasts, before wrapping her shawl around herself.

'Thank you. I'll see to them and I'll return them once I've finished.' Grace looked at her letter, which was just showing underneath all the mending. 'Can I give you this? Mr McMahon said the post would be collected from the saloon when there's enough to be sent.' Grace reached for her letter.

'I'll put it with the pile already waiting. Harry took the last lot with him when he returned the other day. It might be a month or two before this is sent on its way,' Rosie said and took the letter.

'Did he get away safely, Mr Bloomfield? He seems a good man.' Grace smiled, remembering how well he had looked after them on their journey down the Yukon.

'Mr Bloomfield, he's known as Harry to us – Harry the hound, because he's like an old dog that always comes back home, no matter what.' Tilly laughed and smiled.

'Yes, he went on his way. It'll be spring before we see him again. I wished him well. As you say, he's a good man: too good to be out here.' Rosie looked wistful. She regarded Harry as a good friend and wished he would settle down, instead of risking his life on the river and trading with the locals. 'Now we'll leave you. If I can help with anything, come into the saloon and ask for me. I see that your daughter is helping Martha this morning. I went in for an ounce of snuff and she served me. She'll be alright there – kept on her toes, but Martha will look after her.' Rosie turned, following Tilly to the door. 'It'll take you all time to settle, but we are a close community, and we look after one another. We have to,' she said as she stood in the doorway and looked at Grace's sad face.

'I know, I just miss home,' Grace replied softly.

'We all do, but this is our home now, and we have to make the best of it.' Rosie smiled and followed Tilly out into the oncoming snowstorm, leaving Grace in no doubt that there was no going home unless Ethan struck it lucky.

'It's alright, they don't bite. They are the same as me and you, but this is their land. Show them respect and they will be there to help you and yours.' Martha looked at the horror on Amy's face as three men from the Tlingit tribe came into the shop. Their faces were tanned and lined, and they were dressed in buckskins with feathers in their hair. 'Just serve them like anyone else. They are probably here for candles, that's what they come in for, as a rule.'

Martha was proved right as one of the men pointed to the shelf with candles on it and showed on his fingers how many he wanted.

Amy reached to the shelf and placed the ten candles down on the counter, then watched as he put the correct number of coins down, before leaving with the others.

'He's left the right money without me asking.' Amy picked up the change and was amazed that the indigenous man had American money.

'They come in nearly every other day and remember the price of every item they trade with locals, so they always have dollars on them. If you need dried fish, especially salmon, he's the one to ask. The Tinglits, especially the women, have accepted us whites, but the other native tribe called the Han do not like us. We are on their land and they do not mix with us at all.' Martha observed Amy as she thought about this for a while.

'I wouldn't like it if someone came on my land and took it over, so I can understand the Han. We shouldn't be on their land.' Amy imagined people invading her grandfather's land and how he would have felt.

'As I say, treat them right and they'll treat you right. They trade with me, and I trade with them. Unfortunately some folk in this town have no respect for them, and sometimes it causes bother.' Martha shook her head.

Amy picked up a duster and set about cleaning the shelves. She loved the smell of the shop; the air was filled with the scent of candle wax and paraffin, and every corner contained unusual stuff, ranging from blankets to bear traps, as well as whatever foodstuffs and mining equipment were needed. And the customers were just as diverse, with miners, saloon owners and the saloon's dancers entering through the doors. Working in the shop was a lot more interesting than teaching schoolchildren.

The mood at the table in the Postlethwaite cabin was mixed. Amy chattered away about her day, which had been filled with a mix of people and items she had never seen before. Grace had little to say, as she dished out the soup and placed the unleavened bread on the side of everyone's dish.

Ethan had returned, chilled to the bone and disheartened yet again, and he swore as he sat back in his chair and looked at the supper that had been placed in front of him. 'I thought it would be easier than this! Today even the bloody pick was frozen to the ground; it took an hour to get any fire going, and then there was not a bloody glimmer of any gold. Then I come home to bread that's not fit to eat, and soup that's got nothing in it. And to make it worse, you've been chittering like a box of monkeys. Bloody well shut up, Amy. There's nothing here to be excited about, and I wish I'd never dragged us here.'

Amy bowed her head and fell silent. She knew that her father hardly ever lost his temper, but when he did, everybody had to mind what they said.

'Whisht now, Ethan, it isn't Amy's fault. It isn't anybody's fault. We both thought we were coming to better ourselves. It will get easier, once we are used to Dawson's ways,' Grace said quietly.

'Even you've had to lower yourself to mending tarts' clothes. Your father would have something to say about that. I've made a mistake, but the trouble is there's no way out of this hellhole now. We'll have to make the most of it. I'll keep on doing what I'm doing until spring, but once the thaw comes, we should try and go back home – with money in our pockets or with none,' Ethan growled and then went to his bed.

Amy opened the cabin's door and looked out into the cold night. Above her head, the Northern Lights filled the sky with their beauty, and a lone wolf howled. She sighed as her mother put her hand on her shoulder.

'Come in, Amy, don't let the cold in,' Grace bade her.

'I like it here, Mam, it is wild and free. I don't want to leave,' Amy said quietly.

'We'll have to do as your father thinks right. Now come in and hold your tongue – don't aggravate him,' Grace whispered.

Amy closed the door and felt angry. Her father always had to be respected, even though he often got things wrong. If he had anything about him, he should learn to embrace Dawson, as there was more to life there than gold.

6

Every day through winter the situation in the small cabin got worse. The money that Amy and Grace made barely covered the bills, and there was still no sign of Ethan being made rich with a find. Christmas was barely celebrated and Amy's fifteenth birthday was just another day, with a dinner of whatever the family could barter or scrounge from the locals. Ethan's mood got darker and darker, and Amy stayed long hours at the shop with Martha, to keep out of his way.

Then came the signs of spring: migrating birds flew overhead to the thawing lands further north, and the ice on the Yukon gradually receded. Carpets of brightly coloured crocus carpeted the prairies, while sleepy bears made themselves a nuisance, walking through the city looking for an easy feed after coming out of hibernation. The temperature rose and suddenly life was not as hard. People started to appear from the river, bringing much-needed supplies; and even Ethan's mood lightened, with every pan full of earth that he swilled in the icy waters of the Klondike. There was hope, because small nuggets were found in the waste and were shared between Ethan, Ben and Jimmy.

'Another few feet and we'll have hit the bedrock,' Ethan said with excitement as he ate the first egg that he'd had since arriving at Dawson.

'That's good news. Perhaps you'll strike it rich shortly. See, things are looking up for the better. Amy's eggs, which she bartered with her native friend, are good as well, but Lord knows what bird they came from.' Grace looked across at her daughter and smiled; the girl had made the most of her situation, and now that spring was in the air she knew that Amy would want to wander in the surrounding countryside, and that the work in the shop would make her feet drag.

'They are prairie-grouse eggs, I know they are not so big, but they are better than nothing. I traded my hair ribbon for six of them. So don't reprimand me for not wearing my ribbon. I am too old to wear it now anyway.' Amy looked at both of her parents.

'Don't you get too friendly with those natives. It's not long since they'd have been taking your scalp and doing a war dance,' Ethan commented and caught the frown from Amy, who dared not answer him back. 'I'm going to take the tent with me this morning. It's warm enough to stay at the mine, and I don't want Ben to be one up on me when we finally get to that bedrock and the gold it holds. I'll take one of those mosquito nets as well – the bloody things are everywhere, now that spring is here, laying their eggs in every pond or piece of water they come across. You had better cover the water in the barrels outside, to make sure we are all safe, Grace. We don't want to all come down with malaria from the little sods.'

'I've been drinking and using water to clean with from the spring that runs into the water butt in the street across from us of late. Our water butts are getting low, so I thought it was better I did that, in order to conserve our supply. I'll cover the barrels as soon as you have all gone,' Grace replied and carried on putting Ethan's food supply together.

Ethan got up from his chair and watched as his wife packed him enough food for a week, along with the tent, nets and blankets for the cool evenings. He looked across at Amy. 'You behave yourself: no trailing into the woods or out onto that prairie. There's plenty of wild animals that would look at you and mistake you for their dinner. Look after your mother – make sure she gets rid of that cough she has had recently – and I'll be back at the end of the week.'

Amy said nothing. She'd grown tired of her father's negative attitude all winter and now, with a few little finds and the spring coming, he was back with his head set on gold again. She looked up, after her mother kissed him and said goodbye at the doorway, and then pushed her chair back and made herself ready for another day at the store with Martha.

'You listen to what your father says. Come straight home this evening – no wandering,' Grace said, backing up her husband as Amy reached for her shawl.

'I won't. What are you going to be doing? I see that you have finished all the repairs for this week. Rosie will be calling on you, I expect, although Martha said she had not seen her for a while; and her usual customers said that Rosie had taken to her bed, when she asked after her.' Amy looked at her mother as she coughed and caught her breath. Winter had left Grace a little run-down, health-wise, like many others in Dawson.

'Do you really need to put your shawl on, Amy? I think it is so warm today,' Grace said as her daughter held her shawl close to her, before following in her father's footsteps to work.

'It's not that warm yet, Mam, there's still a chill wind.' Amy kissed her mother on her cheek and felt her warmth as she did so. 'You *are* warm – it must be your cough. You feel alright, don't you?'

'Of course I do. There's nothing wrong with me. Now go on. Martha will be waiting for you, and I have these dresses to take to the saloon. I'm taking them myself, because Rosie told me a new group of dancers and singers are on their way. That will mean more work for me, and I want to check if there is a letter from home. They should know by now that we are all alright and have had time to reply to us, hopefully – if our letter made it home. Now shoo, or Martha will wonder where you're at.' Grace ushered Amy out of the cabin and watched her as she made her way through the muddy street to her work, before closing the cabin door behind her. In truth she did not feel well. She did have a temperature, and she couldn't stop making visits to the earth closet at the side of the cabin. She'd felt unwell for a few weeks now, but had hidden it well. The family's fortunes were just beginning to turn and she didn't want to dampen Ethan's spirits.

'Have you been trailing again? That's the second morning on the trot you have come in late.' Martha looked up at the large oak clock that ticked away the minutes and hours slowly and surely as it hung upon the store's wall, as Amy entered the shop.

'No, I'm sorry I'm a bit late, but I had to say goodbye to my father. He's decided he's camping out at the claim. They are hopeful they will soon be finding a decent vein. So he and Ben are guarding it with their lives.' Amy hung her shawl up on a peg behind the shop's door and smoothed her apron down, before standing behind the counter and waiting for her first customer. 'I also spent a few minutes with my mother. She didn't look well; she looked hot with a temperature, although she assured me when I left that she was alright and was going to get on with her day. I left her sewing me a dress out of the offcuts from one of the saloon girl's dresses. It looks lovely – my favourite colour, red.' Amy smiled and thought of the dress that her mother had promised she would make her out of the red velvet.

'It's to be hoped that she is alright. Rosie came in just before you and has heard that typhoid is raising its ugly head in the city. Not as bad as last spring, because folk that have been here a while know now not to drink from the spring next to you. Lord knows what runs into it; it must be full of sewage and muck, and it should have been closed down long since. Your family doesn't use that, does it? You can't do, else you'd be ill by now.' Martha looked across at Amy and noticed the worry on Amy's face. 'You don't, do you?'

'Father and I don't, but my mother said this morning that she'd been drinking from it, because our own supply was getting low. I hope she's not caught typhoid. You can die from it, can't you?' Amy breathed in and looked out of the window and then smiled. 'There's my mother – she's just going into the saloon with her arms full of her mending, so she must be feeling better. Thank heavens for that. You had me worried for a moment.' Amy looked at Martha, then decided to pack the shelves with new products that were awaiting her in the crates that had come down the ice-free river. The store was going to be busy, and all was well with the world.

'Well, tell her to boil that water, if she will drink it, or stick to your own. And I'd keep an eye on her.' Martha shook her head and hoped that Grace was alright, for the sake of the lass she had grown quite fond of.

'Just look at it: we've darn well struck lucky, Ethan!' Ben wiped his brow and stood back and looked at the gold, glinting along the vein they had dug into. 'Jimmy McMahon will be giving everybody drinks all round, by the time we show him this little lot.'

Ethan held in his hand a nugget fresh from the earth of the gold that he had chased halfway around the world. The soil they had both panned in the freezing clear waters of the Klondike had eventually shown traces of what lay under the cold earth, but he would never have believed the beauty and potential wealth of what he was holding. 'Bloody hell! I was all for giving up a month back. I didn't think this day would ever come. Look at it, Ben, just look at it! I know it's not ours, but a share of it is, and we'll want for nothing.' He walked out of the dirt-filled mine into the sparkling spring sunshine and looked up to the sky, yelling for all the world to hear, throwing his hat up into the air and whooping with delight. His dream had come true; now all they had to do was dig out every last nugget – every last piece of dust that clung to his clothes and stayed in his pocket.

He looked at the linen tent with its washing drying on a make-do line, and the campfire they had sat around, nearly freezing in winter. At the water sluice and the mounds of soil they had extracted over the winter months, when his spirit had nearly broken – all for the glorious piece of precious metal that he now held in his hand. Wait until he told his Grace: she'd want for nothing. He'd even take her back home now, just to show his father-in-law that he hadn't been daydreaming about getting rich. He smiled and imagined driving up the winding station hill in a carriage pulled by the finest team of horses, with Grace and Amy in their Sunday best, and announcing that he had bought a property as grand as The Gate on the road to Sedbergh and that they would want for nothing all their lives.

'Come on, you can dream about what you're going to do with your share when you've dug it out,' Ben's voice yelled at him. 'Don't count your chickens yet – it might not be that big. Only putting our backs into it will tell us.'

Ethan looked at the ore in his hand and smiled as he put it into his pocket. He'd done it: they'd found gold! He could hold his head high when he kissed his Grace and told her of his plans. But first Ben was right; they had to find out how much gold there was, and guard it with their lives, no matter how long that took.

It was early morning as Grace lay in her bed, sweat pouring down her neck and her hair sopping. She tried to focus and answer Amy as she came to her side. She'd been in bed since her return from visiting the saloon, after almost collapsing as she struggled back, with her arms full of mending, but still no letter.

'Mam, Mam, are you alright?' Amy looked at her mother. She'd heard her tossing and turning all night and rambling in her thoughts, spoken out loud as she awoke.

'Help me, Amy, I'm ill – help me!' Grace whispered in a shallow voice. 'Water, can you get me a drink of water? Don't touch my bedding, I don't want you to get this.' Grace felt another bout of sharp pain hitting her stomach and making her retch.

'I'll go and get the doctor. I know we can't afford him, but you need him.' Amy put the mug of water to Grace's lips and tried not to cry as she watched her mother nearly double up with pain as she tried to drink.

'No, no doctor, we can't afford him. Besides, I know what I've got. It's typhoid. Amy, you must not touch me.

In fact go outside and leave me. I don't want you ill. Send someone for your father. Go to the saloon, or Martha's, and ask for their help.' Grace fought for breath as she closed her eyes and concentrated on battling the fever.

'I can't leave you, Mam,' Amy wailed.

'Yes, you can. Now go and get word to your father that I'm not well,' Grace said in a demanding, quiet plea to her daughter.

Amy ran like the wind to the only place she knew would help her, passing people she would usually chat with, in her rush to get to Martha at the store.

'What time do you call this?' Martha looked up at Amy as she entered the store and then, realizing something was wrong, she changed her tone of voice. 'What's up, child?' She could see tears running down Amy's cheeks and that her hair had not been brushed.

'It's my mother. She's ill, she's in bed, and she's boiling up and being sick and dirtying herself. She keeps wandering in her thoughts. She's asked for someone to go for my father. I think she's dying.' Amy broke down and cried. 'She's been drinking from that spring that's been giving folk typhoid. She's not dying, is she? She can't leave me.'

'Oh Lord, I thought as much when you told me her symptoms yesterday. Hush now, child. You stay there and I'll shout for my brother. As luck has it, he called round this morning and is in the back room. He'll ride out and tell your father to come home, where he's wanted. You go and stand on the porch and wait for me. I don't want whatever your mother's got infecting my shop – you might be the next one with it. Once my brother is on his way, I'll come and see your mother with you. The poor soul will need someone with her, if it's typhoid she's got.' Martha sighed and then went to tell her brother to ride the mile or so to the mine and urge Ethan to return home.

Amy went and stood on the boardwalk and tried to stop her tears from falling. She was thankful when she heard the sound of horses' hooves and a male voice whipping a horse into action from the stable behind the store. She watched as Martha came out, looking flustered and worried.

'Has she been ill for a while?' Martha walked briskly by Amy's side, nodding her head at customers who bade her good day.

'I don't really know. She was very warm yesterday, and she's been going back and forward to the toilet a lot lately. She's not been eating much, but she never does!' Amy started to think about how little attention she'd been paying her mother of late. In fact both her father and she were guilty of the same crime; both of them were wrapped up in their own worlds. 'She's got typhoid, hasn't she?'

'It sounds like it. Let's hope she's made of stern stuff and that her heart is strong.' Martha caught her breath as Amy's home came into sight. 'It sounds as if you left her in a bad way. Let me go in first,' she said as they stood outside the cabin door together.

'I want to come in. Please, I want to see my mam,' Amy cried, realizing there was no noise coming from within the wooden walls, and that the moans she had heard as she left had stopped.

'Stop here, and I'll let you in when I know how she is.' Martha lifted her shop apron to her mouth and nose and opened the cabin door. The smell of Grace's body fluids hit her senses as she walked towards the bed that the woman lay in. No movement or noise came from the bed and, as she approached, she knew that Amy was now motherless. Typhoid had no favourites, and Grace's Quaker religion had not kept her safe from the disease that had racked her body. Grace lay, still dressed in her clothes, under the blankets that had been hauled from Skagway and over many a pass with so much hope; but now they were used to cover her face, as Martha gently pulled them over her. She blessed herself and said a prayer, before turning to go out and tell Amy. She stopped short in her tracks and looked at the young lass, who stood behind her with tears running down her face.

'I'm sorry – she's passed over, my love. She's at peace now,' Martha said quietly and watched as Amy broke down in front of her. 'Now you've got to be strong. Your mother wouldn't want all these tears. Let's go outside and we'll wait for your father. He shouldn't be long; my brother was going to lend him his horse to come back on. I hope he can ride?' Martha put her arm around Amy and held the girl's shaking body against her.

'He can, he's good on a horse. I wish he was here. He should have been here! He shouldn't have brought my mother and me to this place. We should be back home in

Dent, and my mother would still have been alive then,' Amy sobbed.

'It was her turn to go, no matter what. God works in mysterious ways, and He sometimes shows us what is most important in our lives in a cruel way. Things will come right. And don't you blame your father for your mother's death, as his head was turned by gold, like many a man in this godforsaken place. The Klondike has a lot to answer for.'

Ethan and Amy stood at Grace's graveside. They were on their own in their grief as they looked around them.

'You know, Amy, I thought when I brought us to this country I was going to better our lives. I thought that if I struck it lucky, we would have everything – we would have the things that matter in life. Now I know that couldn't have been further from the truth.' Ethan looked around at the city built on gold sprawling in front of him, and at the wild open spaces of the Yukon. He put his arm round his daughter and kissed her forehead. 'Your mother and you *were* my gold, if I had but known it. I shouldn't have put her through all that I did – nor you.'

Amy looked up at him. 'I like it here, Father. At first I wanted to blame you for Mam's death, but then I realized I was wrong. My mother always backed you and would have followed you to the end of the world, if you had asked her. She missed home, though. It was so cruel that a letter arrived for us from Grandma and Grandad the day after she died, as she had been waiting every day for one, once we were settled.'

'Aye, well, I've written to tell them the bad news. I doubt they'll ever want to see my face again. Your grandfather will never accept me back into his home. He never did have much time for me, but I know they will both support you.'

Amy looked down into the grave where her mother lay, and then at the two gravediggers who waited to fill the grave in. 'I loved my mam. I don't want to leave her here on her own.'

'She's not there, Amy. She's now forever in your heart, and will be looking down upon you wherever you go. The Klondike will be where she is buried, but she will always be with you. Perhaps now is not the time to say it, but I think we should go home. I've got enough money now to get us back, and for us to start up a business. What do you think?' Ethan looked at his daughter, who had grown up so quickly in the months she had lived in Dawson.

'I don't know. It would be good to go home to Dent and have my grandparents back to love me. But my mam . . .' Amy sobbed.

'Come now, let's walk home and let her be in peace.' Ethan gazed at his wife's grave. 'God bless, Grace. I promise I will look after our daughter. I'll not let you down.'

7

It had been more than a year since Amy had lost her mother and, with time, her grief had got easier, but she had still visited her mother's grave weekly, when the weather permitted. Now that was one of the things she was fretting about, as she looked over the railing of the steamship that was bringing her and her father into the port of Liverpool and back to England.

The crossing and journey home had not been as gruelling this time, as they had the money to travel in a little more style than when they had first gone out to Dawson, taking the newly built train over the White Horse Pass back to Skagway and then catching the steamship and booking into a first-class compartment. Amy had cried when she left Dawson – not just for her mother, but for the place she had grown to love. She enjoyed the wilderness, and now that some of the miners had moved on to Nome in search of a new gold strike, it had become less chaotic. Dawson had been changing; there was no longer gold to be found along the Klondike, and nature was starting to reclaim the disused mines. The cabin that had been their home for their time there had been abandoned, with most of their belongings still in it, her father assuring Amy that once they were back in England, they would start a new life and would not need anything they were leaving behind.

'It's a busy port, Liverpool – look at all the boats coming and going. It's a good job there are plenty of docks.' Ethan leaned over the ship's railings next to his daughter and watched the ships navigating their way into the Mersey basin with their cargoes. 'Are you glad we are home, Amy? Is it not good to see the old country? At least we'll not be freezing to death this winter.' Ethan breathed in the sea breeze and smiled as the ship's hooter bellowed out a warning for a small vessel to get out of its way.

'We aren't home yet. Liverpool is still a long way from Dent. Grandma and Grandad do know we are coming home, don't they? You did write, as you promised, and say that we were on our way home?' Amy asked, as she watched the deckhands throw ropes down to the men on the docks to help secure the ship as it manoeuvred into the dock.

'I did write to them. But I told them that we might be staying in Liverpool for a while before journeying back. I thought I might see if there's any employment for me here. You might be wanted back home in Dent, but I definitely will not be. Your grandparents might have sounded sympathetic in their penned letters to me, but I fear they will never forgive me for taking your mother away from them. Besides, it will be a new experience for you, completely different from Dawson. This place is full of shops, markets and sights to see. A few days in the port will do us both good, if I have to deliver you back into their arms.' Ethan looked at his daughter, hoping she could not detect his deception, as he had not the slightest intention of going back to Dent or of facing his in-laws' wrath, which he knew was waiting for him, from the sharp letters George Oversby had written to him. Oversby might have been an understanding Quaker, but he was unforgiving with his words, of late.

'As long as we can go home eventually, I don't mind staying a day or two. You are right, I can go shopping – that is, if you are willing to give me some money.' Amy looked at her father bashfully and gave a cheeky smile. 'A new hat and coat, and perhaps a dress.' She started thinking about what she could really do with, now that she was back in civilization.

'Now wait a minute. I'm not squandering all this money we have made. It's to be put into a business to support us both. However, I think I can manage new clothes for the pair of us. We do look a bit bedraggled. Dawson wasn't known for its fashion sense.'

Ethan grinned. At least he could treat his daughter to a new outfit, before concentrating on business. He was not exactly loaded, but by the time they had mined what ore there was on Jimmy McMahon's strike, and divided up the shares, he had enough to set himself up nicely, if it was spent with care.

'Grab your bags – we can disembark. It'll soon be evening, and we need to find a hotel to stay the night, if not longer.' Ethan looked across at the deck below them and watched as the gangplank was lowered to the dockside and secured. It was soon swarming with fellow passengers jostling in the queue to get onto firm land after the long sea journey. 'Watch yourself – there's plenty in Liverpool, like there was in Skagway, that would help themselves to anything they can sidle away with, without you noticing. And close your ears to some of the dockland talk, as it's not for the faint-hearted.' Ethan had kept his daughter at his side since her mother had died. Amy was more precious to him than life itself, which was another reason for him not encouraging her to go back to Dentdale.

Amy held on to her hat and her bags as the wind whipped across the docks. She smelt the salty sea air mixed with the smell of the docks, spices from the East, newly caught fish and the sweat of the hard-working dockworkers. She grinned at the young lad who took her hand as she stepped down from the gangplank onto the dockside, her legs feeling like jelly as they compensated for the sea swell.

'Thank you,' she said politely as she looked up at him and noticed how tanned his skin was and how blond his hair, from the bleaching of the sun and the salty air.

'You are welcome, Miss.' The lad smiled and then went about his business as his shipmates catcalled and made fun of his rescue.

'Bloody chancer! This dock will be full of them, so

mind what you are doing and stop with me. You are far too young for what's going through his, and his dirty mates', minds,' her father growled as he took her bags and put his arm through Amy's. They walked along the dockside, passing row after row of moored ships and their cargoes.

Prince's Dock, Salthouse, George's, Trafalgar, Queen's – Amy read all the dock names off as she passed them, and watched as people scuttled past her with every sort of container, sack and box. Horses were pulling carts and trailers packed high with goods from all over the world, and she noted every colour of human being and every accent as they walked past a queue of people waiting to board the next Cunard ship bound for America.

'Do you think we should tell them there's nothing different from what there is here, and they should save their money?' Ethan said as they passed the queue and saw the excitement on people's faces.

'No, don't spoil their dreams, Father. Everyone has to have a dream. Besides, you did alright by leaving. You made money.'

'Aye, made money, but lost my wife. I don't think that was a good trade. I should have been content with my lot,' Ethan replied as they walked out of the docks onto Water Street. 'Now, we need somewhere to stay for a while, until we find somewhere to buy or even rent. I don't know Liverpool, but it's a busy port – we are bound to be able to make a living here. I can turn my hand to most things, and you are of an age when you can help me, or even get a job if you have to.' Ethan spoke his thoughts out loud as he looked around him at Pier Head and the busy docks and loaded ships that lay in front of him.

'I'm not staying. You talk as if I'm not going to return to my grandparents', yet you know they want me back home,' Amy protested.

'Aye, well, we will see about that. I know they are wanting you home and you'd like to go, but if I buy a business that demands two folk – like a grocery store or suchlike – I might need you to serve there.' Ethan strode out, leaving Amy looking at him and not believing her ears at her father thinking she would be happy to stay in Liverpool.

'You promised me I could go back to Dent if I wanted to.' She ran to catch her father up. 'Please, Father, I'd rather be there than here. Besides, you don't know what you are going to do yet.'

'Look at all these folk, Amy. They all need feeding and watering. There's money to be made, and we have the brass to set ourselves up in a good position to do just that. You want nowt with going back home – there's nowt there, lass.' Ethan marched on with Amy following behind him, struggling to carry her bags. Now that he had brass in his pocket, he was going to make the most of it. He'd no intention of going back to the Dales, and if his lass could help him make money, then that's what she would do, whether she liked it or not.

'You promised me, Father, you promised. They are waiting for me back at home,' Amy yelled, in between catching her breath as she followed in his footsteps.

'Aye, well, I've changed my mind. I'm your father, and you'll do as you are told if I deem fit that you are needed here.' Ethan made his way through the built-up streets, with people jostling past him, busy in their own world.

Amy knew better than to answer him back, but she felt herself swear under her breath. She'd wanted to see her grandmother and grandfather so much, as they were the nearest thing to her mother that she had.

'This place will do.' Ethan stopped outside a tall town house called Grosvenor House. It had scrubbed steps that looked as if they had been bleached every day of the week. In the window was a sign saying: *Rooms to Rent. No dogs, No Irish.*

Amy stared at the sign and wondered why the Irish were not wanted. They'd always seemed pleasant enough when she happened to come across them. She followed her father up the scrubbed steps and through the dark oak door with the polished brass fingerplate, into the darkness of the house, and stood behind him as he rang a small brass bell on a table in the hallway. The house smelt of lavender polish and was fussily decorated with china everywhere, and a large aspidistra plant in a brass planter in the corner.

'Yes, can I help?' A prim-looking woman in a long black skirt and a pin-tucked white blouse appeared from a room to Amy's left. Its window looked out on the busy street, while the room itself was full of chairs and a grandfather clock, whose tick seemed to break the uncomfortable silence of the hallway.

'I'm looking for a room for my daughter and myself.

You look a clean enough place – as long as you've no fleas, you'll do,' Ethan said roughly and put his bags down.

'Excuse me, you'll not find any fleas in my establishment.' The owner, Mrs Mounsey, folded her arms under her breasts and pulled a face. 'May I ask what your occupation is, and do you think you can afford my prices? This hotel is quite well-to-do and my other renters will expect me to keep up my standards.'

'Standards, is it? Well, I'd hate to bring your standards down, but I think perhaps, despite our looks, we are a respectable pair. We've just returned from the Klondike, where I struck lucky. I could probably buy this place from under you, so you've no problem with brass. Now have you got a room, or do I have to take my money elsewhere?' Ethan stood and stooped to pick up his belongings from the tiled hallway.

Mrs Mounsey looked at Amy and then turned to Ethan. 'I have a room, or should I say two rooms – they are interconnected – right at the top of the house in the attic. I could rent you those. I need payment up front, of course!' She moved to a desk in the darkest corner of the hallway. 'How long will you be staying with us?'

'That I don't know. I'm after buying myself a business in Liverpool. Do you feed your guests as well?' Ethan looked at the guest book, which had suddenly appeared in front of him along with a tariff card, which made him think twice, after seeing the price he was about to pay for a bed for the night. However, he wasn't going to back down in front of the old snob.

'I do. Breakfast is at seven a.m. sharp, and the evening meal is at seven p.m. Both meals are served in the large dining room to your right. To the left is the drawing room, where you and your daughter may sit at any time of the day. Some of my guests enjoy a game of whist or rummy and read the evening paper after being at work. I don't encourage alcohol to be drunk on the premises.' The woman glared at Ethan, judging him by his rugged looks and expecting this to dissuade him from taking the rooms.

'That's no problem. I don't drink. I find drinking a waste of money. Your problems are still there the next morning, no matter how drunk you get, from my experience long ago when I worked on the railway. I may look a little rough around the edges – you would too, if you'd been mining in the Yukon for the last few years – but I can assure you I am house-trained, if that is what your problem is,' Ethan said as the woman's face implied that she had a bad smell under her nose. He reached into his pocket and put a handful of notes down on top of the desk. 'Let me know when our rent runs out and, if we leave early, I expect some of that back.'

The landlady looked at the pile of cash in front of her and changed her opinion of the rough-and-ready man and his daughter. 'Thank you, that will be more than adequate for quite a few months, by the looks of it. I will of course refund anything that I owe you. Now, young lady,' she turned and smiled at Amy. 'You'll find a bathroom on the second floor. We are one of the few boarding houses in Liverpool to have a bathroom, and I'm sure you would appreciate a nice soak after your long journey. You'll find towels and soap, and just say if you need anything else. Be sure to lock the door behind you, though.'

'That'll be grand. Now if you can show us to our rooms, we'd both be grateful. It's been a long journey, as you so rightly point out,' Ethan said and watched as the landlady reached for the room key from behind the desk, then started to walk up the stairs, with Ethan and Amy following.

'Was she hinting that I was mucky? The snotty old cow!' Amy said as she looked round the rooms high in the attic of Grosvenor House.

'I think she likes to think herself better than she is. Every so often her voice changed from posh into her Scouse accent. Nobody's better than anybody else, so I wouldn't let her bother you.' Ethan unpacked the two bags that held all his worldly possessions and placed them in the drawers, then lay down on his bed. 'Go and get your head down for an hour or two. It is grand to have a proper bed to sleep in, and to be warm and back in civilization. Tomorrow we'll look around the streets and see what's for sale – a shop of some kind. I can see us both serving customers. There's always profit in food, and folk will always need it. Look at your old boss, Martha; she was worth a bob or two.' Ethan closed his eyes.

'Father, can I go home? Please can I go home,' Amy pleaded, but got no reply as Ethan rolled over onto his side and went to sleep.

Instead of doing as her father told her, Amy decided to treat herself as the landlady had suggested and wandered down the flight of stairs to where the bathroom had been pointed out to her. The boarding house was quiet; all the other renters were at work or about the city, so she thought now was the ideal time to sneak downstairs and take a luxurious bath. A tin bath had been purchased just before they left Dawson, but it was such a faff filling it up with warm water and making sure her father didn't walk in on her that she'd preferred not to use it. Now, as she gazed at the pristine white-enamelled bathtub and the brass tap, which at a turn was filling her bath with lovely warm water, she could have cried with happiness. There were fancy soaps at the side of the bath and talcum powder on the sideboard, beside the flushing toilet, which was decorated on the inside with a transfer of chrysanthemums and butterflies.

Never had Amy seen such a bathroom. She was going to take her time and enjoy every minute of her luxury, she thought, as she stepped out of her clothes and dipped her toe in the water to test the temperature. It felt glorious as she lay back in the warm waters and washed herself. Bending her head and soaking her hair, she slathered it with the perfumed soap, which got into her eyes and made her reach for the nearby towel. As she was doing so, she froze in fear. She'd forgotten to turn the lock, she realized, as she saw the door open slightly and a young man's face appear, with a look of shock upon it as he caught sight of her, naked and vulnerable.

'Sorry – I didn't see a thing. Sorry, I just needed the

toilet!' The door closed as fast as it had opened, and a voice yelled from the other side and then went quiet as the man went away.

Amy grabbed the towel and stood up in the bath, her long black hair dripping down into her eyes, as she stepped out and over her dirty clothes to lock the door quickly behind her. A young man had seen her with nothing on – the shame of it! She felt herself blushing from head to toe, then grinned as she thought about the look on his face. He'd been as shocked as she was. Whoever he was, she hoped she would not have to meet him again, else she would not know where to look, she thought, as she dried herself quickly, dressed and made her way back to her room. Still, he had been quite good-looking and young, she decided, as she lay on her bed and gazed up at the attic window, her hair still damp upon her pillow as her thoughts, and sleep, overtook her.

8

Amy and her father sat at the breakfast table, and around them were the same people who had joined them for dinner the previous evening. All were men who worked in Liverpool: two bank clerks, a hospital warden and a ledger clerk from the docks. All had been polite and had enquired who the new guests were, and had introduced themselves and been eager to find out more about the life of a gold miner and about the Klondike. Ethan had told his tale of life in Dawson, and Amy had added her account, when asked, and had hoped she had given an accurate version of her time there. This morning, however, no one had time to talk. They were all in a hurry to make their way to work, and left Ethan and Amy planning the day ahead. Amy was simply relieved that she had not seen hide nor hair of the young man who had glimpsed her for a brief second in the bath; nor had she told her father of the incident.

'The first thing I need to do is go to a bank. The fella

that works on the docks told me that all the main banks are on Cook Street, just along the road from here.' Ethan placed his teacup down and looked at his daughter. 'Do you want to stay here while I do that bit of business, and then I'll come back and pick you up?'

'I can do, Father. I'll wait in the room that we were shown yesterday, rather than go back upstairs. I noticed that it catches the morning sun, so it will be nice to sit there and wait for you. I believe there's a market just behind here, and that the best shops are to be found on Bold Street, or so the gentleman from the hospital told me. Perhaps you could have a walk down the street there while I spend some time in a shop that might take my eye.' Amy smiled and wrinkled her nose up, hoping to persuade her father to give her some money for the clothes that he had promised her.

'I suppose you'll be wanting some of my brass? I could do with getting a new suit of clothes myself. We've been away from the real world a bit too long and it shows, from what we're wearing. If we are to be in business, we'd better smarten ourselves up. Besides, that would suit Mrs Snooty over there, who keeps looking at us as if we are going to pinch her silver.' Ethan nodded at the landlady and grinned. 'The bank will open at nine, so I'll see you in another hour. I'll be back as soon as I can.' He pushed his chair back and left Amy sipping her tea, before she wandered into the dayroom to wait for his return.

'Ooh, I must stop doing this. Or you must stop doing this!' A voice came from behind Amy as she sat silently, looking out on the busy street in front of her. 'I thought this room was empty. It usually is, at this time of the morning.'

Amy turned round to face the young man who was standing in the doorway, his hands laden with a tray full of silver and a polishing cloth to clean it with. She felt herself blush as she realized who it was that was talking.

'At least you are dressed this time. That saves embarrassment! You don't mind if I sit down next to you, do you? I hate cleaning my mother's silver. It will pass the time if I've someone to talk to.' The young man sat down next to Amy and put his tray of silver-plated condiments on the table between them. 'You can save your blushes – I've seen it all before. I've two older sisters and they were always showing off their bits, thinking I couldn't see them, so don't worry.'

Despite the lad's words, Amy blushed even more. 'I forgot to lock the door. I was so excited about having such a lovely bath. I'd never been in a bath like that before,' she said quietly.

'Oh, it's my mother's pride and joy. She had it put in last year. I swear she thinks she lives in Buckingham Palace. I'm Percy, by the way – skivvy to everyone, and general dogsbody to my mother. The Dragon, as I know everybody who lives here calls her. She's really a softie, but don't say I told you.'

Amy stifled a snigger and looked at the blond-haired lad. 'I'm Amy – Amy Postlethwaite. I'm staying here with my father until we find somewhere to live and a business to run. Although I'd rather go and live with my grandparents back in Dentdale, if I had my way.'

'Mother was saying that you have just come back from the goldfields in the Klondike. Did you make a lot of money, and find a lot of gold? That sounds more exciting than cleaning the house silver on a dreary morning in September.' Percy had a gleam in his eye as he thought romantically about the adventures he had read of the Klondikers, and envisaged nuggets of gold in Amy's father's room.

'It was a hard life, but I grew to love it. That was, until my mother died. Even then I loved it, but the winters are so hard over there, and there is hardly any food. And the gold is not as plentiful as folk would have you believe. Father was lucky, although he and two others shared a claim, so he only had a small cut, when they did strike it. We are not rich, but we're comfortable for the moment, so Father says.'

Percy looked at Amy with a sneer. 'Comfortable enough to be looking to buy a business – can't be that poor. Not like half of the folk on the streets of Liverpool.' He wrinkled his nose and shook his head. 'This is a good area, but go a few streets further in and you'll see how folk really live.' He sniffed and looked down his nose as he thought about the slums of the city. 'My mother wouldn't last a minute in some of the slums. Keep out of Toxteth and "Greatie", as we call it, even though there is shop after shop and an open-air market. The houses there are rundown beyond belief, with more families living on top of one another than you could imagine. If your father's after a pub, Scottie Road is where he wants to be. There's plenty down there, and all the locals call in after they have shopped at Paddy's Market. I don't know why he wants to open a business here. I'd bugger off any day.' Percy spat on his duster and polished extra-hard at a stubborn mark on the silver teapot.

'It'll not be a pub my father's after, as he doesn't believe in drinking, and neither did my mother. I don't know what he wants. I don't think he does, either.' Amy sighed.

'He'll soon turn to drink, living here, else he'll not survive. Even my mother has her "one" glass of sherry on a night.' Percy winked.

'So, who's this you are gabbing with?' Ethan walked in on Amy and Percy's conversation and looked at the young man who was busy keeping his daughter company.

'This is Percy – he's Mrs Mounsey's son. He was just giving me some advice on where not to look, when we are searching for a business.'

'Was he now? Let's be away, if you want to shop. And I want to have a look around these streets, so we'd better get a move on. There's folk forever out there this morning,' Ethan said curtly.

'Bye, Percy, perhaps I'll see you later?' Amy rose from her seat and smiled at the lad who had kept her company.

'Yes, perhaps. Has my mother told you that this room will be closed until dinnertime tonight? We've got a funeral tea being held here. Mrs Lund from the corner of Deane Street is burying her husband this afternoon, and they are to come back here for a tea. The family are

Methodists, so it'll not be the usual drink-till-you drop Catholic wake that many families in Liverpool have, so my mother said she could accommodate them. Besides, he was our milkman, so it is the least we could do for him.' Percy stood up and looked at Ethan as he took Amy by the arm.

'Thank you, we'll stay clear of the bereaved and go to our rooms on our return,' Ethan said and then escorted Amy out onto the street. 'My God, he can talk. He gossips like an old woman.' He walked out with Amy by his side.

'He works for his mother. He has two sisters, but they must have left home, by the sound of it. He told me all sorts about Liverpool, though,' Amy said.

'I bet he did – you couldn't get a word in edgeways!' Ethan said. 'I now know all about Mrs Lund and her family problems. Now, I hear Lord Street is the best shopping street. What if I give you some money and leave you there until, let's say, two o'clock? I don't want to go into the shops you will want to visit, and you won't want to trail around looking for a property with me. Besides, if I think I've found the right place for us, we can always have a second look together.'

Amy dragged behind her father, taking in all the shops and stalls on their way.

'Come on, these shops are nothing compared to the ones on Lord Street, so the girl in the bank told me,' Ethan said to his daughter as she gazed in a cobbler's window at the latest in button-up boots.

'I'm coming. Yes, leave me, because you hate shopping,' Amy said as they reached the wide stretch of Lord

Street, with the largest selection of shops she had ever seen in her life. It was a million miles away from the wilds of Dawson City. They both stood and looked along the street at the tall spire of St George's Church and at the horse-drawn trams travelling up and down. Arched gas lights ran down the centre of the street, and people gazed in the many shop windows and entered the shopping arcade.

'I'll meet you in three hours: here outside this shop, Hope Brothers. I could do with having a look into it myself, see what they can do to make me look a little smarter. By the looks of the shop window, they should be able to do that – they seem a decent outfitter. Watch out for those trams, they'll not stop for the likes of you wandering in front of them.' Ethan looked at his daughter, wondering if he should leave her on her own in such a big city, but she had her head screwed on and she knew enough about life to take care of herself.

'I'll be fine, Father. Just give me some money please. I can't shop with thin air.' Amy smiled and couldn't wait to go from shop to shop with whatever money her father gave her.

'Here, take this, but spend it wisely and don't let anyone rob you. You'll not be getting that sort of money to spend on yourself very often. Although I know you've done without for a long time, so you can be a little extravagant.' Ethan pulled his wallet out and passed Amy enough money to ensure that she had a good day, buying what she needed.

'Thank you, Father, I love you.' Amy kissed her father

on the cheek as she put the money in her dolly bag, then started off with a spring in her step down Lord Street.

'You love my brass, more than me, you mean.' Ethan shouted after her and smiled as he watched her disappear into the first shop that caught her eye. He shook his head, then made his way down the opposite street in search of any business that might fit his requirements, although he was beginning to feel like a countryman at odds with the city. He didn't think much of the sharp dressing, the shops and the bustle of the streets. Maybe Amy was right; perhaps they should go back to Dentdale and he could always set up in business there.

Amy couldn't believe her father had given her so much money. She was going to have a few hours of heaven, buying clothes that she so badly needed. Her mother had always been there to talk to, when she had needed underwear or to alter her clothes, but of late she had been seeing to her own needs, even altering some of her mother's clothes to fit herself. But the material was beginning to look faded and washed out, and she was finding it hard to keep up appearances. Today she would make sure she dressed herself from head to toe, and she beamed as she entered a shop that caught her eye, selling ladies' wear. She'd start with her undergarments and work her way to her outer garments, she thought, as she looked at the rows of beautiful drawers full of ladies' undergarments, stockings and handkerchiefs.

She smiled at the mannequins modelling the latest corsets, moulding ladies into shapes that were not at all natural. She was in no doubt that she would not be buying those; just two sets of the best bloomers, two camisoles, two sets of wool stockings, along with suspenders. She had no time of day for the torturing restrictions of a corset, which she did not need as she was already slim. She smiled at the shop girl and asked her to show her all that was on her list of 'wants', watching as the girl pulled out drawer after drawer of garments for Amy to look at and choose from: satin, cotton, chambray with lace and without lace – the choice was endless. She decided to be practical and select what she really needed in order to be warm and comfortable with the onslaught of winter around the corner, and still with the hope of returning to live with her grandparents.

Her undergarments were soon parcelled up, and Amy looked around her, adding six embroidered handkerchiefs to the pile, before paying for the lot.

'Would you like us to deliver this to you, Miss?' the shop assistant asked when Amy passed her money to pay for the items.

'Yes, please, it would save me carrying them. I'm currently living at Grosvenor House on Harrington Street – the name is Amy Postlethwaite. How soon will they be delivered?' Amy couldn't wait a day longer than she had to, to change into her new underwear.

'They'll be with you later this afternoon. Harrington Street is not that far away for our delivery boy.' The shop assistant placed the brown paper-wrapped order to one side, with details of Amy's name and address upon it.

'Thank you.' Amy closed her bag and moved on to her next shop. She'd heard that in the bigger establishments there were now ready-to-wear dresses, which she was determined to find and buy, as her sewing skills were no way comparable to her mother's neat stitching. She needed two new dresses and a winter shawl, and then she would look and feel a million dollars, as they said in America. She wandered down Lord Street and gazed in wonderment at all the shoe shops, barbers, hairdressers, cafes, haberdasheries, hat shops and flower shops, and a large glass-covered arcade full of everything she had ever dreamed of. It was there that she bought her two dresses and a blouse, and a hobble skirt, which she was told was all the rage, but which she regretted buying as soon as she had left the shop, knowing that it was not practical to stride out in.

Her father's money was disappearing quickly as she bought herself a new shawl instead of a coat, thinking that if she bought a shawl, she could just afford the pair of boots that she had seen in the shoe shop next to Hope Brothers, where she was to meet her father. That was after she had bought a bottle of lily-of-the-valley perfume that she held in her hand, and the glittering hairclip that had caught her eye and would look so lovely in her black hair. By the time her three hours had come to an end she was laden with bags, as well as having some delivered to Grosvenor House. She made her way back up to the top of Lord Street and stood outside the window of Hope Brothers, trying to peer in and see if her father was already inside.

'Have you finished then?' Ethan said, as he came up behind her and tapped her on the shoulder. 'You don't look to have a lot of packages with you.'

'I got most of them sent back to Grosvenor House. It saved me carrying them, and both the dress shop and the milliners offered to deliver.' Amy turned and looked at her father. 'Have you found somewhere for us? How far have you walked? You look shattered.'

'I've trailed all over this city and there's nothing that takes my fancy. It's either too dear or in a bad position, no matter what the business is; or there's no accommodation, so it's of little use. I'll go further afield tomorrow, but I needed a business in the centre of the city, not out on the outskirts or in the slum areas, like your new friend was talking about.' Ethan sighed. 'I'll have a look in here on another day – there's plenty of time for me to smarten myself up.' He cupped his hands to his face and peered in through the shop window. 'They look as if they could fit me out, no bother. And I'm not the fussiest dresser, unlike you, Miss.'

'I've had a marvellous time. I bought myself two new ready-made dresses. My mother wouldn't believe you could buy clothes that fit you perfectly and you just take them off the pegs they hang on. I tried them on while a real posh salesperson waited for me in the fitting room and commented, when I looked at myself in the mirror they supplied. I felt a bit awkward at first, but I loved trying the new styles on.' Amy related her experience in the clothes shop, as excited with that as with the actual purchase of her dresses.

'Aye, well, whatever makes you happy. Now, we'll go back to our rooms. You can look at your buys and I'll have five minutes to myself. Have you eaten? Did you think of going to a cafe for a bite to eat or were you too busy spending my money?' Ethan turned and asked as they made their way back to Grosvenor House.

'I haven't eaten, but I'm not hungry. Besides, all the women and girls of my age are so thin. I'll have to watch my figure if I am to live here,' Amy said as she tried to keep up with her father.

'Oh, you've decided you are going to live here, have you? I thought you wanted to go back to Dent?' Ethan remarked.

'I could do with the best of both worlds, now that I know there are shops in Liverpool, the like I've never seen before. But I do want to see my grandmother and grandfather,' Amy added quickly.

'You can only shop like you have today if I find a profitable business, so don't take this treat for granted. It'll not always be like it is today. We'll both have to work long hours, and the money I've made won't keep us forever.' Ethan stopped and waited for his daughter to catch up with him, before climbing the steps into Grosvenor House.

'Somebody's had a busy day – all these parcels have come for you, Amy.' Percy, who was just passing the doorway, showed the packages that had been forwarded to them for their latest guest. 'I can't stop. I'm about to take sandwiches in to the funeral tea. But help yourself to the parcels from off the table, else you'll be waiting for them this time tomorrow, because I'm run off my feet.' He disappeared into the kitchen, leaving Amy and her father to carry the parcels up to their rooms.

'It looks like it is quite a big funeral,' Ethan commented as they passed the room where the mourners were gathered. 'He must have been a well-respected man.'

'I suspect a lot of them will be customers, if he was a milkman,' Amy remarked, as she balanced her parcels. She couldn't wait until she unfurled the brown wrapping paper from around the contents and placed them in her drawers and wardrobe, ready to wear in the coming days.

'Now, a milkman would be a profitable trade, but you'd need to be out in the countryside for that. There's nothing but terraced houses and back-to-backs here as far as the eye can see, from what I've seen today.' Ethan stood for a second and looked at the funeral attendants, all dressed in black, sitting down waiting for tea to be served, before he climbed the stairs with his daughter.

'My grandfather would be laughing at you thinking about becoming a milkman. You were never to be found, when he wanted you to milk the cow. My mother or I milked the cows back at home more than you,' Amy joked.

'You just hold your tongue with your cheek! I'd done a day's work by the time I got home from the station. Besides, there were only two old roan shorthorns – they were no work for anyone, they were that placid,' Ethan scolded her. 'You get to your room and admire your purchases and leave me to have a nap on the bed. My legs are aching from the distance I covered today. Walking the streets is harder on the feet than walking in the country, and I covered a few miles in the time I was out and about.'

'I'll not disturb you then until dinnertime. I'll surprise you and wear some of my new clothes.' Amy left her father and went into her room, closing the door behind her. She was glad to have some time to herself, as it gave her a chance to admire her purchases and try on her new clothes. She'd go down to dinner in her hobble skirt and blouse, which was the outfit that made her look quite the lady. She would like to impress Percy, if he was still serving downstairs, she thought, as she held the blouse up to herself and smiled.

9

Ethan stood in the doorway and felt as if his world was caving in around him. They had been in the city just short of a week, and every day he and Amy had scoured the streets looking for a property that they could call their own and make a profit from, but with no luck.

'I'm going downstairs, Amy. I'm going to stand outside and get myself a breath of fresh air, if you can in this busy city,' Ethan yelled through the bedroom door to his daughter.

'I'll join you for dinner shortly, Father.' Amy opened the door and watched as her father left her alone in the rooms by herself.

Ethan went downstairs, passing the now-empty room where the funeral tea had been held earlier in the week, and was surprised to see the widow back there and still dressed in black, sitting with Mrs Mounsey. They were both deep in conversation as he went past the doorway, without making himself known to them. He stood just down from the steps and leaned back, with one leg balancing him against the wall, and looked around him. Liverpool was a big city, perhaps too big for his liking; possibly Amy was right and they should go back to the Dales. Perhaps it was better to be a big fish in a little pond than a minnow, and unknown, in this mighty city.

He watched as folk scurried home along the streets after a full day's work and as the street's gas lights were lit, in readiness for the coming evening. He turned to enter his temporary home. City air was nowhere near as clear as the Dales air or that of the Klondike – it did nothing for your lungs, being filled with smoke and grime from the industries of the town. He waited for a second or two as the widow of the late milkman made her way down the steps past him, her face covered with a black veil secured under a large-brimmed hat.

'I'm sorry for your loss. Please accept my condolences.' Ethan took off his cap and looked at the woman.

'Thank you.' Gladys Lund lifted her head and stared at the face, which she was shocked to realize she recognized. 'Ethan – Ethan Postlethwaite! Is that you?'

Ethan tried to look through the lace veil at the woman. 'Sorry, do I know you? I'm not from these parts.'

'Ethan, it's me: Gladys Metcalfe from Garsdale – or that's the name you will remember me by. I am now Gladys Lund. I married Ted, and we came to be cowkeepers here in Liverpool. Surely you remember me, or did I mean so little to you?' Gladys pulled her veil back over her hat and showed Ethan a face that he remembered from years ago: older now, with a few wrinkles and greying hair, but still the face that he once had known so well.

'Gladys, I didn't recognize you! So you married Ted in the end.' Ethan gazed at the woman, who looked pale and tired, without the rosy glow that was once in her cheeks when he had courted her, before he had met Grace.

'Aye, I did. But he's gone now, leaving me here on my own, with a business to run and no family to help me.' Gladys sniffed and fished for a handkerchief from her sleeve. 'But what are you doing here? Are you on your own, or are you too married with family perhaps?' Gladys looked at the man she had once loved.

'I, like you, am widowed. I lost my wife while I was over in the Yukon. I'm here with my daughter. We've just arrived back in the country, and we were aiming to put our roots down in Liverpool, rather than go back to Dent.' Ethan remembered the days he had spent with Gladys before he had met Grace. The days when he had been working on building the railway through the Dales, and when he had been able to have the pick of any local lasses that took his eye. Gladys was one of them, until her father and brother had put a stop to him calling at the family farm.

'The Yukon, did you join the gold rush? I can see you being caught up in that adventure – you always were dreaming about bigger and better things.' Gladys smiled and gazed down at her feet. She couldn't bear looking into the eyes that she still felt long-buried love for, especially not long after her husband's funeral.

'Aye, I joined the gold rush. I nearly gave up on it, and it wasn't as glamorous as it was made out to be. A lot of cold, hungry days, and then I lost Grace, which made me realize what is important in life.'

'Grace – I don't think I know a Grace. You say you have a daughter. Is she here with you now?' Gladys looked at Ethan.

'I married Grace Oversby, from the farm up the steep hill at Cowgill, the last farm before you drop into Garsdale, just after the station. I don't think you will know her, as she wasn't one for attending dances or the like, as you and I did. Aye, I've my daughter here with me. Her name is Amy, she's nearing seventeen and all she can think about at the moment is the new clothes that I treated to her to the other day. She spent the brass I gave her like sand trickling through her fingers, but she's not had a lot for a long time, so she did right.' Ethan looked at Gladys as he listened to the church clock strike seven. 'I've got to go. Mrs Mounsey is a stickler: dinner will be out on the table, and Amy will be waiting for me. Do you live far from here? Should I come and see you tomorrow?'

'You are staying here?' Gladys asked and blushed again.

'Aye, it looked a decent enough place to stop until we find somewhere to live,' Ethan replied.

'She can be a right old devil – she likes her money and thinks herself better than anybody else. She'll not have a good word for me, because I've had to tell her that I'll have to pay her next week for some of the funeral tea. I hadn't expected that many folk turning up for Ted's funeral. So I warn you,' Gladys said, as Ethan waved at Amy as she looked out of the window at her father talking. 'Is that your lass?'

'It is, and she'll wonder why I'm talking to you and why I'm not coming in, so I'd better join her.' Ethan decided to accept that he was not going to get an invite from Gladys for him to visit, as he stood on the top of the steps and looked down on the woman he had spent many an hour with.

'Bring her and yourself to see me in the morning, if you like. I live on the corner of Deane Street and Ranelagh Street, just across from the central station. Ask anybody who lives on that row for the cowkeepers – they all know me. However, I'll warn you that my brother Fred is with me until next week, until I get into the swing of things and find someone to help me. So he'll not be happy to see you.' Gladys looked back and closed her eyes, thinking of the bad timing of meeting Ethan Postlethwaite the week of Ted's funeral, and hoped she had not been too forward with her questions. She had loved Ethan and had been broken-hearted when her father had put a stop to the dalliance. Twenty years on, she had become a wiser, harder woman, wed to a man who had been second-best in her eyes, and one who had been unwilling to give her the child she so longed for. Perhaps fate was smiling on her, she thought, as she walked back to her home and milking parlour in the centre of the city.

'Who was that, Father? Do you know her?' Amy asked as Ethan drew up his chair and sat down next to her, avoiding Mrs Mounsey's glare at his lateness to the dinner table.

'Aye, it so happens that I do. She's from Garsdale. She's just buried her husband this week, and she lives further up the street near the main station,' Ethan said calmly as he unfolded his napkin and thanked Percy, who placed a bowl of soup in front of him. 'She's asked us to visit her tomorrow.' He picked up his spoon and hoped Amy would not ask how he knew Gladys. 'She runs the dairy.'

'Oh, that's a coincidence – someone from Garsdale in the middle of Liverpool, and you bump into them. We must go and visit her. She'll have news of home, she's bound to know the same families as us, especially as Percy said earlier that she was a Methodist.'

'Aye, I wouldn't hold much store by that, our Amy. They might have been Methodists, but I don't think Gladys and her husband have practised their beliefs so much. If I remember her husband, he was not like the rest of his family. He might have had a quiet funeral here, for the sake of saving his soul, but he was not a good man, from what I remember. Gladys will not have had a happy life, married to a man like that.' Ethan sipped his soup and thought about the man, who had had the temper from hell and had been the talk of Garsdale, where he would bet and take on any railway navvy in a fight for money. Ted Lund had been a hard man – one Ethan had avoided, when he found out that Ted was courting Gladys, with her father's approval. She'd have been better off with him, but Ethan had been just a railway navvy and not a farmer, unlike the red-haired Ted Lund.

'Oh, the poor woman. Has she been left with a family to raise?' Amy looked across at her father who, since his meeting with Gladys, had not even commented on or noticed that she was wearing a new outfit, and that she had taken more care with her hair than usual.

'No, she has no family. Her brother is staying with her at the moment. He's a man of few words, so don't be surprised if he doesn't make us welcome tomorrow.' Ethan sat back in his chair, after finishing his soup. 'Is that outfit what you bought the other day? You've got your mother's brooch pinned on your blouse – don't be losing it.' He looked at his daughter. She was growing up and the pristine white blouse and long, tight skirt made her look older than she was. He'd soon be losing her to a young man who would come and take her away from him, and then he would be left on his own.

'I won't. She loved this brooch.' Amy touched the brooch in the shape of a bluebird that she had fastened on her collar.

'You look grand. Perhaps a little too grown-up, but then a father never wants his daughter to grow up.' Ethan watched as Percy winked at his daughter as he cleared the soup dishes away. He was right; she was growing up and he would soon be left on his own.

Gladys Lund took the pin out of her hat and placed it down on her kitchen table and sighed. She looked around her and wiped tears away from her eyes. Her tears were not shed for the death of her husband, but in memory of the days she had wasted being married to a man who had bullied her, all their life together. The accidental meeting with Ethan Postlethwaite had made her think of the life she once had, and had stirred long-forgotten feelings for the man she should have married, if her father had not intervened. She looked around her at the kitchen, which was functional, but had never had any love spent on it, like the rest of her home – and her life.

'You are back then?' Fred, a dour Dalesman of few words, entered the kitchen and looked at his sister. 'I still can't get over the turnout that our lad had at his funeral, although a lot seemed to go back just for the tea.' He took off his jerkin and put it on the back of a chair and then sat down. He looked dark and moody as he said what had been on his mind ever since the funeral. 'I've milked the cows and delivered the evening supply. What I had left is in the dairy, ready for mixing in with the morning's delivery tomorrow.' Fred looked worriedly at Gladys, knowing that what he was going to say next would upset her further. 'You know I can't stop here forever. You are either going to have to sell up or hire somebody to do the milking and deliver for you.'

Gladys reached for the kettle and placed it on the hearth to boil. 'Half of those at the funeral, as you say, only came for the tea – Ted wasn't thought that much of. Give them something free around here and they'll bite your hand off in sympathy. Nobody came from up home, I noticed.'

'You couldn't expect them to, our Gladys. It's a bloody long way to stand around a grave with a body in it that they weren't particularly fond of. Now, what are you going to do? You need at least one man to look after those twenty cows out in the yard. They take a lot of feeding, and there's heavy work to be done when the feed comes in from Silcock's.'

'I'll manage. You can get yourself home, if you don't want to be here. I've milked those cows nearly every day since we came here, and I can deliver the milk as well, if it comes to it,' Gladys snapped. 'I'm not coming home, if that's what you're thinking. I'd be stuck looking after father and you two brothers, and would never get out anywhere. Here I'm independent and I'll be my own woman.'

'You've changed, our Gladys. You loved being at home. I was only thinking of you and what is best for you.' Fred shook his head as she put a mug of tea in front of him.

'Aye, well, I know what's best for me, and that is staying here. Liverpool is my home now. It's where I'm used to, and I'll manage my beasts.' Gladys stared at her brother. She wasn't going to go home and look after her ageing father and two unmarried brothers – not when Ethan Postlethwaite had walked back into her life.

10

Amy and Ethan stood outside the walled yard of the corner house on Deane Street and looked up at the sign above the large yard gates: *Ted Lund, Cowman and Dairyman.* 'Well, this must be the place, Amy. What would your grandfather say to keeping cows on a terrace like this?' Ethan looked at the wall, which had been partly taken down and replaced with large gates that were in need of painting, and at the terraced house that had once been two dwellings but now was just the one, with its unused doorway bricked up, but not rendered. In the back yard Ted had built a cow house, called a shippon, to home his animals, leaving a small space of the yard for them to stretch their legs in. The house looked unloved – a bit like Gladys had.

'I heard Grandad talking about the cowkeepers in Liverpool when I was little, but I didn't believe him. How can a cow live in a back yard without any grass to eat?' Amy asked and stood behind her father as he knocked on the green-painted door and waited until it was opened.

'I don't know, lass, but you'll soon find out, as I'm sure Gladys will show you.' Ethan pulled his waistcoat down and held his breath when he heard Gladys yell, 'I'll get it' as she came to the door.

'Ethan, I didn't know if you would come or not. After all, it's been a while.' Gladys beamed as she opened the door to let her visitors into her home.

'Nay, I said I'd come and introduce our Amy. I've been telling her all about you and have explained that we knew each other a long time ago.' Ethan stood back to let Amy speak for herself.

'Good morning, Mrs Lund. I'm sorry to hear of your loss,' she said politely as she looked at the woman that her father had talked about with warmth in his voice.

'You are the only one who is sorry, my lass. I can't say I'm going to miss Ted,' Gladys replied and then turned to Ethan. 'You found us, then. If you'd followed your nose it would have been easier. I'm the only one with a muck-midden in my back yard on this street.' She laughed.

'Aye, I must admit Amy and I have been talking about that. We can't weigh up how you feed cows in the middle of Liverpool.' Ethan and Amy followed Gladys into the kitchen and looked around at the sparse living conditions.

'When we first came here, Ted bought two terraced houses and made sure that the yards had good out-houses, which he made bigger. So the cows are in that, and that's where we milk them, while next door has been turned into a dairy and where we keep the hay and feed. It's full to the brim with hay that's been delivered from down south. Thank God that came just before Ted died, else I would have been struggling,' Gladys said, and looked at Amy.

'You mean all the house, even upstairs, is full of hay?' Amy asked, amazed.

'Aye, apart from a spare bedroom, where the travellers that deliver stuff to us stay if they need a bed for the night. It's only like a barn back home, and it keeps it lovely and dry. I feed my cows hay in a morning and cattle food, ration, of an evening. I've got to keep my girls happy, else they won't make good milk, and then I'll not be happy.' She smiled. 'You don't take after your father, do you, in looks? It must be your mother you favour.'

'I don't know who I look like – a bit of both, I think,' Amy said politely.

'She's as pig-headed as me, Gladys. Once she's set her head on something, she's got to do it, but she does favour her mother in looks. Which is not a bad thing; better than looking like this old devil that stands in front of you.' Ethan stopped talking as Fred Metcalfe walked into the kitchen.

'What's he bloody well doing here? There's nowt like a death in the family for the worms to come out of the woodwork! Have you come to stand back in Ted's shoes? If you have, then you can bugger back off where you came from. You weren't good enough for our lass back then, and you still aren't.' Fred Metcalfe swore under his breath and looked daggers at Ethan, whom he had recognized instantly.

'Hold your breath, our Fred. I met Ethan by accident yesterday. He was staying where I held the funeral tea. I didn't know he was there. I bumped into him as I was leaving. This is his daughter, Amy. Isn't she a bonny lass?' Gladys tried to change the conversation as she watched Ethan's daughter attempting to make sense of what her brother had just said.

'So, somebody was daft enough to marry you, then?' Fred said as he sat down at the table and looked at the father and daughter.

'It sounds as if you've not changed, Fred. Can't we let the past be? We've all grown older and moved on and, as you can see, I have a daughter now, although sadly I lost my wife the other year. As Gladys says, it was a sad coincidence that we bumped into one another.' Ethan stood and looked at the man who had always thought him not good enough for his sister.

Amy stared at Gladys and Fred. It was obvious that Fred did not like her father because he had been sweet on Gladys. Had that been before her mother, or when he was married to her? She hadn't known any of this.

Gladys noticed the worried look on Amy's face and smiled. 'Your father and I were good friends, long before your father met and married your mother. Then I met my husband, and that was that.'

'Oh, I see,' Amy replied and glanced up at her father, hoping for confirmation from him. Instead he just glared at Fred, who sat shaking his head.

'How about if we go and have a look at my cows and dairy? I've twenty cows in my shippon – they are all shorthorns and good milkers. They all have names, and I milk them twice a day.' Gladys opened the back door to her yard, which was now a farmyard. Ethan could see that the two outhouses had been extended into a long barn, the shippon, and in the corner of the yard was a muck-midden from the cows' daily waste. 'It does get a bit fragrant out here in summer, but the muck is collected weekly by a market gardener from the Wirral. He pays me for it, so it's a good arrangement, and we both gain from my old girls.'

Gladys walked across the clean yard to the shippon. 'Here they are, my girls. They all have their own stalls or boskins, as I call them, and they are all quite content.' She patted some of the cows on their backsides. 'There's my faithful Dobbin over there in the corner. He's my fell pony from home, and he hitches up to the milk float morning and evening when we deliver the milk to the local streets.' Gladys looked at Ethan and Amy and smiled. 'A farm in a city – that's what we are.'

Amy looked around her. The smell and the sight reminded her of her grandfather's shippon, especially the smell of the hay, which she had missed for so long.

'You've got everything here, Gladys. How many folk buy your milk?' Ethan looked around at the white-washed walls, and at the brush and shovel that kept the gangways clear. It was like any farmer's shippon in the Dales, except that, like she said, it was in the centre of Liverpool.

'Around a hundred or more. I've never actually counted. I supply around twenty streets around here. We cow-keepers have our own patches, and we respect each other. Richard Harper from Sedbergh is a few streets the other way from here. We keep in touch with one another, because we are all originally from the same area. We are all competitive as well, and have organized our own show for the best milker and fat cow. I make butter with the leftover milk – over there in the dairy. That sells really well, because my customers know that it has just the right amount of salt in it to make it tasty, and keeps a little longer than the grocer's.' Gladys beamed with pride at her inside herd; she had no intention of returning home to Garsdale. Now that she had lost her uncaring husband, she would stay and make her own way in the world, if she could, although she felt pressured by her brother to sell and move on.

'But how are you going to manage all this on your own, or has Fred been living here too?' Ethan asked, knowing how long it took to milk a cow, without counting how long it would take to supply twenty streets of households.

'Oh, he's been telling me to sell up. He's only been with me this last week – he's going home at the end of next week. I'll be glad to see the back of him, as all he has done is moan. I'll find somebody to help me. I can always learn a young lad how to milk and to take Dobbin out on delivery, but I'd have preferred to keep to my own ways, if you know what I mean.'

Ethan looked at Amy as she stroked the mane of the

small but strong pony. She was back in an environment that she was happy with, he thought, as he heard her whispering in the pony's ear.

'Would you sell your business to me? It's what I'm in Liverpool for. My lass misses the open fields of Dent, and this is the nearest thing that I'll get to it, if I am to encourage her to stay with me here in Liverpool,' Ethan asked and then wondered if he'd acted hastily. But he knew how to milk a cow, Amy had made butter with her grandmother and, between them, they could sell the milk up and down the streets of Liverpool.

Gladys stared at Ethan. She hadn't thought he would be interested in cowkeeping, as he'd never been a farmer in the past. 'I don't know, Ethan. I don't even know how much the whole thing is worth. I've put my heart into this over the years – it gave me somewhere to escape to when Ted was in a mood. I'll think about it. Can I let you know? She smiled. 'Don't say anything in front of Fred, because he will think I've planned this or will make me sell to you at a top price, and I need time to think about your offer. I just need to work out if I could cope on my own, once he's returned to Garsdale.'

'No, I'll not say anything. It'll give us both time to mull things over. I might have been hasty, but it seems like a good idea for us all.' Ethan watched as Amy came over from stroking the pony.

'What's a good idea for us all?' Amy asked, curious about what her father and Gladys had been talking quietly about.

'Gladys is thinking of selling this dairy, and I'm

wondering if we should be buying it from her. But nothing's been settled yet, so you keep quiet.' Ethan put his finger to his lips as he noticed Fred standing at the kitchen door watching them.

'Right, I'll not say a thing.' Amy glanced quickly at Fred. She didn't know him, but if her father didn't like him, then she didn't, either.

The visit was soon over. Ethan wasn't going to stay long, with Fred listening in to every word, but on his way back to their rooms he had a spring in his step and whistled as he walked next to his daughter.

'Father, can I ask you something?' Amy caught her breath, wondering if she should ask the next bit of her question.

'Depends what it is.' Ethan looked across at his daughter and waited for what he knew she was going to ask.

'Did you court Gladys Lund, Father? It's just that I was thinking about what her brother said, and he really doesn't like you.' Amy waited, hoping she hadn't stepped out of line in asking her father such a question.

'Aye, I did – long before I met your mother. We courted one another all one summer, until Ted Lund came along with his money and farming background. And then Gladys's father and brothers decided I wasn't good enough for her. It seems Fred still thinks that way. That's why I told you not to shout about it,' Ethan replied as they walked along.

'But you'll not be marrying her. You'll only be buying the dairy and cows, so he shouldn't mind you doing that.'

Amy tried to get to grips with the thought of her father courting somebody other than her mother.

'That will not make any difference to Fred. He hates my guts.' Ethan stopped at the boarding-house steps. 'What are you going to do now? It looks like rain, so I'm going to my room to have a think about whether I should buy Gladys's dairy, although I don't think she really wants to sell it.'

'I'm coming in, too. I think I'll write to Grandma and Grandad, if you don't mind; and to Joshua – I haven't written to him for so long, he'll wonder what's happened to me, and we used to be such good friends. Can I mention in my letter that we have looked around a dairy and are thinking of buying it? I needn't mention whose it is, if you don't want me to.'

'You can say that, but don't mention that it belongs to Gladys, else your grandparents will jump to conclusions, like the rest. So you still think of Joshua Middleton, do you? He'll be grown-up now and helping his father farm.' Ethan smiled at Amy. She never forgot anybody and was always faithful to those whom she made her friends, just like her mother.

'Yes, Joshua and I were good friends and I'd like to see him, to find out what he looks like now.' Amy smiled, remembering the day they had sat on the top of Rise Hill, eating the sweet wild strawberries that grew there and watching the steam trains disappearing into the tunnel below them. They had both been only ten back then, but they had made a pledge always to be there for one another, which they had sealed with an innocent kiss. Joshua would always have a place in her heart. He was her first love, and the thought of her father courting Gladys before her mother had made Amy think of him.

'He'll not be flash, like that Percy in here – he's a right townie.' Ethan grinned. 'He wants to know the far end of a fart and where it's gone to, sneaking about and grinning at you. But try not to encourage either of them.'

'Percy doesn't grin at me. He's just being pleasant,' Amy retorted.

'Aye, well, keep it that way. I wouldn't want him knowing you any more than that,' Ethan growled as they made their way up to their rooms.

'Father, I don't know what you mean!' Amy said, pretending to sound shocked.

'Tha does. I remember when I was sixteen and I had looks. Trouble was, I knew nowt. Don't encourage Percy, that's all I'm saying. There will be plenty of lads once you are old enough – and you are not old enough yet, believe me. Your mother would have told you all this. I'm not as good as she would have been.' Ethan opened the door to his bedroom, took off his jacket and hung up his flat cap.

'She did. She told me things like that, so don't worry. I know what you are trying to say.' Amy felt awkward; things like that were always skirted around at the best of times, but when her father was broaching the subject of sex, she was totally embarrassed.

'Aye, well, I'll say no more. Now leave me to fathom out how much I should offer Gladys for her dairy, while you write your letter back home.'

*

Amy sat on a chair with a pen and a bottle of ink, and a blank piece of paper in front of her, as she wondered what to write. She didn't want to hurt her grandparents by saying that she would rather stay in Liverpool, with all its shops. Now that her father was going to buy a dairy, she would have the best of both worlds and would be able to work for him, looking after the cows, just as she would have been doing if she lived at home in the Dales.

Grosvenor House
Liverpool

Dear Nanna and Grandad,

We are now in Liverpool at the address above and will be here for a while yet, I think. It's a boarding house and we have the top two bedrooms. It's very clean and the meals are quite good, although the landlady is very strict. Her son Percy, who looks a little older than me, is pleasant enough and even he calls his mother a dragon! Which makes me laugh.

Now for my big news. Father has found a dairy that is up for sale, so we might be buying that. I'm quite excited at the thought of having our own cows in Liverpool and supplying milk to all the streets. You never would have dreamed of my father doing that, would you, Grandad?

Father also let me go shopping with my own money the other day. I spoilt myself something terrible, buying all sorts. I bought three outfits,

Nanna, all ready-made for me, that look and fit me perfectly.

I miss the Klondike, though it was so remote and wild, and I miss Mrs Black – she was very kind to me when Mother passed away. It broke my heart to leave my mother buried there, but she is buried in a lovely place, so don't you two worry. The graveyard is high on a hill and looks down upon Dawson City and the surrounding countryside. There are wolves and buffaloes that wander the prairie nearby, and the mountains reach so high you'd think they were touching the sky.

Perhaps, when we are settled properly, I will make my mind up whether to return to you both, and I know that you would like me to return to you. I do miss you both and I often think of you and my old home.

Is Joshua alright? I was going to write to him, but my father gave me a lecture about not being too forward with boys. If you could pass on my love to him, or perhaps that should be my regards, I'd be grateful. Tell him I'm asking about him.

I love you, Nanna and Grandad. I often think of you both and I hope to see you in a while.

Your loving granddaughter,

Amy xx

Amy read the letter through, then folded it and put it in the envelope to place in the postbox in the hallway. She'd have to find Mrs Mounsey or Percy and buy a stamp from them, in order to send it on its way. She walked into her father's room. He was busy writing at his own table.

'Can I have a penny to post this letter to Dent, please, Father?' Amy waited at his side patiently.

'Just the one? I thought you were going to write to that Middleton lad as well as your grandparents?' Ethan said, reaching inside his pocket for some money for Amy and noticing the address on the envelope.

'I thought better of it. I might never see Joshua again, and he'll probably have forgotten me anyway.' Amy sighed.

'Aye, he might have done. You've been away from Dent a while now, and he'll have got on with his own life. His father will have him farming and have his eye on a good farmer's lass, if I know the folk up there. Just like you have your own life to lead now.' Ethan passed Amy the money and watched disappointment come over her face.

'You are right, although we were only childhood friends. We have both grown up. I'll go down and post this in the letter box downstairs and perhaps sit in the lounge for a while. There's usually a newspaper to read in there, and I like to watch the people passing by. Even though it's raining quite hard now, the street will still be busy. Do you think that you can afford the dairy?' Amy looked down at the figures her father had been working out on his piece of paper.

'It depends what Gladys asks for it. We'll see.' Ethan returned to his accounts as Amy left him to his thoughts, which weren't solely about the business, but also about

Gladys, who had once held his heart for quite a while. That was, until he met Grace and experienced deep and true love, and then Gladys had been placed at the back of his thoughts. However, now she was back, and if he could rekindle the feelings they had for one another once, then perhaps he could have her love back again and the business. That would suit them both, if Gladys was willing to sell and still had feelings for him.

Amy stood in the lobby with her letter in her hand. She had rung the bell that usually brought Mrs Mounsey out of her living quarters, but this time she had not appeared. She was about to give up on the purchase of a stamp when Percy appeared.

'Sorry. I was reading my book and I wanted to finish the paragraph. What do you want? Is everything alright?' Percy smiled at the girl who had taken his eye.

'I need a stamp, please. And can I put this in the post-box – has the post gone for today?' Amy watched as Percy opened the drawer in the table, which seemed to hold anything that the tenants might require.

'Yes, you can still send it this afternoon. I usually take everything to the post office around four. That'll be a penny, please. Are you writing to your beau then, telling him where you are?' Percy tried to read the address on Amy's letter as she stuck the stamp to it.

'That would be telling.' She grinned, posting the letter before he could see it. 'Do you think I have a beau? If I have, he's not to be seen here, so I must have left him behind in the Klondike,' she teased.

'Then more fool him, for letting you out of his sight,' Percy said and looked Amy up and down.

Amy smiled and decided to go back to her room and keep her father company. Percy was not her cup of tea; he was of weedy build, pallid in colour and too forward for her liking. Her father needn't worry about her encouraging him. She had no intention of doing so, even though she had kept him guessing as to whether or not she was courting yet.

Percy emptied the postbox and looked purposely at Amy's letter, before taking the mail to the post office. So her letter wasn't for a boyfriend, by the look of it. Perhaps there was hope that she might take a fancy to him. Time would tell.

11

The postman pushed his bike up the station hill, stopping every few yards to catch his breath. Of all the days for a letter to arrive for the Oversbys, it would be today, he thought, as the wind blew in his face and the rain pelted down on him. It was rare that they got a letter, especially from Liverpool, so it must be important. Before the last push, he stopped on Dent's station bridge. It boasted of being the highest station in mainline Britain, and Edmund the postman could easily verify that, as he looked down on the line and watched as an engine followed the curve around the fellside over Dent Head viaduct and then Artengill viaduct to pull into the station, spilling all its passengers out onto the hillside.

Those passengers unused to travelling the line stood wondering where Dent village was, not realizing it was two miles further down the dale and that they would either have to walk there or take the donkey-cart that usually met the passenger train. Edmund stood until the train was ready to set off again and was about to cover him with steam and soot from its chimney if he did not move. Then he continued a few yards further along the Coal Road that led to Garsdale. He stepped over the gully by the roadside that was beginning to fill with water, to the field gate that led to the home of the Oversbys at Gill Head, propping his bike up beside the limestone wall. As he knocked on the door, he could see that the rowan tree that grew outside the house was losing its leaves in a battle with the wind.

'Edmund, you must be wet through, coming up to us on a day like this. Whatever it is, it could have waited.' Ivy Oversby opened the door to the drenched postman and bade him enter the kitchen, to dry off and deliver whatever he had for them.

'You've got a letter, and I know you've been waiting for one from that Ethan or Amy, and it looks like a woman's handwriting from Liverpool, if I know the postmark.' There was nothing that evaded Edmund Irving's scrutiny; he knew exactly who wrote to whom, and who was where.

'Liverpool! Thank the Lord – it will be from Amy. She said she would write as soon as they were safely back in this country, when she last sent a letter from the Klondike. Which is a lot more than Ethan ever does. We hardly ever hear from him. If it wasn't for Amy, we would have lost them completely. I'm sure she is the one who makes her father write to us.' Ivy held the letter and smiled. She could at least trust Amy, who always kept her word.

'Are you going to open it then, woman, or are you

going to look at it?' George knocked the ash from his pipe into the fire burning in the grate and turned to the postman. 'You might as well sit down and have a warm-up, Edmund. You'll no doubt want to know the news, just like us.' He smiled to himself, knowing that Edmund knew all the Dales business and was the main source of folk's news, as well as being the postie.

Edmund didn't need any encouragement to have a warm-up next to the fire and hear the news from young Amy Postlethwaite, who had been brave enough to survive the wilds of America. So he took his satchel from his shoulders and sat down, enthralled to hear the contents, as Ivy read word-by-word the letter that Amy had penned.

'Well, at least they are back in the country, although I wish they were back here.' Ivy wiped a tear away from her eye as she finished the last line and folded the letter.

'Ethan buying a dairy! I've heard it all now. It'll not last – it'll be too much like hard work.' George sat back and thought about it.

'Amy's missing the Klondike,' Ivy said. 'Or should I say her mother, that's buried there. A father never suffices instead of a mother.'

'Is that what you think? Her father might not, but I'd do my best,' George said. And then, with a glint in his eye, he turned and looked at the nosy postman. 'Edmund, now you've heard our news, perhaps you could be of use to us? If I change this farm's name, do I have to tell anybody, like the Post Office?

'Nay, I don't think so. Anyway, it's always me that

brings your post and I know who you are. Why do you ask that?' Edmund enquired.

'I've got a liking to change the farm's name from Gill Head to Klondike, to remember our lass by. Then folk will always wonder why a farm up the Dales is called "Klondike" and Grace's name will never be forgotten when they tell the tale to one another.' George puffed on his pipe and thought about the contents of the letter Amy had written.

'It sounds alright by me. I'll know where to go to.' Edmund nodded his head and lifted his satchel back onto his shoulder. He'd heard what he wanted to, so he'd be on his way and tell the rest of the dale the Oversbys' good news.

'Amy would like that. It might get her to come back to us, before the shops and bright lights turn her head. She's still sweet on Joshua Middleton, she's not forgotten him, although it sounds as if her father is curbing her feelings towards him. Joshua asks about Amy nearly every day when he checks his father's sheep in the fields next door.' Ivy smiled. 'She'll be at the age when lads will start to look at her.'

'I'll tell Joshua that she's asking after him – even sending her love, by the sound of it.' Edmund chuckled. 'The Middletons are my next port of call and they always make me a brew.'

'Aye, you do that. And make sure you give Joshua her new address: Grosvenor House, Harrington Street, Liverpool. If he starts writing to her, it might encourage Amy to come home where she belongs, before she's trudged off somewhere else, because her father's no dairyman. It's too much like hard work. It'll never last.'

'Right, leave it with me. There's nowt I like better than playing Cupid.' Edmund winked as he opened the door to the weather. 'And aye, I think "Klondike" suits this place – it's just as wild, on a day like today.'

He disappeared on the rest of his round, leaving Ivy and George discussing their granddaughter's letter and what it meant to them.

'I don't know, the milk nowadays keeps getting later and later, and it is Mrs Lund herself delivering it. She still owes me money as well. I'll not be forgetting, if she thinks I will – I've got to make a living as well as her,' Mrs Mounsey moaned to her son Percy as she filled the milk jugs up for the breakfast table, where everyone was sitting around waiting.

'It's here now, Mother. I'll tell them it's not your fault.' Percy took the filled jugs into the dining room and sighed. His mother had no sympathy when it came to someone falling on hard times. Probably because she had brought up her family on her own, after her husband died young from pneumonia. Percy made his way into the dining room, where everyone looked with relief at the sight of the milk to put into their first cup of tea in the morning.

'Sorry, everyone. Mother sends her apologies for the wait, but our dairy recently lost the main man there, and things are a bit slow since his death.' Percy placed the jugs on the table and left the tenants discussing how inconsiderate the milkman was to make their milk late by his death.

'I think we'll have a walk up to see Gladys,' Ethan whispered to Amy. 'She's struggling to deliver, so that means Fred must have gone home. She was never that strong when she was younger, and she'll be finding it hard work running the dairy on her own. Her mother used to always cosset her, but never told me what exactly was wrong with her, apart from that her health was not as expected. Now's the time to make an offer.'

'Are you still determined to go through with this, Father? It's just that you have never shown a liking for farming in the past, and cowkeeping is exactly that.' Amy looked at her father. She'd had time to mull over his idea, since the initial visit to Lund's dairy, and no matter how she tried, she couldn't see her father milking cows and making butter.

'Aye, it'll make us money and it's a job for you – one that you'll like, seeing as you helped your grandfather a lot when we were in Dent.' Ethan stirred his tea, not noticing the look of disappointment on Amy's face. Since she had been in Liverpool she'd noticed how other people lived, and she would rather have worked in one of the shops on Lord Street and not have to get her hands dirty any more. However, whatever her father said, she had to do; she'd do it for the meantime.

Gladys wiped her hair out of her eyes and looked around her. The cows needed mucking out, the butter needed churning and when she'd done that, she would have to milk the cows again for the evening delivery around the streets. She was tired and tearful. Although she wanted to be her own boss, she knew she couldn't be, as she didn't have the strength. Fred, her brother, had gone back home in a bad mood after she told him that she would not be returning with him, and that she was going to try to run the dairy herself. But now she was beginning to regret it.

She leaned on her muck-fork and thought about Ethan Postlethwaite. She'd nearly asked to see him when she delivered milk to Grosvenor House, but the sharp-tongued Mrs Mounsey had complained so badly about the lateness of the milk. She slapped one of her cows on its backside now and shook her head, trying to sort her thoughts. She didn't want to sell her herd and dairy to Ethan, but at the same time it would give her money to do as she wanted.

She smiled to herself. Ethan Postlethwaite was still a good-looking man and when he'd said hello to her, she'd felt her heart beat just as it did when he first looked at her. They were both too old for romance now, and he had a daughter he seemed to love dearly. Gladys found herself swearing as a cow nearly peed on her skirts and its tail caught her cheek, making her almost cry. She'd have to sell; she wasn't managing and things would only get worse. The only other option, she thought, was for her to persuade Ethan to come and work at the dairy, to see if it was what he wanted. It would also give her time to get to know him again. And, who knows, perhaps to rekindle old feelings between them. She had loved Ethan all those years ago, and perhaps now she had a second chance of making them both happy. That was the better option, she decided, as she forked the manure and sawdust bedding into her wheelbarrow to be placed in the midden in the corner of the yard, catching her breath as she did so. That was what she would do, and she would even offer Ethan the room above the dairy to stay in. His daughter, Amy, could have the spare bedroom in the house with her; she'd be more comfortable there, and the neighbours couldn't accuse Gladys of living over the brush with Ethan. Now all she needed was for Ethan and Amy to appear and still want the dairy.

Amy waited downstairs in the entry hall of Grosvenor House. Her father had decided to go up and change, before they walked up to see Gladys Lund. A suit that he had recently ordered from Hope Brothers had arrived, and he said he might as well give it an airing, seeing that he was going to visit Gladys on business. Amy had smiled to herself. Her father couldn't fool her; he was wanting to look his best for his former girlfriend. And that was exactly what he was doing as he came downstairs in a sharp city-cut suit and a new bowler hat.

Amy didn't know how she felt about her father's old love. She struggled with the thought of anybody ever being in his arms, other than her mother. Plus Gladys Lund was completely different from her mother; she said it like it was – unlike quiet, respectful Grace. However, none of that would matter if they bought the dairy and Gladys went on her way, leaving them to it.

'Don't you look dapper? A right man of the city. You've even tidied your sideburns.' Amy stared at her father. He looked like one of the gamblers they had left behind at Skagway: a different man altogether from the one who had been standing in front of her an hour ago.

'I thought it was time I tidied myself up. After all, you went shopping and now look the part. In fact you look far too old in the clothes you bought. I've seen the heads you turn when we walk together down the street. Your mother would have something to say about it.' Ethan regarded himself in the hallway mirror, and admired the cut of the suit and his father's pocket watch and Albert chain hanging from his waistcoat. He looked quite the gent.

'Mother probably would have something to say about the pair of us. She liked us to look tidy, but never gaudy. Will Mrs Lund like the new you?' Amy tried to hide the smirk. It was obvious her father was going courting, even if he wouldn't admit it.

'I don't know why you say that – she's nothing to do with it. It is only business, like I said. I'm not dressing to impress Mrs Lund in that way, just to show her that I do have money to buy her property, and that I am what I say I am. After all, she knew me when I was a navvy on the railway, and you can't get rougher-looking than that.' Ethan gave himself a final glance in the mirror, content with what he saw, and took Amy's arm. 'Right, let us see if she will sell to us, or at least come to an understanding about the business.'

Amy took her father's arm. They both looked like

they had never done a day's work in their life, but that would all change if they were to run a dairy. The tight hobble skirt would be of no use to her when mucking out and milking cows. She would have to wear more practical clothes, and so would her father. So he'd not always be impressing his old flame Gladys, she thought, as they walked up the cobbled street to the dairy on the corner of Deane Street.

'Oh, Ethan, you caught me by surprise, I wasn't expecting anyone today.' Gladys came to the door looking as if she had been pulled through a hedge backwards and was hesitant to let in her visitors.

'I thought I'd come up and see if you'd come to a decision about selling your business. I hear that you are struggling, since Fred left,' Ethan said as he stepped forward into the house, noticing that the fire had not been lit, even though it was mid-autumn and the wind was blowing bitterly down the streets.

'Who's said that? Let me guess: old bag Mounsey. Just because I've been late with the milk delivery recently doesn't mean I'm struggling. It's simply getting used to things, now I've no man to help me.' Gladys caught a piece of her long hair, which was hanging over her brow, and tugged it back into place as she gazed around her, knowing that her house was in a mess. 'It'll take a while. I don't think I want to sell, so you might have wasted your time.'

'You might not want to sell, Gladys, but you look as if you could do with a hand about the place. You'll not have to let things slip with your milk supply, else you'll lose customers or even have the authorities hounding you. Why don't we go back home, change into some work clothes and help you out?' Ethan looked at Amy and then turned back to Gladys. 'It's no skin off our noses to help you out. And if you do decide to sell, then I'll have a taste of what I'm in for, as well?' Ethan said and caught the disappointment on Amy's face. He had promised her afternoon tea in one of the fancy cafes, but instead he was lining her up to work.

'Would you do that for me? You shouldn't feel beholden to me just because we've known each other in the past.' Gladys slumped in her chair and smiled wanly at Amy and Ethan. It would be good to have him helping her, and it played into her hands. Perhaps if he came to help at first, she would tempt him back into her arms, where he always should have been.

12

Ethan and Amy had been going back and forth to the dairy for a fortnight, helping Gladys milk in the morning and deliver in the evening. Amy had taken over the making of the butter and cleaning the dairy, things she had done often with her mother and grandmother, churning the creamy milk in an up-and-over wooden churn until her arm ached, then adding a good handful of salt, before patting the butter into half-pound bricks and wrapping it in greaseproof paper, to be sold on the milk float by her father and Gladys.

Gladys had shown Ethan the streets she delivered to, with her trusty pony and float, loaded with large oval churns that the customers came to with their milk jugs, to fill at a price of thruppence ha'penny a quart. Ethan shouted loudly that the milk was on their street and waited for all the housewives to come out of their terraced houses. Many a mile was walked each morning and night, with a brief respite in the afternoon when all three of them took time to themselves. Deliveries of ration – the feed for the cows – and the disposal of the manure filled most days, and Ethan was starting to realize that cowkeeping in Liverpool was not easy work, as he sat back at the kitchen table with a mug of tea in his hand, looking around him.

'Mrs Mounsey wasn't so suited with us last night. We went to the dinner table before changing, because we hadn't time. She complained that we smelt of cow muck and that the other renters were starting to complain about us. I wouldn't mind, but neither Amy nor I has sat and had breakfast with them for the last few weeks. And if they can't put up with the smell of honest toil, I pity them,' Ethan grumbled and looked across at Gladys. 'You'd never have managed to run this place on your own. No wonder Ted went to an early grave.'

'He died from pneumonia. The cowshed gets that hot, he got to sweating, and then he would go out on the streets of a frosty morning and catch a chill. It damaged his lungs over the years, he couldn't fight off the flu when he caught it. You'll need to wrap up warm when delivering this winter. I don't want to lose you the same way,' Gladys said, observing the man she was growing to love more each day.

'Who says I'll be staying that long, Gladys Metcalfe? I might have had enough.' Ethan smiled at her and winked at Amy.

'I'm not a Metcalfe any more, I'm a Lund. And you can suit yourself what you do – I'll not tie you down,' Gladys said sharply, holding back the tears, as she thought Ethan was going to say that he was planning to be off, fed up with all the work and no play.

'Now, Gladys, you'd never tie me and our Amy down. We'd soon be off if we didn't want to be here. However, I was going to suggest – if you ladies are in agreement – that we move in. I could sleep next door with the hay, above the dairy, and then there's no funny business; and Amy could sleep in your spare bedroom.' Ethan looked at the surprise on Amy's face, and at the look of relief on Gladys's. 'We must nearly have run out of money by now at the Grosvenor, so it's as good a time as any to leave, and we might as well be living here, as we are never away.'

'So are you going to buy here, Father? Then it will be ours,' Amy asked, thinking if he was suggesting that, he was about to make an offer.

'Nay, not yet, if Gladys here doesn't mind. Besides, she loves this bloody place. I couldn't take it off her.' Ethan smiled at Gladys, knowing full well that she knew what his game was.

'It makes sense. You might as well live here, as you say. As long as you sleep next door, I don't mind, and Amy can have the spare bedroom. It's all nicely decorated and it's warm, because it is over the kitchen.' Gladys sighed. 'It would be good to think I have a man staying on the premises of a night. There's plenty of ruffians looking for an opportunity to thieve or do mischief on these streets when it's dark. What do you think, Amy? It's your life as well.'

'It would be more like a home. At the moment I feel we are not wanted by the Mounseys. Even Percy has stopped talking to me, although that is probably because I've given him the cold shoulder of late.'

'I wouldn't fret over that. You know what I think of him,' Ethan mumbled. 'Right, we will move in at the end of the week. It will be for the best. We can't have bankers and the like sitting with folk like us. We only make the world go round, while they sit in their offices counting our money.'

Amy packed her clothes into her bag. She would never wear her fancy skirt again: what a waste of money, she thought. The dresses were fine, they were nice and warm and practical, but her skirt was no good for a milkmaid. She looked at her features in the mirror with disdain. She'd never get a beau as a common old milkmaid. Not that she wanted one yet, but it would be nice for a boy to notice her, for once – other than Percy, whom she had no desire for whatsoever.

'Are you ready?' her father said as he entered her bedroom.

'Yes, I'm ready. I'm just a little worried that if we get some post from home, it will not be passed on. Grandma and Grandad haven't written back yet, and I gave them this address.' Amy picked her bag up and gave her room a last look round.

'I'll tell them downstairs to pass on to us whatever comes in the post. They should be able to do that – we'll be delivering milk here every morning and evening. It's not like your grandparents not to write back straight away. They will have been waiting for your letter, if I know them, and will have penned a reply at once.' Ethan looked worried.

'I know. I've been thinking that. I'm sure there will be a good reason, and a letter will be on its way. I'm going to miss it here. It was the most comfortable place I've lived in, always nice and clean, and we have been well fed, even if Mrs Mounsey is an old bat.' Amy gave a sigh.

'Aye, well, it's back down to Earth now. We couldn't have stayed here forever – you know that. It was only meant to be a stopgap. We'll be alright with Gladys, although I don't think she will ever sell to me. My money is safe in the bank, and we have a roof over our heads and our bellies full, and she's not a bad soul.' Ethan took Amy's bag from her hand and smiled. 'It doesn't hurt to keep your feet on the ground. Now, let's go. It's no good looking back; you've all your life ahead of you.' He walked down the stairs with Amy not far behind him, stopping to talk to Mrs Mounsey and make sure all was in order, before he left her for their new home.

'Here's your keys, Mrs Mounsey, and thank you for your hospitality. Have I any change from what I gave you when I first came, as we are going a little sooner than expected?' Ethan looked at the landlady, knowing that he had not spent all the money he had given her, and she should still have some left, if she was honest.

'You have indeed, Mr Postlethwaite. And here it is, along with an invoice that I have marked as paid and settled. The post has just delivered two letters for your daughter this morning. I hope that you'll ensure that in future they go to your new address.' Mrs Mounsey passed Ethan his change and the letters, and gave him a dry smile as he thanked her and picked up his bags.

'We will indeed, Mrs Mounsey. Thank you once more,' Ethan replied.

'Mr Postlethwaite, if you are going to live with Mrs Lund, can you please remind her that she still owes me for her husband's funeral tea. It's been quite a while now, and I could do with the money,' she said sharply.

'I'll do better than that, as we can't have you going without. How much does she owe you? I'll settle her bill.' Ethan put the bags back down and reached into his pocket.

'I was only saying. I didn't expect you to pay for her,' Mrs Mounsey replied as she looked into her debtors' book. 'She owes me two pounds, sixteen shillings and thruppence ha'penny.'

'Then here's three quid. Unlike you, I'm not down to a ha'penny here and there, and I'll not have her being talked about for her debt.' Ethan placed three pounds in the landlady's hand and stared at her.

'It'll not be her debt that'll be talked about, as my business is kept within these walls. However, you going to live with her so soon after she's buried her husband is another matter.' Mrs Mounsey pulled a poker face and placed the notes in her money box.

'My father's not living with Mrs Lund. He is to live next door, above the dairy,' Amy intervened sharply. 'Stop gossiping about us.'

'It makes no matter. I will not be buying my milk from her any more. Good day.' Mrs Mounsey bustled off into her back room.

'She's an old bag!' Amy said crossly.

'She's only saying what folk will think. However, we know different. I tell you, these letters look as if they've been here longer than just this morning. I bet she's had them here more than a week. It's a good job we are leaving. Mrs Mounsey and I were heading towards having words, so I'm glad that's the back of her, no matter what she thinks of us. Here, the letters are both for you. I'm out of favour with your grandparents as well, it would seem.'

Ethan passed both letters to Amy as they walked out of the boarding house, up the streets to Gladys and the dairy, ready for the evening milking.

'Now, this room isn't so bad, is it? I've always kept it fairly nice. I thought it would be a room for my own daughter, but we were never blessed with children. You treat this house like your own. I'm grateful to you and your father for coming to my aid.' Gladys stood in the doorway and watched Amy as she sat on the edge of her new bed and looked around her at the sparsely furnished room.

'Thank you. I'll try and earn my keep until we find somewhere else to live, and you are back on your feet.' Amy smiled. She didn't know what it was, but she could not warm to Gladys, no matter what good words her father said about her.

'Aye, well, there's plenty for you to do. We are never quiet. I'm expecting a delivery of sawdust from the joiner's yard tomorrow. The lad usually comes on a Thursday. I don't give him much time, and he's a cocky little bugger. I don't know why Henry Morphet keeps him on. If he comes when your father is out with the milk and I'm washing down the cows, you can deal with him, if you want – save me biting my tongue.' Gladys looked at Amy. She was glad she had Ethan staying, but she had never really wanted his daughter as well, as she could get in the way of any romance that might yet bloom.

'I'll do that. He can unload the sawdust for the cows' bedding and then be on his way. I can put up with whatever he says – he can't be that bad.' Amy wanted to read the letters that were in her pocket in the privacy of her own room and unpack her clothes, but not while Gladys was there.

'That's what he'll do, while telling you how smart he is and that he could be a lot better than a joiner's apprentice, clever little bugger. Anyway, I'll go and see if your father's alright next door. At least we will be altogether of an evening and at mealtimes, and he's not far from you, just the other side of the wall; you'll probably hear him snoring of a night.'

Gladys smiled and left Amy, who quickly fished the letters out of her pocket. One was definitely from her grandparents, but she didn't recognize the sprawling handwriting on the other as she tore into it. A thousand memories of home flitted threw her mind as she read the few lines that Joshua Middleton had written to her, in barely legible handwriting. He told her that all was well, that he was farming with his father and he'd just let the tup out with his ewes. Amy smiled, knowing that all he had ever thought about was farming with his father. And now he was nearly a grown man and doing exactly that.

Joshua told her how he'd often walked down the dale and stood on the bridge at Lea Gate and looked up at her old home, and had missed her when he'd gathered the sheep in the fell above her home. But it was the last line of the letter that caught her heart and made a tear come to her eye as she read:

> *Do you remember the strawberries we picked together on Rise Hill tunnel? Well, since you have been gone, they have not been half as sweet.*
>
> *Your friend always,*
> *Joshua*

Amy blew her nose and held the letter in her hand. She missed Joshua, she missed home and, most of all, she missed her mother. Her father might not think she had seen what was going on, but she had. An old flame had been lit in front of her eyes and she could tell that, given time, Gladys would take the place of her mother. It would be a substitute that Amy would not welcome. Gladys was harder than her mother, and she knew that Gladys would never totally welcome her, no matter how she tried to show her love.

Next, she opened the letter that she knew was from her grandparents, only to find a piece of white heather fall out of it. She knew exactly where that had been picked as soon as she saw it. High above Stone House viaduct was the only place that white heather grew. She remembered that she had always brought it home for her mother at this time of year. She smelt it and placed it on the table next to her bed, then read the letter with all the news of the dale in its sheets, the love spelled out in every word and the disbelief that her father was actually thinking of buying a business that meant hard work. Finally she read that her grandparents were renaming the old farm "Klondike", both for her when she finally came back to them and in memory of her mother.

Amy lay back on her new bed and hugged the pillow near her. She loved her grandparents, and they would not be happy with what her father was up to. Perhaps it would be best if she told them in her next letter that he'd bought the dairy, and didn't mention Gladys Lund. She didn't want to give them cause to worry. One day she would return to them, with her father's blessing or without.

'They'll be the laughing stock of Dentdale, calling the farm "Klondike",' Ethan scoffed as Amy told her father the news when he sat down to eat his breakfast after delivering the morning's milk. 'Folk won't even know where the Klondike is in a few more years, and they'll look like fools.'

'They called it that in memory of my mother, and I think it's lovely. Besides, it is wild and on its own up there, just like the Klondike.' Amy stood her ground.

'I suppose they are asking you to go home to them, and are not saying a good word about me. I hope you told them that you want for nothing, and that we are doing very nicely. Bloody hypocrites! They were the first ones to tell me not to go and make my fortune in the Klondike, and now they call their farm after it.' Ethan was tired from his milk round. He'd been up since four in the morning, and now he was listening to Amy full of the news that her grandparents had fed her, in an attempt to lure her back home.

'I always say we are doing well. Why should I worry them? We are doing alright, so I'm not lying.' Amy looked at her father as he ate his porridge. He never did like her getting letters from her grandparents, but at the same time he knew it made her happy, so he put up with it. 'I'll go and finish churning the butter. You'll be having a doss after doing the round, I suppose, while Gladys and I finish off cleaning the dairy. And then I've to see to the sawdust delivery from the joiners – Gladys asked me last night.'

Amy turned for the door to the back yard and then looked at her father. When they were at the boarding house he had looked and acted like a real gent, but now he had returned to his usual self, apart from when Gladys was about, and then he'd smile and flirt, no matter how tired he was. The truth was that her grandparents were, unfortunately, right in what they had written in her letter: her father did not like work and he'd probably tire of the hours needed to run the dairy. Only time would tell, she thought, as she closed the door and went to the dairy to finish churning the butter.

'Mind what you are doing when you open the gates for the lad from the joinery. Watch this one – she's an old devil, and if she thinks she can make a run out of those gates, she will.' Gladys slapped one of the roan-coloured cows as she walked past them, after letting them out in the yard for their daily exercise. 'She's got a mind of her own, has that one.' She stood next to Amy with her hands on her hips. 'Have you churned the milk: is there enough butter to supply our regulars? The milk yield has dropped a bit lately. The hay this year is not as good-quality. In fact your father said it was too green and that it shouldn't have been put into a confined space yet. There's always a danger of fire when it hasn't dried out properly and sweats and gets too hot. It's a good job he's living with it, as he can keep his eye on it.' Gladys sighed.

'Yes, there's enough. I've just got to pat the butter into shape and package it, and then it will be ready for delivery. I'll watch the cows when the sawdust comes, don't worry,' Amy replied as Gladys took off her apron and folded it over her arm. She was a hard worker; she had milked all the cows before her father was even awake and up, and had cleaned out the shippon, buckets and utensils and was now ready for a break. Amy had made breakfast and a pie for dinner, as well as tidying the house, before churning the milk. Everyone in the new household was playing to their own strengths and making sure that all ran smoothly. It was back to being a good business, for the time being, and would support all of them if they all continued to work as they did.

'I'll go and spend a few minutes with your father. Don't take any cheek from that Billy O'Hara when he delivers the sawdust. He'll give you some, I know, as he's full of blarney, telling his tales,' Gladys said and looked at Amy. 'He's always saying what he's done and where he's going, and it's all shite.'

Amy watched as Gladys went back into the house and

decided that when Billy O'Hara came with the sawdust for the bedding, she would make him welcome, out of spite towards Gladys. She'd no right to say who Amy should welcome and talk to, whether he gave her cheek or not.

'Is my lass busy? She'll not be coming in, will she?' Ethan held Gladys in his arms and ran his hands through her hair, before kissing her with a passion.

'She's busy in the dairy, and I've told her to keep an eye on the cows and see to the lad that comes with the sawdust. We are alright for a short while.' Gladys returned Ethan's advances and ran her hands down his neck to his chest, unbuttoning his striped twill shirt and kissing his neck.

'Not here, Glad. Amy might come in and catch us at it,' Ethan whispered as he ran his hand up the inside of her leg.

'Come on then, let's go upstairs. I've heard Billy and his horse and cart arriving at the gate. He'll keep her busy talking for a good while, rather than doing any work.' Gladys pushed Ethan's hand down from her skirts and took firm hold of it, pulling on his arm to join her upstairs. 'I've waited for this for so long,' she whispered as he followed her to her bedroom and started to undress. 'We both have, I think – this was meant to be.' She lay on the bed and waited for Ethan to make love to her, as he had wanted to all those years ago. 'We are together at last, and nobody is going to part us.'

*

'So who are you? Has she taken you on to help her out here?' Eighteen-year-old Billy O'Hara cursed as he tried to get his horse and cart into the back yard, which was full of doe-eyed cows looking for better pastures, then he quickly closed the yard gates before one escaped down the street. He turned to the black-haired girl who was rounding up the cows and herding them back into the shippon until he had unloaded his cart of sawdust and had left.

'I'm Amy. My father and I are living here with Mrs Lund. My father knows her from years back.' She looked at the jet-black-haired lad who stood in front of her. His eyes were as blue as forget-me-nots and he had the longest black lashes, which Amy could not help but think were wasted on a boy, as he grinned at her.

'By God, she's not wasted time finding a new replacement for her old man. She must be kinder to her fellas than she is to me,' Billy laughed.

'It's not like that. She and my father are just friends,' Amy said quickly.

'And I'm a monkey's uncle – that's what they all say.' Billy reached for his shovel to unload the wood shavings from the back of his cart and place them in their usual storage. 'Where are you from then? You are not from around here, else I'd have seen you before.' He leaned on his shovel and looked at the lass that had caught his eye.

'Well, that's a bit debatable. I was born in a place you'll probably never have heard of before, called Dent, but we have recently returned from the Yukon. My father went searching for gold, and took me and my mother with him.' Amy leaned against the wheel of his cart and looked at Billy as he stood in front of her. He had a certain swagger about him, dressed in his corduroy trousers, a tweed jacket with a striped shirt underneath and with a spotted neckerchief around his neck.

'That's where you are wrong, Miss Clever-clogs, I know where Dent is. I deliver to all the cowkeepers around the back streets of Liverpool, and most of them come from Dent, Garsdale or Sedbergh, and they never shut up about it, in their Dales twang. Now the Yukon, that's interesting. When I've saved up enough I'm going to book a passage to New York and go and make my fortune. Your father can't have made his, else he wouldn't be here looking after cows with old bag Lund.' Billy grinned and lifted his shovel and started unloading the shavings.

'He made enough. He was going to buy a business, but then he met Gladys, who had just lost her husband, and we've ended up here instead. My father knew her before he married my mother.' Amy watched as Billy easily unloaded his cart without breaking a sweat. 'Going to America is not all it promises to be. You still have to work hard for your money, and nothing is as easy as it seems.'

'I'm still willing to try it. Anything's better than delivering sawdust all my life and having Henry Morphet yelling at me if I don't do a job right. I want to be my own man, start up my own business. I'm a good joiner, if I don't have somebody looking over my shoulder all the time. I've nearly saved my fare. I want to be on my way by next summer. I've nobody and nothing to keep me here.' Billy jumped down from the cart after cleaning out the deepest corner and put up the tailgate.

'Have you no family? You can't be on your own – you must have a mother or father.' Amy watched him and wondered what sort of life he had had.

'My mother died back in Ireland, and as soon as I was old enough to look after myself, my father buggered off with another woman. One who didn't want me. So no, I've nobody to care about except myself – and the cat that keeps me company of an evening, although it's on its last legs, the scraggy old fleabag.' Billy wiped his brow with his neckerchief and grinned. 'You're a bonny lass. I suppose you are courting somebody. I couldn't have been that lucky to find somebody as bonny as you that's unattached.'

'Mrs Lund warned me that you were full of blarney, and now I know she was right – true blarney, seeing as you are Irish and all. But no, I'm not courting. I'm not that bothered about having a beau.' Amy blushed.

'Well, you can always have me as a friend. We needn't be as serious as to say we are courting. How about I come round on Sunday and pick you up, and I'll show you the sights of Liverpool. I bet you came in straight from the docks and have never been anywhere else, if you are like the rest.' Billy winked and waited for a reply.

'I don't know. My father wouldn't like that. I've walked and shopped down Lord Street anyway, so you can stop your cheek,' Amy replied.

'Sure, you look as if you shop on Lord Street.' Billy grinned, looking down at the old boots that had served Amy well when she was in the Klondike, and the worn skirts and apron that she wore when doing her work in the dairy.

'I'll show you, Billy O'Hara! I will come with you on Sunday, and I'll catch other men's eyes when you've got me by your side. I can dress just as good as the next lass in Liverpool – you'll see when you pick me up,' Amy replied quickly, then regretted her words, wondering what her father would have to say about her first walking-out with a lad that she had already been warned about.

'Right, eleven o'clock at the end of Lord Street. I daren't face your father or old bag Lund – she'll give me such a mouthful – so it'll be better there.' Billy got hold of his reins and started to turn his horse and cart round in the small yard, as Amy opened the dairy's gates.

'Eleven o'clock. I'll be there and you won't recognize me, I'll be that swanky.' Amy grinned and watched as Billy got up into the driving seat and flicked the reins across his horse's back.

'Eleven o'clock it is, and no looking at any other fellas while I'm not here.' Billy winked again and left her standing with the yard gate open, staring down the street at him.

Amy's heart fluttered in her chest. Billy O'Hara was full of blarney, she had been warned, but she couldn't resist the smooth talk and the blue eyes that looked at her with a glint in them. How she was going to explain her meeting with him on Sunday, she didn't know, but she wasn't going to miss her day out with him, no matter what.

13

'You are not going out on your own with a lad I don't know. Gladys says he's got the cheek of the devil, and we know nowt about him,' Ethan shouted angrily at Amy as she stood her ground over her insistence on spending Sunday with Billy O'Hara.

'I am going, Father. He's alright, I know he is.' Amy stood across from the kitchen table. 'You are not going to stop me. I've promised Billy and, besides, I never have any time to myself. How am I supposed to make friends when I'm forever working here at this dairy?'

'He's a wrong 'un, Ethan, she wants nothing with him. He's Irish, for a start, and even his father has nowt to do with him.' Gladys added her four pennyworth, needing Amy to do her duties in the dairy, whether it was Sunday or not.

'What does that matter? He's shown me kindness, that's all that matters,' Amy answered back and glared at Gladys. She had no right to say anything about her life, and she was not her mother. 'You'll be able to have time with my father on your own, anyway. I thought you'd want to take advantage of that, seeing as you are more than friends,' she added, sharply letting slip that she knew exactly what was going on.

'Amy, be careful what you are saying. Gladys has put a roof over your head and has fed you this last week or two. Don't say things you will regret.' Ethan looked across at Gladys as she shook her head and scowled at the lass who had come as baggage with her father. 'I'll come and meet Billy with you, and if I think he's alright, you can go with him. I'll give him the hard word that he's got to look after you, and not take advantage of your age.'

'Oh, Father, I'm not that innocent. I know what goes on between men and women. My mother told me all I needed to know when I was younger. If that's what it takes for me to be able to walk out with him, then I suppose you'll have to do it. Although I'll feel like a child when you do.'

'You are still a child, in my eyes. My daughter that I need to protect, whether you like it or not.' Ethan reached for his flat cap and pushed his chair back. 'Away, let's meet this man of yours. But if I don't like him, I'll tell him so and send him back with his tail between his legs.'

'Thank you. Don't worry, he'll not take advantage of me. I'll make sure of that,' Amy said, ignoring the sarcastic sounds coming from Gladys.

'You bloody well make sure he doesn't, else I'll have

his balls served on a plate – and I'm going to tell him that to his face,' Ethan growled as he watched his headstrong daughter walk out in her much-loved tight skirt, a shawl around her shoulders, wearing her favourite hat with cherries on the side. She was right; she was no longer a child, she was a young woman. And she had made them both understand exactly what she thought of the relationship between him and Gladys.

'By God, your father laid into me. I thought at one time he was going to punch me – he really laid down the law. I don't know if I even dare look at you,' Billy joked as they walked down Lord Street to get a hackney cab to where he had told her father he was taking her. 'Still, it was good of him to give us the brass for a cab to and from the park, and money for something to eat. I didn't expect that. It is a fair walk to Sefton Park, but I'd have shown you the sights on the way.'

Billy looked at Amy as she struggled to keep up with him in her tight skirt.

'It is perhaps a good job he did give us the brass, as we'd have taken all day with you wearing that skirt you've got on. It might be fashionable, but it's not practical.'

'I thought I'd wear it to show you that I can look as good as all these posh lasses in Liverpool. I thought that you'd like it,' Amy said as she hitched her skirt up to climb into the cab, pulled by a horse that was chomping on its bit, wanting to go.

'Sefton Park, please,' Billy said to the cabbie as he laughed at Amy showing her ankles to all the world as she fell into the back of the cab. 'It makes no difference what you wear – it's you I took a liking to, not your clothes.' Billy sat down next to her. 'It's a bit cold for a stroll around Sefton Park, but there's the warmth of the Palm House to walk around in, and we can visit the Aviary. They serve tea and cake next to the bandstand, so we can sit back and listen to some music if the band is playing.'

'Sounds lovely. I'd no idea there was all that here in Liverpool. All I've ever seen is row after row of terraced houses and the busy docks. Plus the shops – I enjoy the shops.' Amy smiled.

'We have everything here in Liverpool. We are the next biggest city to London and have just as many impressive buildings. And there are plans to build even more. It's a good city. Everyone looks after one another, but there is a lot of poverty in the back streets,' Billy said with feeling in his voice.

'I saw St George's Hall. My father pointed it out to me. It's a big city, the largest I've ever been to. I was hoping that when we returned from the Klondike we would come home via New York, but unfortunately we didn't. I've always wanted to go there. However, I like Liverpool. It's different from my home of Dent, and even from Dawson City. The folk are a lot sharper in their ways. I feel a real country bumpkin when I walk down the street,' Amy confessed.

'Well, you shouldn't because, with it being a port, it's a mixture of folk that have either always been here or, like yourselves, find themselves here because it's a port. A bit like New York. That's why I want to go there, just like you, but I want to make a new life for myself, where nobody knows me or my family. Look, we are here now. I hope the weather doesn't turn.' Billy jumped out of the cab after it had rattled its way a good distance through Liverpool's busy streets. 'May I take your hand, milady,' he joked and took Amy's hand as she stepped down from the carriage.

'I don't mind if you do.' Amy smiled as she took it, then slipped her arm through Billy's as they walked through the large iron gates into the green park and onto the paths within. The park was filled with people in their Sunday best admiring the gardens, even though the summer flowers had now died back. Billy led Amy down by the boating lake.

'We should have brought some bread for the ducks. I didn't know we were coming here.' Amy watched as the ducks and swans flocked around her feet.

'I thought of that. Here, feed them with this.' Billy pulled a paper bag out of his pocket. 'It's a handful of the horse's oats from work that I helped myself to yesterday.' He put his hand in the bag and threw the oats out to the squabbling birds at their feet, before passing the rest to Amy.

'Thank you, I love feeding the birds.' Amy threw the oats and smiled and laughed at the greedy ones squabbling, and the swans looking as if they were far too superior to argue with the likes of the ducks.

'Come on, I'll pay for a boat for us, and we'll have a row across the lake. Can you manage in that skirt?' Billy asked as he pulled on Amy's hand to get her to join him.

'Of course I can: watch me. The last time I was in a boat like this I was going down rapids, and we were all fearing for our lives on the way to the Klondike. I clung to my mother for dear life,' Amy said sadly and wiped a tear away.

'Hey, this is a happy day. I didn't mean to make you cry. We needn't go if you don't want to,' Billy said as they reached the jetty and looked at the man renting out the boats.

'No, it'll be nice to go boating. It's just me with my memories.' Amy smiled and took Billy's hand as he paid for use of the boat, then steadied it while she stepped hesitantly into it, as it rocked gently on the pond.

'We'll not stay long – it's too cold to be out on the water for long. We'll come back in the spring when the park is all green and fresh, and the trees have new leaves on them. I don't like this time of year; everything is dying back for winter, and soon all it will do is rain and snow and it will be hard to keep cheerful.' Billy grabbed the oars and looked across at Amy, who smiled at him as he pulled on the oars with a glint in his eye.

'I don't mind what time of year it is, but I must admit I do like spring, when all the life comes back to the world. I used to like watching the lambs being born with my grandfather. We'd sit behind a wall and talk to one another and watch the sheep drop the lamb, then gently nudge it and lick it into life, making sure it was strong enough to get its first feed from her.' Amy smiled and thought about her grandfather as Billy glided them across the pond. He was handsome. He had been worth falling out with her father for, and she'd be willing to stand her ground over him again, if he asked her back out.

'Why don't you go back to your grandparents? You seem to talk about them with such love – surely they'd welcome you and your father?' Billy asked as he rowed, slow and sure.

'They don't like my father. They blame him for my mother's death and think that he's lazy and likes to make easy money. Although if they knew what we went through in Dawson, they'd think differently of him.' Amy hung her head. 'I wanted to go home when we first landed in Liverpool, and I still do some days, but Father's content, when he's not tired. And I realize there's a lot more to life than open fells and sheep. I like the shops and the vibrancy here, when I get a chance to see outside the dairy's walls.'

Billy looked at Amy. He felt sorry for the lass who sat across from him, as her life had been equally as hard as his. 'Well, I'm glad you are here. I think I'm going to turn back now, and we'll go and get warm in the Palm House – it's always pleasant in there.' He stood up, rocking the boat and making him unsteady on his feet. 'Swap seats; be careful, though. Don't move suddenly, else we will end up in the brink, and then your father will have something to say to me.' He grinned as he stood balancing, while Amy shuffled over carefully to sit on the opposite plank of wood, making Billy sway as if he was going to fall overboard. Amy gasped, reaching out for his hand as he stopped himself and the boat from overturning.

'Lord, I thought we were all going to fall in then, you

idiot,' she said, looking into his blue eyes as he balanced opposite her.

'Would you have jumped in after me and saved me?' Billy chuckled.

'No, I would not. It's too cold and you can probably swim, and it's not that deep,' Amy scoffed.

'And there was me, thinking you were a caring, kind lass who actually liked me,' Billy teased.

'I do – I do like you, else I wouldn't be here, and I wouldn't have fallen out with my father over you,' Amy said quietly.

'Well, now I know we had better get back to shore. Look, it's starting to rain, so the sooner we get into that Palm House, the better.' Billy nodded in the direction of a huge glasshouse that could be seen on the other side of the park. 'We can sit in there for as long as we want. I think the bandstand and the fairy dell I was going to take you to are not on today, but we can always come back another time.'

He glanced across at Amy. She looked beautiful, sitting there in the boat, with her long black hair spilling down over her shoulders and her cheeks rosy in the cold air. She was everything a lad could want, but he must not get too attached. He could not afford to take two of them to New York, and that was a dream he would fulfil, whether he had to leave her behind or not.

'Well, at least he got you back for milking time.' Gladys glared at Amy. She'd had no peace from Ethan, who had been worrying about his precious daughter all afternoon.

'Is that all you are worried about? Me being here to make sure your butter is made and the dairy cleaned?' Amy snapped, as she took off her sodden shawl.

'You know it isn't. Your father has worried himself sick, thinking what could happen to you with a lad you barely know. Look at you: coming back home like a drowned rat.' Gladys sneered at the girl as she shook her hat free of rain and hung her shawl up on the airing rack above the fire.

'I suppose my father's already in the shippon, and then he'll be going out in this weather with the milk, while you are snug in here,' Amy answered back.

'That makes no difference. He said he'd do everything today. With it being Sunday, there's not as many customers. Not that you'll be bothered, but I've not been feeling well this afternoon. So hold the sarcasm, young lady!'

Gladys watched as Amy climbed the stairs up to her room to change. Ethan worried far too much about his daughter. She was old enough to stand on her own two feet and make her mistakes, if she was that foolish. Gladys wanted Ethan all to herself, not shared with a spoilt brat from a marriage he should never have made in the first place.

Amy unbuttoned her high-necked white blouse and stepped out of her unpractical skirt, hearing her mother's words of 'Pride comes before a fall' as she did so. She loved the skirt, but it caused her no end of problems. Next time she walked out with Billy she'd wear her ready-made woollen dress and her warmer shawl, now that the days were turning colder. She smiled to herself, thinking of the words 'walking out with Billy'. She'd never dreamed of that when she set out that morning, but they had agreed to meet again the following Sunday, regardless of the protests that would come from her father and Gladys.

Gladys could say whatever she wanted; it was nothing to do with her what Amy did with her life. But her father was a different matter. She'd have to ensure that he realized Billy was not a bad lot, and that he had been the perfect gentleman all day. He'd made her laugh and forget her worries, with his Irish humour and his dark good looks. They'd sat under the luscious spread of the palm trees and exotic plants listening to the rain pounding on the huge glass panes above their heads, and talking about their dreams and their hopes for the future. Billy's head was set on crossing the Atlantic and making his fortune in America, and Amy had not wanted to dash his hopes by telling him that things in life would be no different, no matter where he lived. He'd still have to work for his living.

She pulled on a drier pair of black stockings and a warmer skirt and blouse, before sighing, thinking that she would have to go through the kitchen and probably be tackled by Gladys again for being so cheeky. Gladys's attitude towards her had changed of late; it was almost as if she was jealous of Amy having her father's attentions. If the woman thought her spiteful words could drive a wedge between them, she was wrong. Amy loved her father, and he loved her. She wished he had never set eyes on Gladys Lund and her dairy, as she walked down the stairs and quickly made her way out of the empty kitchen and across the yard to make the supply of butter for Monday, before the day was done.

'So you are back. Did he behave himself? I'd have taken to my heels and run, if a lass's father had given me the same dressing-down as I did Billy. So he must have set his head on walking you out.' Ethan leaned in the dairy's doorway, after dropping two or three buckets of creamy milk off to be made into butter the following day.

'He was the perfect gentleman, so you don't have to worry.' Amy took a break from churning the morning's milk, after skimming the cream from the top, and looked at her father. 'Have you finished milking? I thought Gladys would have been helping you. You need to wrap up when you go out with this evening's delivery, as it is cold and wet. The streets are really dreary – nobody's out and about.'

'Gladys has had an afternoon off. She deserves it just as much as you. I'll be right. Folk will need to top their milk up, no matter what the weather is like. I'm a bit knackered myself, but the thought of the meat-and-tattie pie Gladys promised me for supper will keep me going.' Ethan smiled. 'She's worried to death over you going out with that Billy. She's nearly made herself ill over you. She's such a good woman.'

'Father, do you think we've done right to come and live here? It isn't turning out like I thought it would. I thought that you'd have bought it by now, and Gladys would have taken the money and gone back to Garsdale. Can we not look for somewhere else, now you've got her back up and running? She should be looking either to selling it to us or finding somebody else to help her run it, and then we could be on our way.' Amy had dwelt on the words she and Gladys had said, and had come to the opinion that her father might be happy with Gladys Lund, but she was far from being enamoured. Gladys was a hard woman; she'd no airs and graces, and had no sympathy when it came to the love between father and daughter.

'Aye, lass, we're alright. What's brought this on – this lad that you've been with? Gladys said he had too many opinions for her liking.' Ethan scowled.

'No, it's nowt to do with Billy. I just thought you could do better than working all the hours there are, for a woman who happen doesn't appreciate either of us. She doesn't like me, of that I'm sure,' Amy replied quietly.

'"That woman", as you call her, is a grand lass. As I said, she worried all day about you coming home. And I know I sometimes moan and growl, but that's only because I'm tired – like I would be if I worked anywhere else. Now don't talk so daft, and be right with her.' Ethan glowered. 'I'm off out with the milk. I'll not be long this evening; it's hardly worth hitching the horse up for. I want a decent atmosphere when I sit down at that kitchen table and we have supper together, so clear out of your head any daft thoughts of Gladys not liking you.'

He stomped off across the yard, and Amy could hear him swearing under his breath as he put the harness on the horse and lifted the kits on the back of the float. His head had been turned by his old flame and, no matter what Amy thought, he would not see her in the same bad light as she did. She'd have to be careful what she said about Gladys, else she would lose her father as well as her mother, and she couldn't have that.

The atmosphere around the kitchen table at supper time could be cut with a knife.

'There weren't many folk wanting milk this evening – there never is on a Sunday, from what I've seen,' Ethan said as Gladys placed a white-and-blue enamelled pie dish on the table, with steam rising from it. 'By gum, lass, that looks good. I've looked forward to eating this all day, as I smelt that beef simmering away.'

'I remembered it was your favourite. Can you recall when I used to walk to Mossdale viaduct when you were working on the line, with a pie specially for you? All the other fellas used to be so jealous of you, when you sat down to eat it.' Gladys smiled at Ethan as he helped himself to a portion, as well as taking a good spoonful of the pickled red cabbage that was in the jar on the table.

'It wasn't the pie they were jealous of, it was me having a lass like you on my arm. I got many a jibe,' Ethan answered with his mouth full, and looked across at Amy's face as she waited, last in line to help herself. 'Tuck in, Amy, it's bloody good – it's better than your mother's used to be. This 'un's got a decent amount of onion in it.'

Amy reached forward after Gladys had got her portion and put some on her plate. How dare her father say that Gladys's cooking was better than her mother's!

She'd not have used such a cheap cut of meat when they were back in Dent, and the pastry would have been better, she thought to herself as she picked the fat away from the lean of the meat.

'You are a kiesty thing. There's nowt wrong with that meat you're leaving.' Gladys looked at Amy's plate, and the meat that was unfit to eat, as she ate around it. Your mother's spoilt you, I can tell that.' She smiled at Ethan. 'Have some more. If this one's not eating, that means you might as well fill your boots.' She spooned another helping onto Ethan's plate and put her hand on his, as Amy looked with disdain at the two lovers.

'I've had enough. I'll go to my room, if you don't mind. I've letters to write and it is Sunday, so that's what I usually do, or read a book.' Amy pushed her chair back and stood up.

'Well, you could have done that and posted them, if you hadn't been trailing with that Billy. The light will be bad now – there's only one candle in your bedroom,' Gladys said as she took her plate from under Amy's nose.

'I'll manage. I need to reply to Grandma and Grandad, and Joshua. It was Joshua who wrote to me just before we left the lodging house, and they will all need to know where we have moved to.' Amy looked at her father.

'What, another lad in your life! How many do you want?' Gladys scoffed.

'I haven't seen Joshua since we left Dent. We were childhood friends,' Amy said quickly.

'You needn't mention Gladys in your letter, Amy. It'll

only upset them at home, although you can say we are living here.' Ethan looked up at his daughter and hoped she did not ask why.

'Why? Are you feeling guilty? If nothing is going on between you both, it shouldn't matter what I say,' Amy replied angrily.

'Your grandparents will read more into it, just like you are. Now don't you bloody say anything, and don't test my patience again today,' Ethan snapped and looked up at Gladys, after glaring at his daughter.

Amy didn't reply as she left them to each other. But halfway up the stairs she heard Gladys say, 'You've spoilt that lass. She wouldn't speak to me like that if she was mine. She needs a good slapping.' But her father never replied. She continued up to her bedroom and sat on the stool, looking at herself in her bedroom mirror. It had been a wonderful day with Billy, but now she was back to reality – the reality that Gladys Lund was making up for lost time away from her father, and that she was weaving him into a web he would never escape from.

14

'Are you alright, Amy? Did your father say anything after you returned home?' Billy asked and looked around him as he unloaded the week's sawdust supply for the yard. He'd no intention of being chastised by either Gladys or Ethan, if he could get away without meeting them.

'It was *her* that was worse than my father, and *she* can't tell me what to do.' Amy leaned against the wheel of the cart and watched Billy shovel his load down with ease. She was admiring his muscles and his dark hair, which hung just over his shirt collar.

'Well, I told you she was an old bag – she never has a good word for anybody. Lord knows what your father sees in her. Are we still alright for this coming Sunday? I thought we'd have a walk along the pier head, or perhaps take the ferry across to Birkenhead if the weather is decent.' Billy jumped down from the cart, stood beside Amy and smiled at her. 'Since I met you, it's done nowt but rain. Perhaps it is trying to tell me something.' He laughed.

'I could say the same myself. It could be a warning for me not to bother with you. But that sounds good to me. I like the sea, even in wild weather. I'll have to go now, else words will be said if I don't get the dairy cleaned and the butter packaged. I'm in slavery to them both, I think, like the poor devils who landed on Liverpool docks all those years ago.'

'No, don't give me that. You will never be as bad as them, they really did suffer. You have got a lot to be thankful for. Now, eleven o'clock in the same place as last week, and try not to bring your father this time. I'll have to be on my way as Henry Morphet wants me back quick. I've to deliver a new batch of coffins to the workhouse on Dukinfield Road – they are his best customer. There's always somebody dying there; it's always full to the brim with folk that has no way to make a living or are dying in poverty. I hate the bloody place, and the coffins I take there are made of the worst wood ever, not like the posh folk's coffins that he takes care of sanding and polishing,' Billy said sadly as he touched Amy's hand. 'I'll see you Sunday. I'll look forward to it.'

'Yes, I'll close the gates after you. Mind what you are doing.' Amy looked at Billy and felt the urge to kiss him, but as he showed no inclination and she knew that if she was caught by either Gladys or her father she would not hear the last of it, she decided against it. Instead she watched him turn the horse and cart around, and felt a moment of sadness as she closed the gates behind him.

'What had he to say for himself then? I watched you both from my bedroom window,' Ethan said as he walked through the dairy's door and joined Amy in the yard.

'He's walking me out again on Sunday. We are going to cross the Mersey and visit Birkenhead – whatever's there. I think it's the trip on the ferry he thinks I'll like,' Amy said and looked at her father's face cloud over.

'Is he now? So that's what you've planned together. What if I say you are not going, if I have my way? He's a townie, Amy, and you can do so much better. Believe me, I used to know lads like him when I was a lad back in Burnley. He's no prospects; he's a dreamer, just like Gladys says.' Ethan looked sternly at his daughter.

'But weren't you a dreamer? You dreamed of going to the Klondike. He's no different from you. Billy's kind-hearted, which is the main thing. Besides, he's only a friend, like Joshua back in Dent, and you never complained about me going walking with him,' Amy moaned.

'No, I didn't because you were bairns, but it hasn't escaped my notice that I have a young woman for a daughter now. One that doesn't know much about men,' Ethan said with meaning.

'Oh, Father, I'm not a child. I know what some men are after, but Billy isn't one of them. He's going to America next year, so he's not going to be wanting to put down ties here, and we both know it is just a friendship.' Amy lied to herself because, in the innermost secrets of her heart, she hoped Billy would become more than a friend. He made her feel like she had never felt before. Her heart had been a-flutter when he'd walked in, and she was counting the seconds till Sunday.

'Aye, well, I'll be watching the bugger. And if he takes advantage, I'll kick his arse all the way to America, you can tell him,' Ethan growled. 'Now, get on with packaging that butter. I'll need some for this evening, and Gladys will be on your back if it's not done.'

Amy watched her father going into the kitchen. Gladys would be waiting for him; she'd cleaned and washed the shippon out a good hour ago and had gone into the house, out of Amy's way, before Billy arrived and before her father had returned. Only the barest essential conversation was passing between them, and it was making life awkward for all.

The rain was pouring down as Amy took her shawl from behind the kitchen door and argued with her father that she was still going to wait for Billy at the top of Lord Street, no matter what the weather.

'He will be there. You are not stopping me from going,' Amy yelled, as Ethan said the weather wasn't fit to let a dog out in, let alone his daughter.

'Don't be stupid, lass, he'll not be there. Even he's got the sense on a day like this to keep in and stay warm.' Ethan watched as his daughter, with a wild look in her eye, opened the door onto the street, which was deserted and empty. 'If you are off, you need more than that shawl to keep you dry, you stubborn-headed devil. Take my oilcloth coat, which turns the rain,' Ethan shouted. 'He'll not be there lass, don't be so daft.' Amy banged the door shut behind her, leaving Gladys shaking her head at the lass who would not listen to sense.

'She needs a good hiding, Ethan. She'll be sodden before she gets to the end of the street. That lad has really turned her head. There's no making any sense of her at the moment. When she first came she was so quiet and polite, but of late, I'll be honest, I'm beginning to find her hard work.'

'Aye, well, I think she's upset over you and me. She's not daft, she realizes we think something of one another. She'll be thinking you are about to replace her mother.' Ethan sighed. Bloody women, they had always ruled his life, he thought, as Gladys came over to him and kissed him on the lips – a kiss that he took pleasure in. And he soon forgot about his daughter, as she pulled on his hand to lead him upstairs to her bedroom.

Amy stood in the doorway of Hope Brothers, cold and shivering, looking down the usually busy shopping street to the tall spire of St George's Church. The rain was bouncing off the paved street and even the trams were not running along the tracks, as everybody gave up on the bitterly cold November day.

She was soaked through to the skin, feeling unloved and a little foolish, knowing that her father was right. Billy would have more sense than to come out on a day like this. She wouldn't admit that, though, when she returned home, she vowed, as she heard the clock on St Peter's Catholic Church chime twelve. How had her father been so sure that Billy would not be waiting for her? Had he been and warned Billy off again? The more she thought about it, the more plausible it seemed, as she stood with her hair dripping down over her neck and tears running down her face. That's what he'd done, she thought, as she made her way back home. Billy would not let her down, no matter what the weather. He'd promised to meet her, and a bit of rain would not put him off. It would be her father who had put him up to it, and Gladys swayed his every thought at the moment.

Amy grew more and more convinced that her father was responsible for Billy's no-show, as she walked through the dairy's gate and threw open the back door to find the kitchen and living room empty. From upstairs she heard the voices and laughter of her father and Gladys as they made love, thinking the house was empty. She climbed the stairs unheard and stood in the doorway, looking like a wild banshee as she glared down at Ethan and Gladys, lying in one another's arms.

'You told him not to come! You can have your pleasure, but I can't. I hate you and I hate her, I wish you were both dead,' Amy yelled with hatred in her eyes.

'What are doing back so early? And what are you blathering on about?' Ethan shouted as Gladys hid herself under the sheets, pulling his shirt over her head.

'Billy – he didn't show. You told him not to come, I know you did. You are determined to spoil my life,' Amy shouted.

'Amy, stop it – I've never seen the lad! He's not turned up because of the weather. Don't talk so soft. You are upset.' Ethan sat up in bed and pushed Gladys away. 'I'm sorry you have found us like this and, aye, I should practise what I preach.'

'You did, you warned him off, I know you did,' Amy cried, not wanting to see her father in a state of undress, as he pulled his breeches back on while Gladys lay in the bed and stared at her.

'You ask Billy, when he comes on Thursday with his delivery, if he's seen me. He'll tell you that I've not seen hide nor hair of him. It's just the weather. I've nowt against him. But I don't want your heart to be broken by a town lad that will know a lot more than you do about suchlike.' Ethan moved towards the sobbing Amy, who was now feeling foolish and embarrassed about the situation she had found her father in.

'You don't love me any more – you only listen to her. You've forgotten my mother these last few weeks; me and her are not of importance any more.' Amy sobbed and nodded her head at Gladys, who was keeping quiet as she watched Ethan go and put his arm around his shaking, sodden daughter.

'I'll never forget your mother and I'll never stop loving you. The feelings you have for Billy are new to you. I've been there in the past, and it's hard. You do get a little selfish and wrapped up in your own world. Perhaps Gladys and I are so at the moment, after finding one another after twenty years. We had the same feelings as you when we were your age, but you must believe me. I said nowt to your fella.'

Ethan held Amy close to his chest. She was wet and frozen, and disappointed at being let down both by Billy and by him.

'I love you more than life itself, and don't you forget

it.' He kissed her head and felt her sobs and shivers. 'Now, go and get changed into something dry and warm and join us downstairs. There's some lamb roasting in the oven and a pan of tatties waiting to be boiled. We'll not mention this again. I'm sorry you've found Gladys and me in bed together – it was wrong of us.'

'I don't want any dinner. I'll go to my room,' Amy said without looking into her father's eyes, before walking shakily to her bedroom. She had shown herself to be a selfish piece of work, and had said words she didn't really mean. She loved her father, but she could never forgive Gladys for being the temptress that she was. She'd never, ever replace her mother. And Amy was not about to apologize to her for the words said in haste.

Life at the dairy had been fraught all week. There was an unseen tension between the three of them, and Amy still had her doubts about why Billy had not turned up for their date, not quite believing her father's words and not forgiving him for falling so easily into Gladys's arms.

She was in the dairy, cleaning and making the milk into butter as usual, and felt her heart beating fast and her stomach churning just as much as the milk. It was Thursday morning, the day of Billy's usual delivery to the yard, and she needed so much to speak to him. Her heart pounded as she saw the dairy gates open and Billy leading his horse and cart into the yard. She watched as Gladys came out of the shippon and gave him his instructions, before going back to clean out the cow stalls. He was early, Amy thought, as she washed her hands under the icy-cold water tap and decided to talk to the lad who had her heart pounding and her head thinking irrational thoughts. She regretted the words she had said to her father, but she wanted to ask Billy why he had not shown up on Sunday, thinking that a drop of rain would not keep him from meeting her.

'Now then, my lass, what are you up to?' Billy shouted across the yard, seeing Amy walking across to him.

'You are early. Have you wet the bed?' Amy said, with a hint of sarcasm in her voice.

'Nay, I thought I'd come here as soon as I could, to explain why I didn't show my face on Sunday. It was too bloody wet to turn out. I hope you did the same. Nobody in their right mind would have wanted to walk around Liverpool on a day like that.' Billy grinned but, from Amy's face, knew instantly that she had been there waiting for him. 'You didn't – you'd be wet through before you got to the end of the street!'

Gladys walked past them both as she made her way back to the kitchen and, overhearing, added her four pennyworth. 'She did, and then she played hell with her father for you not turning up,' she said, stopping to listen to their conversation from outside the kitchen door.

Amy bowed her head and said quietly, 'I thought he'd told you not to come – warned you off me.'

'Oh, Amy, he's never been near me. It was the weather, you silly bugger. Now I'd better unload this before I get into bother, but before I go we'll make arrangements for this weekend, providing it isn't pouring down.'

Gladys shouted from the kitchen door, 'You'd better not

skulk about on a street corner in future. Come and knock for her on the door next time. Her father says I've to tell you that, although why he is encouraging you, I don't know. I'd be kicking your arse back home.' She shook her head and watched as the young couple smiled at one another, before she entered the house to do her chores.

'I don't expect my father really told Gladys to ease up on us both.' Amy grinned.

'Sure, I'll call on you. But, Amy, we will just keep it as friends; we can't be any more because I won't be here forever,' Billy said and knew he was lying to himself. The lass in front of him had pinched a piece of his heart already.

'Of course, I never thought we were courting. Friends it is,' Amy lied. 'I'll not keep you from fulfilling your dream of America. Dreams are precious.'

'Right then, I'll knock on your door on Sunday, whether it is raining or the sun is shining. You'd better apologize to your father, poor devil.'

'I will. I feel daft now, as I got upset over nothing.' Amy sighed. 'I'll get back to the dairy. I don't want to tempt fate, and for Gladys to come out and tell you to get on with your job. I'll see you Sunday, usual time.' She smiled. Billy might want to keep it at friends for the moment, but if their relationship grew deeper, she'd not be complaining.

'Now then, lad, tha'd better come in. It's a bit wet out there. Gladys has the kettle on and Amy's made some biscuits. I said you were welcome to stay in here instead of trailing the streets. Gladys said you could go into the front room for an hour or two, if that's alright with you.' Ethan opened the door to the lad who had caused so much heartache between him and his daughter.

'Thank you, Mr Postlethwaite, that would be better than us walking around the streets on a wet day like today.' Billy took off his cap and screwed it up in his hand, as he looked at the man who had taken him to task about walking out with his daughter. He walked into the kitchen, to be met by a beaming Amy; and Gladys, who was sitting by the fire darning socks.

'You came, I'm so glad,' Amy said and then looked at her father. She'd apologized to him and admitted that she'd made a fool of herself. However, she was still not happy that her father was treating Gladys as his wife now, but she was in no position to comment, if she wanted to carry on seeing Billy. 'The fire is lit in the front room. Follow me and I'll bring us some tea and biscuits.' The front room was the only half-decent room in the house, and was reserved for special occasions. A chenille-covered oak table took pride of place, and two velvet-covered armchairs sat directly opposite one another. It was warm and homely, and Amy grinned and made her way past her father and Gladys as Billy followed her hesitantly.

'Go on, lad, we'll not bite. You are better here than getting up to no good on the streets. I said my piece the other week and it still stands, so take heed.' Ethan looked at Gladys, who shook her head in disbelief at having Billy O'Hara under her roof.

'Thank you, sir. You needn't worry, I'll not step out of

line. I've told Amy that we are to be just friends, nothing more. She knows I've set my head on America, and nothing and nobody is going to stop me,' Billy said and looked at Gladys.

'Aye, well, as long as she knows that. I wouldn't want to see her with a broken heart when you go sailing over that ocean. She's had enough in her life already.' Ethan watched as Billy followed Amy into the front room and hoped that the lad would behave himself.

Amy reflected on her few hours with Billy in the sitting room as she lay in her bed, trying to sleep. They had talked about their dreams. Billy was full of the adventures he had planned in his head, once he landed in America. He'd talked about things being different for him in New York than they were in Liverpool. He had something to aim for, rather than dreary days working for the joiner who didn't appreciate him. She'd told him about her days in the Klondike and her days growing up in Dentdale, realizing how much she missed both, and that Liverpool was a poor substitute for the wide-open spaces she had been used to.

It was not only thoughts of the day that were keeping her awake. Down in the kitchen she could hear her father and Gladys arguing – over what, she didn't know but, feeling paranoid, she guessed it would be about her and Billy. Her father had obviously put his foot down, so that she had been allowed to entertain Billy in Gladys's home. Things were not quite as her father had planned, and she could see that perhaps, with time, he would not be feeling quite as enamoured with his old love, despite making her bed his own.

Whatever they were arguing about, she'd had a good day with Billy, who made her feel special. And her heart beat that little bit faster when he looked at her with his deep Irish eyes.

15

Gladys was reading the local paper when she turned to Ethan. 'Here, Ethan, we will have to go to this. We have always attended the Great Liverpool Show and shown our best cow there. Ted was dead proud when he won second-best dairy cow. I usually ask his family to stay with us and go to the show. It's a big event for us cow-keepers.'

'I don't know, Gladys. Remember you are still supposed to be in mourning – it will not look good. Besides, have you got a cow good enough to show? Daisy is the best-looking one, but I don't know as much about beasts as you. I hope you are not thinking of asking Ted's family to stay this year, as it'd be a bit awkward.' Ethan looked across at Gladys as she studied the categories for the show.

'No, I'll not be asking them. They'll not want to come anyway, now Ted's passed. But I will enter a cow, and it will be grand to see folk from back home. It's a chance to catch up with folk, more than anything. Do you think we should enter the Best Kept Shippon or Milkhouse category? Although I wouldn't want any of those judges snooping around, and the shippon could really do with a lick of limewash on the walls. On second thoughts, we'll stick to entering a cow,' Gladys said excitedly. 'I can dress up in my finest and enjoy myself for once. I'm not wearing black. I've worn it long enough now, and I can't say I've mourned Ted's passing, anyway.'

Ethan looked across at Gladys. Sometimes she was so hard, and he could understand why Amy and Gladys did not see eye-to-eye. 'Those from up the Dales will think little of you if you do that, especially if I'm on your arm.'

'Well, you'll be showing my cow. I'm not going to stand there with it on a halter and walk it around North Haymarket, for all to see me. Bluebell is our best cow. She'll fit into the Best Cow in Calf or With Milk category, and she weighs under eleven hundredweight, which is what they want.' Gladys felt no shame. She was going to show off her cow and her new man to one and all, knowing full well that Ethan and she would be the talk of the Dales when all the visitors returned to their homes. It would be a chance to prove that, even without Ted Lund, she could run a good dairy and own fit cows.

Amy stood in the usually open space called North Haymarket. It was full with the bustle of cowkeepers, dairymen and farmers, their wives and their families. The air was redolent with the smell of cattle, pipe smoke, roasting chestnuts and baked potatoes from the many food-sellers around the edge of the market. The women were all dressed in their Sunday best. It was a time for the Dales folk of Liverpool to celebrate and show off their finest beasts, as well as themselves.

All around her she could hear the sound of her own Dales dialect being spoken, a dialect where sentences were cut short and mixed with a smattering of Norse, from when the Vikings had made their homes in the Dales. It was an accent that reminded her of home, of her grandparents and of the place she had thought so much of during her childhood. In the centre of everything was a hastily made ring of cleared ground, where the cows stood patiently, waiting to be judged, with their proud owners by their sides.

'What'st think o' that 'un then? It hardly looks wick to me,' one farmer said to another, pointing at a cow that had just lain down in the middle of the show ring.

'Aye, it leuks like it's deeing, lying out like that. Does tha ken that fella? I've niver sin him afore,' the other farmer replied.

Amy smiled. She knew they were commenting on the cow looking ill and asking who the owner was, in the Dales tongue she had spoken and heard since her birth, and that made her feel warm inside.

Now she held her breath as Bluebell, the roan-coloured shorthorn that had been washed, scrubbed and powdered until she was spotless, made her way into the ring. Her tail was combed, her horns and hooves polished with linseed oil. And now, after being led through numerous streets in Liverpool, she stood looking doe-eyed, with Ethan holding her halter, as the judges walked around her, felt her udder and ran their hands along her flanks.

'We don't stand a chance. It is Robert Raw from Bootle that's judging, and he never favours me,' Gladys said with a quick look at the man.

'Surely it's the cow he's judging, not the owner,' Amy replied and smiled at her father, who looked a bit lost, standing with all the other cow-handlers, who had a lot more experience than him. Robert Raw looked the business, dressed in a white smock and with a checked tweed cap on his head. In his hand he held a switch of a stick, which occasionally he tapped across the cow's backside.

'I should have shown it. They are asking your father something and he hasn't got a clue what to reply with – we'll not win,' Gladys moaned, and shook her head as the judge stood back and looked at the row of milk cows and made his decision. 'Bloody typical! Rowland Harper has won again – he always wins one thing or another. His cow does look more fit than our Bluebell, though, so I can't argue with that.'

The judge, Robert Raw, saw Gladys shaking her head as he handed out the rest of the awards, giving Ethan and Bluebell the reserve prize. He walked over to Gladys and stood and watched, as Ethan led the cow out of the ring.

'It was a near thing, Gladys. Your cow was just not as fit. And I don't know who your cowman is, but he's not good at handling them or answering questions. Thou will happen do better next year,' Robert said and looked her up and down. 'You are looking well – in fact I'd go as far as blooming. That new cowman might not be good with cows, but happen he's better with women. You'll be free to do what you want, now Ted is six feet under.' He winked and grinned at Gladys.

'Mind what you are saying, Robert Raw. You keep your eyes on the cows. Ethan Postlethwaite and I have known one another for a long time. In fact this is his daughter standing next to me. They are helping me to keep the dairy running until I get back on my feet after Ted's death,' Gladys said sharply and turned to look at Amy.

'Now then, Miss. So your father is helping Gladys, is he? But he's not from these parts, so he says. He mentioned being out in the Klondike, but that he'd married a Dent lass, who must be your mother.' Robert looked at Amy and quizzed her for information.

'Yes, sir, we are living with Mrs Lund. My mother, unfortunately, died when we were in the Yukon, and we came back here to buy a business that Father and I could run,' Amy said and watched a smile come across his face.

'Well then, it was fortunate that your father met Gladys here. I'm sure she will have made sure you both want for nothing.' Robert grinned, while Gladys gave him a dark stare and wished him on his way. 'There are a few folk from Dent here today. A load of lads have come down to the show; they came on the milk train this morning and are going back on the mail train later this evening. They will be jiggered by the time they get home.' He laughed. 'There might be some you know. They are over there, looking at the next round of cows to be judged. They are handsome Dales lads, just right for a bonny lass like yourself.' Robert winked and then went off in the direction of the ring to ready himself for the next judging.

'The fond old devil, he only thinks of one thing!' Gladys said as she watched Ethan walking with the cow, still on its halter, back to her. 'It wasn't the cow that let me down, I think it was your father. I should have shown the cow myself. It's my own fault. I should have known better than to let your father show it. I suppose I was showing your father off to the world, as well as my beast.'

Amy glanced across at her father. He'd done the best he could, and he'd never been much good with cows.

'Sorry, I let you down. He asked me stuff that I knew nowt about.' Ethan stood and watched as the cow started to graze on the few stalks of grass it could find.

'I should have shown it myself. I should have known he'd ask you everything about it and that you'd not know the answers. It's my fault. Are you taking it back home and then re-joining us? There's folk here I'd like to have a talk to, so I'm in no rush to return to the dairy. I'll be back before milking time,' Gladys said as she watched Ethan look around him.

'Nay, I'll go home and stay there. I hardly know anybody here, and you forget I'm not a farmer. What are you doing, Amy? Are you staying or coming home? There's plenty to see, and some of these folk will probably know your grandparents. Here, I'll give you a bob or two, and you can spend it on the stalls over there in the corner of the market. Have you seen the organ-grinder with the monkey? He spooked a horse and cart earlier – you should have seen the commotion when the cart loaded with apples overturned. Nearly every young lad in Liverpool was helping themselves.' Ethan placed a few shillings in Amy's hand and then turned to Gladys, who looked with disdain at him for losing her a prize even though she knew it was partly her fault.

'Aye, I'll see you later for milking, because you'll not want to do that,' Gladys said with sarcasm in her voice as she turned her back on Ethan.

Amy looked at her father and felt sorry for him. 'I'll not be long, Father. I'll just have a quick walk around the show, as you say, and see if there's anybody I recognize, although I've been away from home for so long now, they'd have to recognize me first.'

'Aye, you do that, lass. Watch your pockets and bag, as you don't know who's about in this crowd,' Ethan replied as he pulled on the halter and switched Bluebell across her hindquarters with his stick, to get her to move from eating the few blades of true grass she'd had since she'd joined the dairy in the middle of the city.

'I'll not be long,' Amy repeated, as she watched Gladys stop to talk to a gathering of Dales folk that she obviously knew. Her father had not come up to Gladys's standards, and now she was embarrassed by him. How Amy wished that her father would leave Gladys and the dairy behind, and buy the business he'd set his heart on when returning to Liverpool and be his own man. Gladys Lund thought only of her dairy and herself. Any hope of her selling it, and leaving her father to run it, had long since gone. She would never leave that dairy, which she loved more than any man, Amy thought.

Amy laughed at the antics of the monkey on the organ-grinder's shoulder as it clapped its hands and held its small cap out for coppers, while the handle of the heavily painted ornate organ was turned for well-known tunes to come out. She thanked the man roasting chestnuts for a bag of his nuts, which, as well as being delicious to eat, also kept her hands warm as the afternoon grew colder with the onset of evening. She then looked at a stall with embroidered handkerchiefs on it. Buying two with her father's name on them and one, rather grudgingly, with violets on it for Gladys, she'd hide them away to give at Christmas, which was fast approaching. She smiled and peered at some of the farmers and their wives, wondering if she should recognize them or not as they walked past her. Her grandfather would probably know, or know of, most of them, but she had been away from the Dales so long. She was just about to go home when she heard her name being shouted.

'Amy! Amy Postlethwaite, is that you?'

Amy turned and saw a blond-haired lad dressed in a green tweed suit, with a jaunty bowler covering his fair hair. He was running up to her with a smile on his face and stopped next to her, bending over to catch his breath as he glanced up. 'It's me – Joshua. I was fair hoping you'd be here and, when Robert Raw said he'd seen you, I knew I had to find you.' He looked at her intently and grinned. 'My God, you've grown up. Look at you, quite the lady.'

'Joshua, is that really you? I'd never have recognized you. What are you doing here? You should have written to tell me you were visiting.' Amy beamed and then, not thinking, opened her arms to hug the lad she had grown up with, taking him by surprise and making the crowd look at the young couple embracing.

'I've come down on the milk train. It was a last-minute decision with some of the other lads from the dale. We return later tonight. I'll have to be away in another hour. We are to have a pint or two in one of the pubs near the station before we return. I am glad I've found you. I wanted to see you so much,' Joshua said, his cheeks filling with colour as he thought about the hug Amy had so openly given him. 'Have we to sit on that empty bench over there? I'd like to hear how you are doing. Robert Raw is telling everyone that your father's working for Gladys Lund. I thought he'd bought his own dairy, from your letters?'

Joshua took Amy's hand and pulled her to sit down with him, as he couldn't take his eyes off the lass. Last time he had seen her, she had tangled hair and a snotty nose; now she was a young woman whose hair shone, black and beautiful, with rosy-red lips and kind blue eyes. She was everything he had imagined.

'Oh, Josh, it's so good to see you. I don't want to burden you with my news. How's your family? Have you seen my grandparents?' Amy asked, trying to change the subject.

'They are all fine. Now, what's wrong? Because you are not answering my question, and I know you: when something's wrong, you clam up.' Joshua smiled and held Amy's hand, and it was if they had never been apart.

'Oh, Father was supposed to buy the dairy, but instead they have kindled an old love, so we are just living there with Gladys Lund. I hate her, Josh. All she thinks about is herself – she's not one bit like my mother. I'm only thankful my father has not thought about marrying her. In fact I think Gladys might even be wearing a bit thin on him at the moment, so hopefully we won't be there much longer.' Amy brushed away a tear and then smiled at Josh. 'Now your turn: are you courting?'

'Well, I can't beat that! But listen, I'm sure your father will see sense and, hopefully, leave with you, or kick Gladys out if she sells to him. I can't see her doing that, though, from the tales Robert Raw was saying about her. She's not liked, for not mourning her husband. The news will be all around the Dales that your father is living over the brush with her, now that Robert has put two and two together. They'll have something to say about that at the newly named "Klondike", and your grandfather will not be happy at all.'

'I know. I'm going to have to tell them the truth. I sometimes wish I was back home with them. Liverpool is alright – plenty of shops and lots to see and do – but it is not my home. Now, what about you? I can't believe you are sitting next to me.' Amy smiled and held Joshua's hand tightly.

'Oh, sheep, sheep and more sheep. I've bought some land that joins your grandparents'. About twenty acres – it's that big pasture that runs nearly into Garsdale. I've got the best view of both dales, when I'm sitting with my sheep and listening to the skylarks overhead. I see your grandparents at least once a week and say hello to them both. They are always talking about you, and get so excited when you write to them. They aren't getting any younger, though. As for courting, nobody wants me. Besides, there's nobody that takes my fancy in Dentdale.' Joshua looked at Amy and smiled. 'Talking about courting, have you got a beau? I bet you have; you couldn't walk down the street, looking like you do, without somebody admiring you.'

'No, I haven't really.' Amy sighed. 'I have a good friend called Billy O'Hara, who comes with the sawdust for the cows' bedding once a week, but he's just that: a friend. He's saving up to go to New York, so I can't get attached to a lad that is going to leave in another six months. Besides, I'm nothing special. You haven't seen some of the lasses who look like models that walk down Lord Street.'

'When I told my mother I was going to try and find you today, she gave me something to give you, and she remembered that you always liked to eat it when you came to our house. I must admit she had a twinkle in her eyes when she placed it in the paper bag – she always did like you. I only hope that it's not a bag of crumbs.' Joshua grinned as he put his hands in his deep pockets and pulled out a bag. 'Here, this is for you from me.'

Amy took the bag and peered into it. 'Oh, it's kiss-me cake, she remembered I liked it. I do love it, and I haven't eaten a slice of this for so long.' She took the square of shortbread with a jam centre, sprinkled with sugar, and broke it in two. 'Share it with me, like it should be shared between good friends or courting couples.'

'Aye, well, my mother has always called it "courting cake". I think that's why she gave it to me. She thinks it's time I found myself somebody.' Joshua blushed as he watched Amy eating her half. He wanted to ask her if he could court her, but knew she lived too far away. And now there was this Billy, and she must think something of him, else she wouldn't have mentioned him. 'Can I still write to you, Amy? I wish you were back home. We had some good days together, and I miss you,' he said quietly and then bit into the courting cake.

'Of course you can, Josh. You know that now I'm back in this country I'll return your letters. I enjoy hearing from you, and I miss you too. We used to wander all over the fells together, and get hell when we were late back. Your mother blamed me, and my mother blamed you, though to be honest, we were both as bad as one another at keeping time.' Amy wiped her mouth free of sugar and smiled at the lad that she loved like a brother. He'd grown into a handsome man, and she couldn't quite believe it was the same lad that she had walked many a mile with.

'Yes, we were always in trouble, one way or another. Can you remember when we went scrumping apples from Len Sedgwick's orchard at New Closes? Heavens, I did get a walloping when he caught us and took us both back home. My father took his belt to me. I remember you said that I led you on, and you just got a good talking-to by your lot. You always could get away with blue murder, with those looks you have.'

'What looks are those, Josh?' Amy smiled and looked innocently at him, noticing him blushing.

'You know, Amy Postlethwaite – you are doing it now.' Josh looked up at the group of young men walking their way. 'Oh, hey up. It must be time to go with the lads, they'll be wanting to go for that pint before home.' He looked at Amy and wanted to kiss her before leaving her, but knew that if he did, his mates would never give him any peace on the way back. 'I'll write,' he said as he stood up to go.

'I'll write as well,' Amy replied, and looked at the group of lads from Dent. She thought she recognized a few of them, but she didn't know them like Josh. A sudden urge took her and she rushed forward as Josh turned to leave her, and kissed him on the cheek, regretting doing so when all the lads made whooping noises and patted Josh on the back. 'Take care, Josh,' she cried out after him, as his friends teased him and urged him to join them in the pub.

He turned and smiled as he left her, and for a second Amy felt her heart flutter a little more than it did when Billy looked at her. It had been good to see Josh, and how he had altered from the scrawny young lad with holes in his trousers, when she had last seen him. She would write more often, as Josh was the only one who truly knew her.

16

Amy looked at the letter from her grandparents. The news about Ethan had spread fast up the Dales, and now she was going to have to reply and tell them that yes, the rumours were true; she and her father were living with his former love, Gladys Lund. That was one of the things about living in a small community: everyone knew everyone, and sometimes it was a good thing, and sometimes it was a bad thing.

She sighed as she put the letter to one side, and wished that her father would write to her grandparents, to explain the situation. They had sounded so angry with the news, and she didn't want to confirm it. The letter had arrived in the afternoon post and she hadn't opened it until she went to her bed. As a consequence, she had tossed and turned all night, wondering how to reply. Now, as she sat on the edge of the bed, she could hear the low voice of her father talking to Gladys in the next room. She also heard the sound of Gladys being sick in the pee-pot, her retching echoing in the darkness of the early morning. Was she ill? Amy couldn't help but wish that she was. Gladys had eaten enough of the stew last night, and her father had watched when she helped herself to an extra portion.

Amy heard the church clock strike five. She'd have to get a move on. Once Gladys and her father had milked the cows, she'd have to light the fires and clean the house while her father delivered the milk and Gladys saw to feeding and mucking out the cows. She quickly pulled on her clothes, shivering in the cold of the mid-December morning. The fern-like pattern of Jack Frost's beauty was visible on her bedroom window as she picked up her candle and made her way out onto the landing.

Her father had beaten her downstairs and was pulling his boots on in front of the still-glowing embers of the kitchen fire.

'Good, you are up! Gladys is ill this morning, she's got a belly ache and feels sick.' Ethan pushed a kindling stick onto the fire, and it spat and took hold as he placed another one on and some coal, watching the smoke rise up the chimney and then red flames start to lick around the coal. 'The fire's going now. Can you help me milk the cows this morning? Gladys is not up to it, and we need to get the milk out on the streets by seven.' Ethan looked at his daughter, knowing that she was capable of milking a cow, but expecting her to complain.

'If she's ill, I suppose I'll have to. I heard her retching, and she's looked peaky for a day or two lately,' Amy said and noticed the worry on her father's face. 'I've not slept anyway. Them at Dent have heard who we are living with, and they are not happy with us, Father,' she continued, quickly seizing the opportunity of a moment alone with Ethan.

'Aye, well, they can keep their opinions to themselves. We are not doing any harm, and they always did listen to gossip too much. Now, put Gladys's coat on and grab that storm-light – you can't milk in the dark.' Ethan stood up and looked at his daughter in the glow of the two paraffin lights that he had lit. 'Write to your grandparents and tell them what you want. I'm past caring. They never will be happy with whatever I do, so it's no skin off my nose.' He passed Amy the lantern as she buttoned up Gladys's milking coat and looked at him.

'Are you alright, Father?' Amy asked as she followed him out of the house across the yard, picking up the heavy milk pails as they entered the shippon.

'It's just a bad morning, Amy. I'm slow at milking, and you are not much better. Now hold your noise and let's get the job done – the delivery is going to be late enough without you blethering in my ear.' Ethan hung up his lantern and adjusted the flame, making the light shine over half the shippon. 'Can you fodder the cows with some of that oil-cake in that bin at the end? That will keep them quiet until they are milked. And then make a start with Bluebell.' He slapped the back of the first cow and grabbed the milking stool and bucket, then rested his head on the side of the cow as he put his hands on the udder and started to express milk from the animal.

Amy went to the large metal bin where the oil-cake

was kept, delivered weekly by Bibby's and Silcock's. The smell of the pressed grains filled the air as she shovelled a helping to each individual cow, to keep them happy as they were milked. She loved the smell of the shippon. Despite it being a mucky place, it always smelt of hay and feed. It reminded her of home, as she sat down like her father on a milking stool and placed her head on Bluebell's side. Her fingers gripped each teat and pulled hard down until there was no milk in that side of the udder, then moved on to the next side, before starting on the next cow, with her frothing pail of warm, creamy milk. It was in the shippon that Amy knew she could never be a town girl, all clean and petite. She was of farming stock and would always yearn for the open spaces and fresh air, she thought, as she got into a rhythm and the milk pails started to line up, ready for the delivery.

Outside on the streets, the knocker-upper was tapping at the windows of the workers of Liverpool with his pole, and the inhabitants were stirring. They'd expect fresh milk for their breakfasts, so they had to get the milking done – and fast – while Gladys lingered in her bed and felt sorry for herself.

It took a good hour or more to milk the cows, but once Ethan had harnessed Dobbin, he was on his way, after quickly having a drink of warming tea and a slice of bread and dripping. It wasn't his usual breakfast, but it would do this morning. Amy watched as he led the pony and float out of the yard. It was still relatively dark, but she could see the steam rising from the warmth of the pony and the warm milk in the kits, as her father walked down the cobbled streets under the glow of the illuminated gas lights. 'Milko, milko!' he yelled as he turned the corner and walked down the first street on his round, while Amy closed the yard's gates behind him.

She glanced up at the bedroom windows and caught Gladys looking out of them at her. Whatever was up with her, she had managed to get herself out of the bed, now that the cows had been milked, Amy thought, as she walked back into the shippon to let the cows out into the yard before she cleaned the stalls. She untied the tethers and watched as the last cow made its way into the yard for the only exercise the poor creatures would get for the day. She then picked up the shovel and started cleaning the shippon, shovelling and brushing the waste from the cows onto the midden in the corner of the yard, before swilling out the shippon with cold water from the small well in the yard. She then refilled all the cows' drinking buckets and carried hay from beyond the dairy to fill the hay-racks. Jobs done, she went to go and have a brew after changing out of the coat that belonged to Gladys, and before making a start on the dairy.

Amy entered the kitchen to find Gladys brushing the fireplace clear of the old ashes. She looked up as Amy took the coat off and sat down at the kitchen table.

'You've done the milking then? I don't know what is wrong with me – I feel that sickly.' Gladys sat across from Amy with the hearth brush in her hand, and looked pale and wan as she held back another wave of sickness.

'If it keeps up, you'd better go and see a doctor. You

do look a bit peaky.' Amy thought the woman did seem under the weather and felt a little sympathy for her.

'The doctor! I can't spend money on a doctor. I don't even spend money on my cows when they are ill, so I'm not about to spend it on myself, just because I'm feeling sick. Leave cleaning the house and dairy, if you want. Once this bout has gone, I'll be fine. We'll swap jobs this morning.' Gladys sat back. 'Why don't you have a wash and a look around the shops? I'm sure you'll be needing to get a Christmas present for your father, if nobody else, and Christmas will soon be upon us.' She smiled and waited for a reply. 'I could do with some shopping from the market as well. You can save me my legs for once.'

'I could, but you are not well – I can't leave you,' Amy replied and looked at the woman, who was never usually kind to her.

'It's only an upset stomach. Now go, get your tea drunk and have a change. It will do you good to have an hour or two to yourself. Have you enough money? Do you want me to lend you some, as well as giving you the money for what we need? I'll make a list while you change.' Gladys tried to smile as another bout of sickness caught her, making her gulp it back to prove to Amy there was nothing seriously wrong with her, and that she wanted, in all honesty, an hour's peace to do as she wished.

'I suppose I could. I have some money, but my father . . .'

'Never mind your father. I'll tell him when he returns that you've gone out, on my insistence. The shops will just be opening, and you could have a wander around the market. I'll give you some money for some fresh fish. Three good pieces of haddock – your father will enjoy that for his supper. And if you can call at the chemist, get me some milk of magnesium, which will settle this stomach down. Now, go on, get changed. Nobody will want you standing next to them, smelling of cow muck.' Gladys scowled at Amy, hoping that she got the message she was not wanted at home that morning.

'If you are sure, I'd like a look around the market, as I don't usually get the chance. I'll take a look in the shops first and then I'll go to the market. I won't be long.' Amy watched Gladys as she went to the kitchen-dresser drawer and took out her purse.

'Go on then. Get changed and I'll write my list. Then I'll see to the dairy, so there's no need for you to rush back – all's in hand.' Gladys sat down at the table and started to make a list of things she needed on the piece of paper in front of her.

'You are sure you will be alright, and that you'll tell my father it was your suggestion? I don't want him to think I've let us all down.' Amy looked at Gladys as she pushed the shopping list into her hand, along with some money.

'I'll tell him, don't worry. Now just go. Take your time. I'll be fine, and now you are getting what we need for the day, you are doing me a favour anyway.' Gladys sat down in the chair, then watched as Amy picked up her basket and went out of the door. She was thankful the house was empty. She had a good idea what was wrong with her, but what to do about it was another matter.

All her life she had wanted a child of her own and now, at her age, it had happened. It was morning sickness she was having; she was carrying Ethan Postlethwaite's child, at the age of forty-two. Would he stand by her, and would she be able to cope? She'd no idea how to bring a child up of her own. Perhaps she'd be better getting rid of it – as the doctor, she knew, would advise her to do. All her life she had been warned not to risk a pregnancy, knowing that her heart was not strong, and she had heeded the doctor's words. Now that she was actually pregnant, she was scared for both of their futures.

There was a woman who was known to her, from buying salve for the cows' udders; she might be able to help. She lived on the back streets of Liverpool, in the poorest area, and her kitchen was filled with herbs and potions that the poor locally relied upon. She would seek her advice and, hopefully, the woman would be able to help her in the situation she found herself in.

Gladys shook her head, thinking of what her father would have said: 'That's because you've let a new bull in t'field.' She heard him saying it, and it was true: Ted either hadn't, or wouldn't, father a child, but now she knew that Ethan was still very much a virile man. A virile man who would not like hearing that he had a child on the way, if she knew him at all.

Amy walked through the streets towards the market. She'd decided she'd go there first, drop off her shopping at home and then have a dawdle down Lord Street, visiting the arcade, which was filled with small individual shops, ideal for finding Christmas presents for those she loved. The market was best visited first in any case, as the fish would be fresh in, and the bread that Gladys had put down on her list newly baked. She walked amongst the early morning shoppers with her basket over her arm and her shawl wrapped tightly around her. It was freezing, there was a real nip in the air, and folk were wrapped up warm against the cold wind that blew directly off the Irish Sea and up through the busy streets. The market was bustling, with the stallholders all yelling and shouting their wares in order to attract buyers.

She walked up Great Charlotte Street and visited the fish market first, weaving past boxes of newly caught fish with their mouths still agape and their scales shining in the weak winter sun. Boxes of oysters and cockles lined the walkways, as fishermen delivered them to the wholesale market before they were sold to the public market next door. The air smelt of fish, and their entrails stank in the drainage gullies that criss-crossed the market. No wonder Gladys hadn't wanted to come, Amy thought as she watched three pieces of haddock being skinned for supper that night; it was churning her stomach, along with the smell and guts that lay discarded. Noisy, squawking seagulls gathered above her head – it would be feast time when the market closed later in the day and all the surfaces were swilled clear.

She placed the fish in her basket and made her way into the main market, then jostled with the other women buying for their families and haggling over the prices.

Bread bought, she made her way to the vegetable and fruit stall, finding apples and a cabbage; fruit and vegetables were not abundant in December, so it was a case of buying what was there. She paid and watched as a poor woman, down on her luck, begged the stallholder for the leaves he had discarded, to make a broth with. Life was by no means a bed of roses for some people in Liverpool. Amy was just thankful her father had made enough money to see that they were comfortable, although by no means as wealthy as some of the merchants, who lived in the grand houses that had been built on the back of trading goods at the port.

She walked past the tobacco factory. Its smell filled the air, and Amy watched for a brief second or two the delivery of tobacco leaves from countries that she had never heard of, let alone visited. Not concentrating on where she was going, she accidentally knocked into a young boy with her basket and got a mouthful of language, the like of which she'd rarely encountered, then she watched as he dodged his way through the crowds.

'Make sure he's not pinched your purse. He's known for his light fingers, is that little bugger,' said a man as he watched the scene, his cart full of frozen ice that he was taking to the fish market.

Amy quickly checked the contents of her basket and, to her relief, her purse was still there. 'Thank you for warning me – he's not helped himself this time.' She smiled at the fella, who looked her up and down.

'Be more careful, Miss, else he'll be back, if he thinks you are an easy target.' He spat a mouthful of saliva out and then went on his way, pushing his cart quickly, not wanting the ice to melt before it got to its destination.

With those words of warning and the food shopping done, Amy decided to return home and empty her basket before going to look for Christmas presents. She lingered for a few minutes more, to buy a bunch of holly with red berries on it from the flower seller at the edge of the market. She'd place a sprig in each of the windows at home and brighten it up, ready for Christmas, she thought as she walked down the street past the Star Theatre. She stopped to admire a poster showing a woman singing, and longed to be able to watch a show for a change, and have some time to enjoy herself. It seemed that since they had moved into the dairy, all it had been of late was work – that's why she would make the most of an hour's shopping on Lord Street, she decided, as she opened the door to the house and walked into the kitchen to empty her basket.

'Hello, Gladys, I'm back. I'm going to drop the shopping off and then I'll be on my way again,' Amy shouted at the bottom of the stairs, once she realized Gladys was not on the ground floor. However, there was no reply, so she went out into the yard, having put the groceries away. She put her head through the shippon door, but there was nobody there except the cows; and the dairy was likewise empty.

Gladys was not to be found – so much for being ill, Amy thought, as she slammed the house door behind her. There was nothing wrong with Gladys, she decided, as she walked to Lord Street and an hour's shopping without any guilt, now she had found out Gladys was not working, either. She should have known there was nothing wrong with her, the bloody woman.

Gladys pulled her shawl over her head and hoped nobody had seen her leaving the woman's house, feeling that everybody knew what she had discussed with the old herbalist. In her pocket was a potion that the woman said would help her lose the unwanted child, if her instructions were followed. Gladys felt ill just thinking about the conversation she had had; and at the thought that she was to get rid of a child, which a few years ago she had wanted so badly. Now she was a widow on her own, with a man that she knew was growing tired of helping her run the dairy, and who would not be with her forever, no matter how he had felt about her in the past. Besides that, Ethan's daughter would always come first, and her own child would never be favoured as much as his precious Amy.

She put her head down and quickly made her way home. She needed to return to the dairy and start cleaning and making the butter, before Ethan and Amy returned. She'd no intention of telling either of them about the unwanted baby that was growing in her belly. She'd do away with it, and nobody would be any the wiser.

Amy had lingered in Lord Street. She'd enjoyed her time shopping, buying presents for all the family. Some snuff for her grandfather and a boxed set of handkerchiefs for her grandmother. She also watched the young well-to-do women of the city parading down through the shopping arcades, dressed to the nines, and wished that she had grown up in a more elegant family and had more fashion sense. She was in the midst of pondering whether to buy a box of chocolates for Billy, and wondering if it was a bit too forward to do so, when, as if by magic, he appeared, standing behind her.

'They'll make you fat, and then I'll stop walking out with you,' Billy said cheekily as he held his horse's reins and laughed at the surprise on Amy's face.

'I was only looking. Besides, they wouldn't be for me. They were to be for a Christmas present. What are you doing down here – should you not be busy at work?' Amy said, before she realized that in the cart being pulled by the horse was a piece of furniture that Billy was obviously delivering somewhere.

'I'm taking Turner's their new dresser. It's bloody heavy, so I hope there's somebody at the shop to help me unload it.' He scratched his head and lifted his cap to reveal the curly black hair that Amy loved him for. 'More to the point, what are you doing here – has she let you out of the dairy? I've seen your father from a distance up Gable Street. He must have been on his way home, and he looked bloody weary.' Billy leaned back against the shop's wall and looked at Amy.

'Gladys was ill this morning. She was sick, so I did the milking with my father and then she insisted, when he'd gone out, that she would do the dairy and I could have an hour or two to myself. I don't know what game she is playing, because when I went back with the shopping from the market, she wasn't anywhere to be seen.' Amy sighed.

'Aye, I think I saw her as well. She was nearly running as I came out of the yard. She looked to have been coming from up Brownlaw Hill. Wherever she had been, it's not the finest of places to visit.' Billy noticed the worry on Amy's face. 'Perhaps she was visiting the pig slaughterhouse – she's perhaps thinking of ordering a ham for Christmas.'

'She's not likely to have been visiting there, after spewing up all morning. Lord knows what she's been playing at!' Amy looked at Billy. 'You'd better get that delivered, else you'll be getting the sack. I'll see you on Sunday, won't I? We'll catch up then.' Amy smiled as he pulled on the horse's reins and the animal snorted all over him.

'Sure, I'd better be on my way. There's a ceilidh to be held at St Patrick's Hall next Saturday. I don't suppose you fancy joining me, do you? It'll be full of us Irish and Catholics, so perhaps your father won't allow you?' Billy looked at Amy and saw her grin.

'A what – a ceilidh! What's that?' Amy asked, as Billy shook his head in disbelief at her not knowing what it was.

'A dance, you idiot – an Irish dance night. To be sure, it'll be a good night. A right good laugh and plenty of good craic,' Billy said and watched Amy's face light up.

'A dance! I'd like to see my father stop me. Anyway, he won't be bothered if you are Catholic, Protestant or

Methodist. He doesn't believe in religion, never has. He'll no doubt give both you and me our orders, and lecture me on how to behave.' Amy hung her head in shame.

'By the sound of it, he happens needs the lecture, if Gladys is being sick in the morning. That's what comes of living over the brush. I bet she's expecting.' Billy was used to the signs. Catholic families were renowned for being large, and he'd often heard the women who lived around him being sick of a morning.

'No, she can't be, she's too old! She'd just eaten something that didn't agree with her!' Amy blushed, as she never talked about such things.

'You'll see. If she's sick for a few mornings on the trot, then your father has a lot to answer for.' Billy grinned. 'I might be wrong, so take no notice, but it wouldn't surprise me.' He pulled himself up on to his cart. 'I'll see you Sunday. Ask your father about that dance and then I'll get us tickets.' He flicked the reins over his horse's back and went on his way, whistling as he went down Lord Street, thinking about taking Amy to the ceilidh. He left Amy thinking about the possibility of a baby brother or sister being on the way inside the woman she really did not like.

'There's your bottle of milk of magnesium, which should settle your stomach.' Amy put the clear ribbed bottle down on the table and looked hard at Gladys as she entered the kitchen.

'Did you have enough money? I see you came back with the shopping while I was out across the way. Mrs

Dougherty yelled, saying she wanted some butter, when I was opening the yard doors for your father to come back through. She would insist that I had a cup of tea with her. She's such a gossip, and she kept me there in her kitchen far too long. I'd only just got back in when your father returned.

'Yes, I'd enough money. The market was busy, but cold,' Amy said, knowing full well that Gladys was lying to her. 'So what had Mrs Dougherty to say for herself? Has her Jimmy come back from the sea yet? She never shuts up about him when I see her.' Amy knew full well that Jimmy was in the China Sea, after talking to her neighbour briefly the previous day.

'She never said, and I never asked. I'm going to the dairy. I need some milk for our dinner,' Gladys replied as she made for the back door, away from Amy's questioning eyes.

17

Ethan sat on the edge of the bed as he pulled his braces on over his shirt and looked across at Gladys, sighing deeply. 'Is there something you want to tell me, lass? I'm not that daft, I recognize the signs. And my Grace did the same when she was carrying our Amy. Tha's expecting, and it's all my fault!' He watched as Gladys was sick once more in the pee-pot and brushed her greying hair out of her eyes.

Gladys looked across at him and tried not to cry. She'd not taken her potion, which she had rushed for in a panic. She'd not had the heart to do away with the baby she had wanted so much over the years, when she had opened the bottle and sat looking at it in her hands.

'I might not be. But I think I am. It's too much of a coincidence that I'm being sick of a morning and my monthly has stopped. I'm sorry. I'll understand if you up and leave me. I didn't mean to tie you down by having a baby. I even went and got this potion off an old crone I know, to get rid of it, but when it came to it, I couldn't do it.' Gladys sat on the edge of the bed and sobbed.

Ethan sighed. 'It's as much my fault as yours. I shouldn't have been so eager to bed you. I thought that with you not having children in the past, you couldn't. It must have been Ted that was firing blanks.' He ran his fingers through his hair and continued dressing, then went and stood in front of Gladys, kissing the top of her head as it hung low, waiting to hear what he was going to do. 'Well, there's nowt for it, is there? We'll have to get married. I'm not having a bairn of mine without my name. Mind you, Amy will not be happy. She thinks I should still have eyes for no one but her dead mother – God rest her soul. She'll just have to lump it.' Ethan sat down on the bed next to Gladys. 'Here my lass, come on, there's no need to cry. I thought you were a hard-faced woman who could take on the world.' He held Gladys tightly to him as she sobbed.

'I didn't think you'd stand by me. I thought you'd be out of that door as soon as you had an inkling!' Gladys wiped her nose on her nightdress's sleeve.

'What, and miss out on wedding you again! It will be right, lass – we'll make a do. It isn't exactly what I had planned for myself, but never mind. A baby needs a father, and it isn't its fault that I think with my dick and not my head,' Ethan said quietly. 'Now, are you up to milking this morning? I don't really want to tell Amy the news until after Christmas, if I can get away with it. She'll be writing and telling her grandparents, and then all hell will be break loose. Although she probably has an idea that something's not quite right, by the black looks that she's been giving me of late.'

'She'll hate you for marrying me. She doesn't like me, even though she does her best to hide it.' Gladys reached for her clothes.

'You are just not her mother. I thought she'd have decided to go home to Dent by now, but then Billy came along, and she's smitten with him.' Ethan smirked and laughed. 'She's a bit of a devil. She walks out with Billy on a Sunday, and yet writes to poor Joshua Middleton at least once a week. There's nowt like keeping lads guessing.'

'Billy will not be here forever, and Amy knows that she'll break her own heart if she's not careful.' Gladys fought back the morning's sickness as she buttoned her skirts in the dim lamplight of the bedroom. 'If we wed, you'll have part share in the dairy. It will be yours as well as mine, so you will come off well.' She pinned her long hair up into a bun and looked at her reflection in the dressing-table mirror.

'I'm not marrying you for the dairy. I'm marrying you for this child growing in your belly. Now stop fretting. I'll stand by you, and Amy will have to lump it.' Ethan put his arms around Gladys's stomach and kissed her neck. 'This should have happened twenty-odd years ago. We are going to be a bit long-in-the-tooth when this one's growing up, but perhaps we'll be none the worse for that.'

'I'm frightened, Ethan. I'm old to be having my first,' Gladys whispered.

'It will be right, lass. I'll look after you,' Ethan said

and put his cap on, making his way out of the bedroom and down into the kitchen, where he sat in his chair for a while staring at the four walls of the kitchen. He'd made a right bugger of it, he thought. If he'd wanted to leave, he couldn't now. He'd wed Gladys, and at least part of the dairy, as she said, would be his. He should never have bumped into her that day. She was beginning to prove not to be the woman he had once loved. And Amy was a better judge of character than he was. Gladys was short-tempered, thought only of herself and showed little love towards Amy. The Lord only knew what she was going to be like when a child of her own was born to her. He was the one who would have to lump it and make the best of the situation that he and Gladys were to blame for, because of their lustful ways.

Amy sat at the table. It was Sunday morning, the only time the three of them ate breakfast at a relaxed pace. Today was different, though; it was quiet, and her father looked worried as he asked her if they were to expect Billy calling later that day.

'I think he's calling. He'll want to know my answer to his question,' Amy said coyly.

'Oh, and what question is that? You are not going to run off with him, I hope!' Ethan looked up and grinned at his daughter, knowing full well she might do exactly that, if the lad asked her to.

'No, I keep telling you, we are just friends. Billy wondered if he could take me to the Christmas dance at the

Catholic Hall this coming Saturday. I said I'd have to ask you first, even though I'm old enough to do as I wish now,' Amy replied, watching Gladys as she struggled to eat the porridge she had in front of her.

'The Catholic Hall, is it? It'll be full of the Irish, I suppose, and everybody knows they like a good time.' Ethan sat back and looked at his daughter.

'It's called a ceilidh, so Billy says. I'd never heard of it before.' Amy hoped her father had nothing against her going.

Gladys looked up from her dish and glared at Amy. 'Those Catholics, all they have to do is say a "Hail Mary" and their sins are forgiven. I don't trust them. They'll be trying to convert you as soon as you enter that hall.' She took her dish to the sink and gazed out of the window, rather than think about her stomach churning.

'He'll walk you there and bring you back?' Ethan asked and saw Amy's face light up.

'Yes, and he'll look after me.'

'I suppose it is Christmas, and we have nowt planned. He'll have me to answer to if he brings you back drunk, or worse than that. Get yourself gone with him. I remember when I was young, I used to like the Christmas dances. I'd walk miles to get a glimpse of the girl I'd set my head on. It's how I met your mother at Dent Memorial Hall. By, she was a good dancer.' Ethan sat back and thought about Grace, and how he had loved holding her tightly.

'You met me at the hall at Lund's on the road just past The Moor Cock Inn. You danced with me all night, too.'

Gladys turned and looked at Ethan. 'It goes to show that not a lot of good comes from flirting and holding somebody tightly on the dance floor. You just bear that in mind when you are in that lad's arms,' Gladys spat.

'Now then, lass, you enjoyed those days back then. Let Amy enjoy her days of freedom – they go fast enough,' Ethan said and frowned darkly at Gladys.

'Aye, they do. And before you know it, you are married and in a life of drudgery with children, and tied to somebody you don't really love,' Gladys said, then opened the back door and walked into the yard to let out her feelings.

'Is she alright, Father? I've heard her being ill every morning of late.' Amy glanced towards her father, who hadn't stirred from his chair.

'Aye, she's alright, just upset over something. And I didn't help by mentioning your mother. You go to your dance and enjoy yourself.' Ethan smiled at his daughter.

'Thank you. Billy is to be trusted. I'll wash the breakfast pots, and then I'm going to write my Christmas cards and wrap up my presents for posting to Dent. I've got Grandma and Grandad's presents to post, and I've bought Joshua a bar of chocolate. I'll post it with his card and letter.' Amy went to the sink, looked out of the window and saw Gladys crying as she stood in the shelter of the cowshed.

'Two-timing will get you into bother,' Ethan laughed.

'I'm not two-timing. Billy is a friend, and we are not courting.' Amy blushed.

'Well, be careful with that heart of yours. I don't want

to see it broken by him – or anyone else, come to that,' Ethan sighed.

'Then you'd better go and see to Gladys, as she looks upset. Happen someone has broken her heart?' Amy said and cast her father a knowing glance, before going into the front room to write her letters and parcel her presents. Gladys was definitely expecting, but when was she going to be told?

'You look as if you are ready for Christmas. Are these all the cards and parcels you are going to send?' Billy picked them up from the table, where Amy had placed them.

'Yes. I thought I would send them tomorrow and then they will arrive in good time. Who do you give presents to? I'd rather give than receive. I love to see their faces when I get the present right.' Amy beamed.

'I've nobody to give to, really. Christmas will just be another day, and it's been like that since my father left. I see you've got a present here for that Joshua you keep talking about.' Billy picked up the parcel and felt it. 'A bar of chocolate, that's my guess. Is that to keep him sweet?'

'It is a bar of chocolate – is it that obvious?' Amy said and looked at the parcel. 'No, it's not to keep him sweet. He's always the same, is Josh.' She smiled and put the parcel back down on her pile.

'I think you like him a bit too much,' Billy said sullenly.

'He's back in Dent, Billy O'Hara, and we grew up together. Besides, what is it to do with you? We have an understanding with one another that we are just friends, and nothing more, if you are to go to America,' Amy replied with a glint in her eye.

'Sure, I know, but I still can't help feeling a little jealous. I bet you write all sorts of soppy things to him.' Billy picked up the cushion next door to him and started to kiss it. 'I love you, Josh, please kiss me, more and more,' he said jokingly.

'I do not. We usually discuss sheep, the weather and our families, and I sometimes tell him my worries. I've written and told him about my father and Gladys, because I think you were right. She is expecting. They've both been acting strange of late, and my father didn't complain once about you taking me to the dance on Saturday when I asked him. Although neither of them has said anything to me.'

'Well, he couldn't complain, else he'd be a bloody hypocrite. You innocently coming to a dance with me, while he goes and gets a widowed woman up the duff,' Billy said sharply.

Amy blushed. 'Billy! That's my father you are talking about. Watch what you are saying.'

'So what do you think he'll do now or don't you know?' Billy looked at Amy.

'I don't know. I thought he was getting a bit fed up with Gladys and her dairy, but now a baby will make all the difference. Besides, we might both be wrong. But she'll have to say something soon if she is carrying a baby, as it will begin to show.'

'Well, at least you'll be with me on Saturday and we'll have a good time. It'll be a noisy affair – it always is –

but it's grand. I right enjoy the Christmas dance, it's a chance to catch up with folk and enjoy the craic. I'll pick you up here at eight. It is only a short walk to the hall.' Billy grinned. 'Don't wear that bloody skirt you are fond of. It'll be no good for the dancing we'll be doing, that's for sure.'

'I wasn't going to. I've a red dress with a lace collar that I've brought back with me from Dawson. I've let the hem down and the seams out, because it was one my mother made for me before she died, so I've grown a little since the last time I wore it. It is my favourite. I always think of her when I wear it,' Amy said wistfully.

'You'll look grand, whatever you are in. We'll make the most handsome couple in the pool,' Billy said and smiled.

Amy looked at him and thought: 'A couple'. We said we were just friends!

'I haven't seen you in that dress since your mother made it, shortly before she died. I remember her sewing it out of some material those lasses from the saloon gave her.' Ethan looked at his daughter in the plush red dress, with her hair hanging loose over her shoulders and a small evening bag under her arm.

'I thought it looked right for Christmas, and I never get a chance to wear it.' Amy smiled and pulled her skirt out, to show herself off.

'You'll have every lad in Liverpool looking at you. My lass has grown up in front of my very eyes,' Ethan said quietly. 'Your mother would be so proud of you.

Hey up, here's your escort, right on time.' He went to the kitchen door and opened it, to find Billy standing on the step, shivering in the frosty night.

'Evening, Mr Postlethwaite. It's a bit nippy this evening.' Billy looked sheepish, expecting a lecture on what was expected of him for taking Ethan's daughter to the dance. He blew on his hands and waited.

'It is that, Billy. She's ready for you, and looking bonny too. You make sure you look after her, or else you'll have me to answer to.' Ethan thought the lad seemed absolutely petrified. He remembered standing in the same shoes, when he was his age and calling on Gladys.

'I will, Mr Postlethwaite. She'll be safe in my hands,' Billy said.

'That's what I'm bothered about, lad. Now get yourselves gone. The door will not be locked, but no later than midnight home.' Ethan turned to Amy and made way for her to take Billy's arm. 'Behave yourself,' he said as she brushed past him.

'I will, Father. Stop your worrying,' Amy said, as she grabbed Billy's arm and gave him a smile, at which Billy did not know where to look because of his embarrassment.

'Has she gone then?' Gladys asked as she came down the stairs and saw Ethan sitting glumly in his chair.

'Aye, she has. I hadn't realized until now how grown-up she is these days. I've got one nicely raised and off my hands, only to find I've another on the way.'

'Don't you be going and having second thoughts about

this baby, Ethan Postlethwaite. You've promised to marry me – don't let me down now,' Gladys said and sat down next to him, reaching for his hand.

'I'll not, but it isn't what I'd planned. I've never been the best of husbands, and I can't say that you and a new baby will change me. We'll get wed and make the best of it.' Ethan picked up his pipe and gazed into the fire. If it hadn't been for Amy still living with them, he'd walk out on Gladys, now that he had been given time to think about the situation he was in. He didn't want this baby. And, more importantly, the love he had once felt for the woman had been tainted by the years away from her, and he now realized that he didn't love Gladys half as much as he'd loved his Grace.

Amy held her breath. She could hear all the noise coming from the Catholic Hall, and young people kept going past them, laughing and giggling and enjoying themselves in the run-up to Christmas.

'Oh, Billy, I don't know anybody. I'm not Irish or Catholic, and I shouldn't be here,' she said and looked up at him.

'Of course you should – you are my guest. It doesn't matter that you are neither of those. The dance is open for everyone. Father Thomas will make you welcome, I've told him you are coming.'

'Father Thomas! Oh, I don't think I should talk to a priest, I wouldn't know what to say.' Amy felt sick at the thought of walking into the hall and nobody knowing her.

'Give over. Now come on, once you've had a drop of the good stuff inside you, you'll not be worried about anything. There's bound to be a drop of poteen being handed around – there always is at these dos, it helps everybody relax. Father Thomas is a grand man. He's offering to find me a family to live with, once I've got my passage to New York.' Billy grinned and took her hand as he walked into the hall, followed by a hesitant Amy. 'Come on, enjoy yourself.' He led her into the middle of the hall.

The wooden dance floor was filled with couples dancing, while around the edge the single girls eyed the single boys across the other side of the room, and whispered to their friends and giggled and blushed when they caught one another's eye. On the stage at the far end of the hall the band played, filling the place with their boisterous sounds. A bodhrán drum set the beat, with the man playing it deftly, twiddling the stick between his fingers as he smiled and shouted encouragement at the dancers, along with his fellow musicians of a fiddle player, a concertina player and a man who looked like a true Irish leprechaun, who ran his fingers up and down a penny whistle.

Amy watched and couldn't stop her toes tapping as somebody grabbed her arm and swung her around in the dance. She laughed and grabbed the next person's arm and soon found herself twirling around to the catchy tunes, which you couldn't help but like, as you were passed from person to person and made welcome by the rest of the dancers. Billy looked across at her as she laughed and smiled, with her black hair shining and her cheeks as red as the dress she was wearing. She was the bonniest lass in the room and she was on his arm, he thought, as she came to his side and caught her breath.

'See, I said you'd enjoy yourself. If you can stand still while this music plays, there's something wrong with you.' He laughed as Amy gasped for air.

'I've never danced like this before. I love the music and the reels they are playing, and everyone is so friendly.' Amy looked up at Billy and knew she felt slightly more than friendship for the lad she'd promised just to be friends with. He was dark and handsome and everybody knew him. He had been slapped on his back and had his hand shaken by all the young men, while the girls eyed him up and down and stared at her, wondering how she had managed to corner him for the evening.

'Here, Billy, take a swig of my mother's finest.' A dark-haired lad passed Billy a silver hip-flask and grinned. 'Give some to your lass an' all, but don't drink it all, you greedy gannet.'

Billy took a quick swig and screwed up his eyes as the potent liquid slipped down his throat. 'Here, Amy, try a bit of Irish moonshine. Not too much, though, I don't want your father playing hell with me.' He passed the flask to Amy and watched as she hesitantly took a swig, then started spluttering as she swallowed the strong whisky.

'Oh, you can keep that – it's like poison.' Amy wiped her chin with her hand and looked at both of the lads.

'That's blasphemy! I'll not be telling me Ma you said

that.' The lad laughed and patted Billy on the back again, then made his way through the crowd, offering people a drink as he went.

'He's a bugger, is that Danny. He'll have half the dance hall drunk before he goes home. He tempts you with a free drink and then sells bottles of it outside around the back of the hall – he does it every year.' Billy took Amy's arm and guided her to two empty chairs, where they sat and watched everybody dancing. 'Are you alright? We'll sit this next one out. I can't do step-dancing.'

Amy and Billy watched as a line of girls did original Irish dancing with their backs and arms straight, while they bent their legs and tapped their feet hard, lifting them off the ground like pawing horses.

'That's amazing,' Amy said and smiled, reaching for Billy's hand to hold as she watched.

Father Thomas walked along the line of his parishioners and noted who was behaving themselves and who wasn't. 'Ah, Billy, I thought you'd be here.' He came to a halt by the lad he'd known since he had come to live in Liverpool. 'And you've brought a friend.' The priest looked down at Amy. 'I don't believe I've met you before. Do you attend St Patrick's?'

Billy stood up. 'This is Amy Postlethwaite – you'll not know her, Father.'

'I see, you are just joining Billy at our annual dance? I hope you are enjoying yourself?' Father Thomas asked and smiled at Amy, then turned to Billy as he noticed the look of love the boy gave her.

'Yes, thank you, Father. I've never been to a ceilidh before. I'm grateful that Billy thought of asking me,' Amy said quietly, as she took in the priest, dressed all in sombre black.

'Yes, he did well to ask you.' Father Thomas smiled and then addressed Billy. 'I'd like to have a word with you before next weekend. Can you call round and see me as soon as possible?'

'Yes, of course I will, Father. Will tomorrow evening at the rectory, around seven, be convenient?' Billy shuffled his feet and knew what was going to be asked of him, and the dressing-down that would probably follow.

'Yes, that will be fine. I'll see you then.' Father Thomas smiled and moved on between the dancers.

'What will he want to see you for Billy? He looked so serious,' Amy said.

'It'll be something for nothing. He'll probably want some kindling sticks from the joiner's yard before we finish for Christmas – he's always after something for nothing, or begging for the Church. Come on, stop worrying. Let's dance!' Billy pulled on Amy's hand and hooked her arm, then twirled her around. Tomorrow was another day, and he'd worry about that when it came.

It was after midnight when the two of them walked back along the empty streets to the dairy. Billy stopped outside the wooden gates under the gas light and looked at Amy. 'We've had a good night, haven't we?'

'Yes, I wished it would never end.' She gazed into Billy's eyes as he reached for her hand.

'Me, too. You looked beautiful tonight. I was proud to be with you.' He smiled and then moved forward as she leaned on the dairy gates. 'I shouldn't do this, but I can't help myself.' He cupped Amy's face in his hands and kissed her, as she had only ever dreamed of being kissed.

They both looked at one another and then smiled. 'So much for just friends, Billy O'Hara,' Amy whispered and kissed him back.

'Very good friends, that's what we are – there's no harm in that,' he said as he kissed her again. 'But now you get to your bed, else we will both be in bother, and I might get carried away.' He let her hand drop and turned to go.

'Will I see you before Christmas?' Amy asked as he walked away.

'Sure, else I'll not be able to give you my Christmas wishes. I'll be in the yard on Tuesday, Christmas Eve, instead of Thursday. I'll see you then,' Billy shouted.

Amy felt her heart racing. She'd never been kissed like that before and she'd liked it. She could quite happily fall in love with Billy O'Hara.

18

Billy stood on the rectory steps and waited until the bell that he had just rung was answered by Father Thomas's maid. He looked up at the Gothic building and felt worried. Father Thomas didn't demand to see you unless there was something wrong, or there was something he thought he should intervene in. Billy knew the priest wouldn't be pleased that he'd taken a Protestant lass to the Catholic Hall, but he'd spoken to Amy, so he couldn't have been that offended.

'Father Thomas has been expecting you – he's in his study.' The maid opened the door and took Billy through the tiled hallway into the book-filled study. Billy stood and looked around him; all the furniture was gleaming and smelt of lavender polish and ageing books. It was a room that made him feel belittled and small. He was in the presence of a learned man and one of the cloth, to be obeyed. As he held his cap in his hands, he watched Father Thomas, looking stern in his black robes and white collar, reach for a letter from his desk.

'Now then, Billy, I suppose you are wondering why I asked you to come and see me this evening?' Father Thomas looked up at the young lad that he'd kept an interest in since he'd lived in his parish.

'I am, Father. I know I haven't been attending Mass and confession as often as perhaps I should, if that's what is worrying you,' Billy said, shamefacedly.

'That's for your own conscience, Billy. Only you will know if you need to attend and seek forgiveness for the wrongs you have done. But no, it's not about your confession – or lack thereof.' Father Thomas gave Billy a piercing stare. 'I've had a letter from a family that I keep in touch with and helped to settle in New York. They've done well for themselves. They went with next to nothing and now have a building firm that's expanding by the day. They've written to me asking if I know anybody who deserves the same break as them, by offering the right person part-passage and a job as an apprentice joiner or, indeed, a time-served joiner.'

Father Thomas stopped and noticed the surprise and excitement on Billy's face.

'They are from Donegal originally, a good Catholic family by the name of Murphy, who live in the Bronx district. They are offering, as I say, part-passage, a job with their firm and somewhere to live, for the right person.' Father Thomas stopped and let Billy talk, as he shook his head and couldn't believe his ears.

'Are you asking me? Do you think it is right for me?

I can't believe it! It is what I've always dreamed of – it's what I've been saving my money for – a passage to America and somewhere to stay, and a job. I can't believe my luck.' Billy grinned and stood up and shook the Father's hand. 'I'll never be able to thank you, and them, enough. I really won't.' He sat back down and listened to what the job entailed, and more about the family, taking in the priest's every word. The Father would reply straight away and arrange part-payment for the ticket on board a ship, as soon as possible.

'Can you afford part-payment for your ticket, Billy? The family wants you to show your commitment to them by meeting them halfway, with your travel costs,' Father Thomas said and looked earnestly at him.

'I can. And I'll have some left to live on for a while. I've been saving up these last few years for this.' Billy sat back and smiled.

'Right, then I'll try and get you on a ship towards the end of January. Now, what about the lass you had on your arm? Is it a serious relationship? She'll not be included in the deal, Billy. It is only for you.' Father Thomas looked at him hard.

'Sure, I realize that. It will be alright, as we are just friends. I asked Amy to join me at the dance because she doesn't get out and about much. She'll understand; she knows I've had my head set for America ever since I met her,' Billy said quietly, and thought it was going to be hard to break the news to Amy after their evening together.

'That's as well. I take it she's a Protestant, and it is

best we keep to our own, Billy. Find yourself a good Catholic girl once you are in America. Now, go and have a drink on the strength of you having a new life set out for you. Enjoy Christmas and look to the future. I'll keep in touch with plans and tickets. Perhaps I'll see you more often at church until you go.'

Father Thomas stood up and went to open his study door and patted Billy on his back as the young man thanked him and shook his hand. He was glad he'd been able to help Billy O'Hara. If the opportunity hadn't arrived as it did, he could have seen Billy staying in Liverpool and marrying his so-called 'friend' and regretting his life when he was older. As it was, America beckoned, and it was up to Billy to build his life there.

Tuesday had not come quickly enough, in Amy's eyes, as she ran out of the dairy and went to greet Billy. She had been counting the minutes till seeing him again, and had made sure that she looked her best, as she rushed across the yard to meet him with a Christmas card and a present in her hand.

Billy pulled back the sheeting on his cart and looked at Amy as she ran to him with a huge smile on her face. He breathed in deeply. He must not show his true feelings, and he must keep her at arm's length if he was not to break her heart, he thought as he turned to her.

'Billy, I haven't been able to stop thinking about our night at the ceilidh. I really enjoyed myself.' Amy stood and watched Billy as he looked at her.

'Sure, it was a good night. I'm glad you enjoyed

yourself.' Billy felt a cloud of sadness come over him. He had started feeling something for the bonny black-haired lass, but not enough to stop him following his dreams.

'Here, I've got you a card and a small present for Christmas.' Amy passed him his card and the gift of a pocket knife, lovingly wrapped up in patterned paper. 'I wondered what you were doing for your Christmas Day dinner? My father says you can join us if you want, rather than be on your own.' She looked at Billy as he fingered the present, before putting it and the card into his jacket pocket.

'Thank you – you really shouldn't have bothered with a present. I've not brought you owt.' Billy looked down at his feet and felt awkward. 'I'll not come to dinner. Next door usually has me, but thank you for asking me.'

'Oh, I was hoping that you would – not that Gladys is making a big fuss of it. If I hadn't put holly in the windows, you wouldn't know it was that time of year. There's no Christmas tree or anything. She's gone to the market and shops now, so hopefully we will have something decent to eat.' Amy sensed that something was bothering Billy. 'Are you alright, Billy? I've not done anything wrong, have I? You don't seem to be yourself today.'

'No, nothing. I'm sorry, I didn't want to tell you until after Christmas, but I better had – it will be for the best. I don't want you to get attached to me. As I said at the beginning, it is best to keep us as friends.' He shook his head and tried to smile at Amy.

'Tell me what, Billy? What's wrong?' Amy held her breath.

'I'll be off to America at the end of January. Father Thomas has got me lodgings and a job in New York with a family he trusts. They have even agreed to pay for half my passage. I can't turn it down, Amy; it's everything I ever wanted.' Billy looked at her with pleading eyes, hoping she would understand that he hadn't meant to bring hurt to either of them.

'Oh, I see.' Amy went quiet and thought about it, as she looked at him. 'Then yes, you must go! We always agreed we were to be just friends, knowing that you were to leave to follow your dreams. I wish you well, Billy. I hope that your new life makes you happy.' She stepped forward and kissed him on the cheek and held him tightly for a second, before stepping back and holding his gaze. 'I'll never forget you, but go with my blessing.'

She made her way into the house, running upstairs with tears in her eyes. She splayed herself out on her bed and sobbed into her pillow. Billy O'Hara would always have a piece of her heart, and she had been a fool to give it to him.

'By, Gladys, that looks a grand goose – you've gone to town on the dinner today.' Ethan looked across at Amy. 'Isn't it a fine spread? It's a good job Christmas comes around only once a year, else we'd all be fat as pigs,' he said as he carved the goose and placed it onto their plates.

'It's the pudding I'm looking forward to. There was a

queue as long as my arm at the baker's for them, so they must be good. However, they'll not be as good as Grandma's were. I can taste it now, with a good covering of sherry sauce all over it.' Amy took her plate from her father and looked at the greasy meat of the goose. She'd have preferred anything but goose, but dared not say as much.

'You'll not be getting sherry sauce here. It'll be cream – take it or leave it!' Gladys said, then passed Amy the Brussels sprouts, which were boiled to within an inch of their life and looked like mush in the blue-and-white terrine. Gladys was no cook; it hadn't taken both Ethan and Amy long to find that out.

'We'll open our presents after dinner. It seems that the big man has brought us all one, if not more, by the look of the pile on the sideboard.' Ethan grinned as he ate his goose and wiped his chin as the gravy trickled down it.

'We'll open them in the front room. I've lit the fire and there's a box of chocolates and a bottle of sherry, if anyone wants a tipple. I suppose we'd better celebrate in some way, although there's not a lot to celebrate, to my mind.' Gladys looked at Amy and Ethan and then set about eating her dinner.

'So I take it Billy didn't want to join us?' Ethan said, knowing that Amy had been down-in-the-mouth all morning over something, and he guessed it was to do with Billy not sitting at their table.

'No, and I won't be seeing him as much of him – if at all. He's sailing to New York at the end of January. He's got a job there and somewhere to live. The priest has organized it all for him,' Amy said, holding back her tears.

'Well, he did say he was planning to go. Never mind, Amy, there are plenty more lads out there. And I never said anything, but Billy wasn't right for you – he's a townie at the end of the day. I see there are two or three presents come for you from Dent. It looks like that Joshua Middleton might have sent you something. I recognized the sprawling handwriting when the postman passed me it yesterday morning.' Ethan smiled as Gladys cleared away the empty plates.

'Why do you mention Joshua – he's miles away. We might write to one another, but that's all,' Amy said sharply.

'I just thought you've been friends a long time, you know each other well and he's obviously thought of you this Christmas,' Ethan said, noticing the scowl on his daughter's face. It seemed he couldn't say anything right at the moment, and it was going to be made a whole lot worse with what he was going to say while they were having their pudding.

Gladys placed a dish of plum pudding in front of Amy and Ethan, then looked at him as she picked up her spoon. 'Well, are you going to tell her our news? Let's make it a Christmas dinner to remember,' she said with a hint of sarcasm in her voice.

'Tell me what? If it's about the baby that I know is on the way, then you needn't bother. I've heard you being sick first thing in a morning, then ailing nothing as the day goes on. So I know your secret,' Amy said and looked at her father and Gladys. She blushed as she said it and pushed the pudding away from her – the pudding she had really looked forward to eating.

'I should have known you are not that daft. Aye, we've made a mistake and now we must pay for it. We can't take it out on the baby that'll soon be with us,' Ethan said and looked at the upset on Amy's face. 'I'm sorry, Amy. I should have practised what I preached. Anyway, I can't see the baby without a father, so I've arranged with the vicar to have us married as soon as he can read the banns.' Ethan sighed at the tears running down his daughter's face. As far as she was concerned, Grace would always be the only wife he should have wanted.

'How could you, Father? Have you forgotten my mother already?' Amy pushed her chair back and stared at Gladys. 'And don't think you will ever be my mother, because she was ten times the woman you'll ever be.'

Gladys shook her head and breathed in deeply. 'Now watch what you are saying, my lass. This is still my home, and I needn't have you under my roof.'

'Gladys, hold your noise! You'll not talk to my lass like that, and she's every right to say what she's said. I don't deserve any kind words. And if you want to marry me, then Amy lives here until she wants to leave and has somewhere else to go to.' Ethan glared at Gladys and then walked over to Amy, putting his arm around her. 'Now, don't be upset. Nothing changes really, as you are still my precious daughter.'

'Leave me alone. You have deserted me, Billy is going away and I have nobody.' Amy pulled her father's arms from around her and ran out of the house into the yard, then through the dairy up to the spare bedroom, which was supposed to have been her father's. If only he had stayed in that room, she thought, as she lay on the iron bed, which creaked with every move she made. It was the worst Christmas Day she had ever had. She sobbed and sobbed, feeling sorry for herself. She'd got used to thinking that perhaps Gladys was carrying her father's baby, but for him to marry her was a step too far, in her eyes. How could he love somebody like Gladys, after loving her mother for so long? She longed to go and cry in Billy's arms, but he'd made it clear that he didn't want her, either. She was on her own and about to have the stepmother from hell. Amy despaired as she cried herself to sleep in the unloved bedroom.

It was dark when she awoke and she had to gather her senses for a moment, wondering what time of day it was, then suddenly remembering the whole terrible event of Christmas dinner. She looked around her. The gas light from the street was throwing shadows on the walls, and the smell of the stored hay filled the air. She sighed; perhaps she had been selfish. After all, what was her father supposed to do: leave Gladys holding his baby? When it came to Billy, she had known from the outset of their friendship that it was just that, and she shouldn't have given her heart so freely.

The cold of the building suddenly got her shivering, and Amy decided to eat humble pie and apologize for her behaviour. After kissing Billy, and feeling the things she did for him, she could understand how her father had ended up in Gladys's bed; after all, she had been his old flame. You couldn't help your feelings and desires, she thought, as she walked down the stairs, through the deserted dairy and out into the yard. The night was still and calm, and she stood for a while listening to the low bellowing of the cows in the shippon and looking up at the star-filled sky. She would pick up the courage to make her apologies, even though they were only half-meant, in Gladys's case.

'So, you've decided to join us, have you? I saw you go into the dairy house, and I thought I'd leave you to it. I knew you'd want time to think things over and make sense of it all. Nobody has gone out of their way to hurt you – it's just the way life rolls the dice.' Ethan was sitting next to the fire in the front room, with a drink of sherry in his hand and Gladys sitting across from him.

'I'm sorry, Father, Gladys. It was one thing on top of another, and now I've had time to ponder everything, I think I was being a bit selfish.'

Gladys gave a sigh. 'A little, my dear. I know you love your father, and that you will probably find it hard to share him. However, you are not a child any more. Another few months or years and you could well have a man of your own to love. And then you'll realize that he's doing right by this child I'm carrying,' Gladys said and looked at Amy. 'Now come and warm yourself; have a sherry and a chocolate. We haven't opened our presents yet. Your father said we had to wait until you came to your senses. As for Billy O'Hara, he had his head set on going to America from the very minute he arrived in Liverpool and you couldn't stop him, even if you tried. Remember him as your first love and let him go,' she continued, with surprising warmth in her tone, as she passed Amy the chocolates and smiled.

'Aye, lass, I'm not going anywhere, and I don't expect you to be going anywhere, either. You will always be my daughter, who I love more than life itself, so stop your worrying and enjoy what's left of Christmas. Now, let's have these presents opened and finish the day on a good note. We'll be back at it in the morning. Folk will want their milk whether it is Boxing Day or not – there's no peace for the wicked.'

Ethan smiled and watched as Amy picked out a chocolate and thanked Gladys as she reached for the parcels from the sideboard. Amy passed her own parcels to her father and Gladys, and looked at the three that were hers. She smiled at her grandmother's handwriting as she felt the parcel, before quickly unwrapping it to find a shawl that had been hand-knitted, with love in every stitch. The green-and-black moss-stitched shawl was finished off with some tassels at each corner, and the weight of it would keep her warm, no matter what the weather.

'Aye, that'll be from your grandmother – she always insisted everybody kept warm and sat many an hour knitting, looking out of the window down the dale.' Ethan smiled and started to open his present from Amy. A smirk came across his face as he realized his present was braces. 'Are you trying to tell me something, lass?' He grinned at his daughter.

'No, what do you mean? I just noticed you needed a new pair of braces,' Amy said innocently, not knowing what he was grinning at.

'I thought you were hinting that I need to keep my trousers on, and up.' Ethan winked at Gladys, who said nothing, but smiled.

'Oh no, honestly, I never bought them because of that.' Amy blushed.

'Well, they are grand. I'll start wearing them tomorrow. Now what's in that lad from Dent's parcel? It felt a bit fragile when I took it from the postman.'

Amy unwrapped the brown paper to find a square parcel wrapped in Christmas paper with robins and holly on it, and a tag that read: *Happy Christmas, Amy. Something to remember me by.* She unwrapped the newspaper surrounding a wooden frame with a photo of Joshua inside it. He'd taken the trouble to travel down to Settle by train to the Horner studio, where he had posed against a mountainous background; he stood there, smiling at her and reminding Amy how much she missed him. She looked at him. Josh was a true friend and wouldn't abandon her, like Billy had, she thought as her father came behind her and looked at the photograph.

'Bloody hell, he's grown up – he's a handsome bugger, isn't he?' He sat back down in his seat and winked at Gladys, as she opened her parcel from Amy and looked at her rose brooch.

'Very nice, Amy. I'll wear it on my wedding day. I don't have a lot of jewellery. You've done me proud,' Gladys said and pinned it to her blouse.

'I didn't know what to buy you, and that just caught my eye.' Amy smiled and felt awkward.

'Go on, you have got a present from both of us. It doesn't look much, but it is. Not many lasses will have anything near it.' Ethan held his breath as Amy opened the small, flat parcel, which felt like a book.

'Oh my Lord, it's a bank book with my name on it.' Amy opened up the savings book from the Yorkshire Bank and stared at the opening balance, made by her father in her name. 'I can't accept this!' She looked at her father with tears in her eyes. She had been so hard on him at dinnertime, and now she was looking at a bank account into which he'd paid fifty pounds for her own personal use.

'Aye, you can. You went through a lot when I trailed you and your mother to the Yukon, and it's my way of making you more independent. Gladys and I are going to pay you for the hours you work in the dairy as well. You've never asked for a penny since we came here, and it is only right that we give you something for the hours you put in. After all, it isn't your fault that your father's getting married instead of buying a business.' Ethan held his hand out for Gladys to hold and gave her a look of reassurance.

'I don't know what to say. My own money – I can't believe it!' Amy grinned.

'You don't have to say anything. You'll earn what money you make, and more besides, once this baby is born. Gladys isn't the youngest mother in the world, and she'll need your help in the run-up to the birth and when it is first born. I hope this mends any bad feelings that you women have between one another. I can't stand another day of sniping and arguing. It will reassure you that I love you with all my heart, and I want nothing but the best for you.'

Ethan looked across at his daughter, whose eyes were full of tears. She had been wrapped up in her own world of late, and he had wanted to leave both women far behind him at times. But now was a moment to stand together and make the best of a bad job, whether he loved Gladys or not. Amy could do as she wished now, but he sincerely hoped she would be faithful and would stay to help him and Gladys run the dairy – the dairy that would be partly his, once he was married to Gladys, and it wouldn't touch his bank balance.

19

'You know, I've not always been this bitter and twisted old woman that you see in front of you,' Gladys said to Amy as they both worked together in the dairy.

'I don't think you are bitter and twisted.' Amy looked at Gladys and then continued to add salt to the freshly churned cream, which had been turned into a bright golden-yellow butter, before patting it into half-pound packages.

'Aye, you do. I know you do, because I'd think that of me. I have a tongue on me that can stab many a person where it hurts, if I put my mind to it. It's life that does that, Amy – you think on that, when you are looking for a man of your own.' Gladys started to cut up the greaseproof paper for the butter to be wrapped in, once the last drops of whey had been patted out of it, weighed and shaped.

'I gave my heart too readily to Billy, if I am truthful. I knew he was leaving and that I couldn't hold him back. It hurt so much to think he'd leave me for a place that is exactly the same as here. There's only land, sea and sky wherever you go; and folk, of course, but they are all the same, from what I've seen of them,' Amy replied. She sighed as she set about taking her thoughts of Billy out upon the butter pats.

'But he doesn't know that, lass. You've been across that sea, so you know what is on the other side. He doesn't; he just dreams of a better life, as all of us do. Sometimes the best things are under our very own noses, but we don't realize it. Perhaps I should have married your father all those years back. However, Ted came along and seemed to be the better man, but perhaps I shouldn't have let my father and brothers bully me. Your father didn't have any money back then and he was a bit of a romancer – as they say, up the Dales. Now he's back, and he looks at me sometimes and thinks: where has the young lass I used to love gone? I know he does. It's because of living with a man for the last twenty-odd years who thought only of money and had no time for the frivolities of love.' Gladys regarded the young woman in front of her, who she knew hated her for pinching her father from her.

'Do you still love my father? Did you keep on loving him, even when you were supposedly happily married? That must have hurt you so much.' Amy looked at Gladys and, for the first time, could feel some sympathy for her.

'Aye, I did love him for a long time. And I couldn't believe it was him, when I met him outside the boarding house. It was if my prayers had been answered, after all these years. However, I hadn't realized that his life and his love had moved on. He remembered me for who I used to be, not who I am now. He doesn't love me; he loves a memory, and his heart belongs to you and your mother, and always will do. He's marrying me for the sake of the child I'm carrying, because one thing your father remains is honourable.' Gladys sat down on the milk stool. 'This bairn I'm carrying will never be loved as much as you are by him. I'll love it, because I've always wanted a child to call my own. And I'll always feel for your father, but not with the same love we felt all those years back, as time has taken its toll.'

'You don't know that. My father will love it, I'm sure. And I'm sure he loves you,' Amy said, trying to sound positive, but knowing that she had seen signs in her father of regret at the situation he was in.

'We'll see. The last thing I wanted to do was become a burden, so we should never have set eyes on one another that afternoon. Then we wouldn't be here where we are now, with you hating my every word and your father having to walk me down the aisle. Take heed of what I say. Make sure you love the man you are to marry for himself, not out of lust. And be sure he loves you for what you are, not just as a fancy who looks good on his arm.' Gladys smiled up at Amy. 'I've laid my heart open to you. Now you must think what you will of me, but I don't want us to be enemies. We both love the same man, but in different ways.'

'Right, a fresh start between both of us. I promise to stop being the spoilt brat, if you promise me that you will always be there for my father, no matter how much he tests us both.' Amy smiled at the woman she had vowed to hate all her life.

'It's a deal. Now, my advice to you is to write to that lad at Dent, because he obviously thinks a great deal of you. Plus, make it right with Billy. Next time he's in the yard, wish him well and then put him behind you. Don't let him still have that piece of your heart twenty years on, and still be thinking "What if?", as I was.' Gladys rose from her stool and put her arms round Amy. 'I'm not such a bad old stick, once you get used to me, and once I start trusting you. We'll make a good family, if we are given the chance.'

'We can but try. My father has a lot to answer for, if he did but know it.' Amy let Gladys hold her tightly.

'He has that, but then he always did set his head on things, regardless of anybody who stood in his way. Now we had better get on with wrapping this butter, else he'll accuse us of slacking when he comes back from his round. And we can't have that. After all, he just delivers the stuff and we do all the work. He's not a cowman, but don't tell him I said that.' Gladys grinned.

'I know. He's no farmer – never will be. He's not keen on work, full stop, but I didn't say that.' Amy smiled.

'It seems we both accept him with all his flaws. As I say, we both love him for what he is, like your mother did, I'm sure.' Gladys watched Ethan come back into the yard with the milk float, and the pony dragging its feet. She'd made her peace with Amy. She hadn't the energy to argue and fight with her. Although she was only a couple of months pregnant, the baby was telling on her. She'd need Amy's help in the dairy in future, and it would make Ethan more settled, once married, if he knew that his precious daughter and she had become friends at long last.

It was late evening and, in the illumination from the gas light, Amy sat writing letters back home. She'd a lot to tell her grandparents and she hesitated with her words, knowing that the marriage of her father to Gladys would not be approved of, especially as it was a hasty one, with a baby on the way. However, she told them the news and pondered on their faces, when they had read her words. She wrote about Billy going to America and how she was going to miss him, and that she missed home, but knew she was wanted here with her father. She looked at her words and thought that all she ever wrote to her grandparents was a tale of one crisis after another, even though she did not tell them everything and held back on how she sometimes did not see eye-to-eye with Gladys.

She sealed the letter in the envelope and kissed the seal on it, before starting to write to Joshua:

My dear Joshua,

Thank you for the photograph of yourself. I have it next to me on my bedroom table. It reminds me of you and home, and helps to keep my spirits lifted. You must have travelled to Settle to have it taken. I used to like visiting there on the train when it was market day.

I hope you had a good Christmas. Mine was marred by the announcement of my father's wedding to Gladys in the next month or so (the date is not yet set). Yes, you would be right to assume it is because she is in the family way, else my father would not be going ahead with it. I don't think he loves her; he did once, but no longer – I can see it in his eyes. It came as a blow to me. As you know, I don't care for Gladys. However, she seems to have mellowed towards me since the announcement of the baby and the wedding. She actually doesn't look very well. Her face is pale and she is tired all the time; she's too old to be having her first baby, if you ask me.

I'm also to lose my good friend Billy O'Hara, who is to pursue happiness in New York. We went to a ceilidh (an Irish dance) together in the Catholic Hall before Christmas and enjoyed ourselves. He's been a good friend, but not in the same way as you are to me. You are never far from my thoughts, and I miss home so much sometimes. I long for the smell of the peat moor and heather, and to watch the clouds scuttle along in open skies, throwing shadows on the fellsides. It is convenient to forget the wet and wild days when it isn't fit to let a dog out. I prefer to remember the days when you and I would wander together for miles and come back home exhausted.

One day soon I will return to you and the dale, especially now that Father has given me my own money. I'm independent, so one day I will do as I please. Do keep writing, Josh. Your letters mean so much to me and you mean a great deal to me, you always have.

With dearest wishes,

Amy

She looked at her letter and wiped a tear away from her eye. She wasn't lying; she did miss home and Joshua. His photograph had worked – it had made her look at him and think about him. He was handsome, faithful and a good person, and she could do worse.

'You don't think Billy has gone already and not let you know?' Gladys swilled the milk kits out in the dairy and watched a new delivery lad arrive with the sawdust, unload it and not talk to anyone as he led his horse and cart out of the yard.

'I don't know. I'd have thought he might have come and say ta-ra, but he'll suit himself, no doubt.' Amy tried to sound unconcerned that she had not seen Billy since the day before Christmas.

'He'll turn up. Bad pennies always do.' Gladys smiled at Amy and then held onto the side of the pot sink as she felt faint.

'You need to go and see a doctor – you don't look well,' Amy said and watched as Gladys closed her eyes and tried to concentrate on her job.

'I'm short of iron, I think. I'll have to eat a few more eggs and cabbage; that'll get me right. I'm not wasting my money on a doctor, when I know it's the baby that's draining me. That and worrying about going to see the Methodist minister at the chapel on Pitt Street. I don't think he'll show either of us much pity for the situation we are in.' Gladys sighed. 'The sooner he can get us married, the better. We are not going to stand on ceremony, and we don't want any fineries, just a ring on my finger and a blessing. We are both too old for any fuss.'

'I hope I'm invited?' Amy said, glancing at Gladys, who really looked tired and washed-out.

'You are bridesmaid. And I suppose I'll need a bouquet of some sort. I'm not bothering with a new dress. I've one that I wear for best that'll do – that is, if it still fits me then.' Gladys had once dreamed of marrying Ethan, but now it felt like a chore, and something she had to do to give his name to her baby.

'I'm sure you will look blooming by then. I understand the first few months of carrying a child are always the worst, and then you are supposed to bloom.' Amy tried to sound positive as Gladys sank once more onto the milking stool.

'Bloom – I don't think I'll ever bloom. My belly might be growing, but blooming is one thing I'm not doing.' Gladys cursed the day she had ever invited Ethan to her bed.

Amy was sitting next to the fire, enjoying the few hours of peace she had to herself. Her father and Gladys had gone to see the Methodist minister, dressed in their best and trying to look respectable, even though they had to tell the minister that Gladys was with child and they wanted to be married as soon as possible. She looked into the fire and decided not to move from the comfort of her seat, and to wallow in the pleasure of her own company. That was until there was a knock on the door, making her go and see who it was, cursing under her breath as she thought of a customer who had run out of milk and had decided to spoil her quiet afternoon.

She opened the door and stood back. 'Billy! I thought you must have gone and left us, as you've not been here this last month or so.' She beamed, glad to see her friend, whom she had not really said goodbye to properly.

'Nay, I sail at five in the morning, but I wanted to come and say goodbye. You seemed upset when I told you my plans, and I wanted to make it right with you.' Billy looked at Amy. He hadn't been able to stop thinking about her since she'd left him standing in the dairy yard before Christmas. He'd seen the hurt in her eyes when he said he was off, and hadn't realized until then how Amy felt about him. 'Have you time to walk down to the docks and pier head with me, for old times' sake?'

'I'm on my own – why don't you come in?' Amy turned and opened the door wider for him.

'Nay, I'd rather take a stroll, please. Just half an hour. You can see the ship I'm going on – it is moored in Albert Dock.' Billy held his hand out for her and waited.

'I'll have to put the fireguard up and grab my shawl. It looks cold out there. I bet it is snowing up at home.' Amy rushed to put the metal fire-frame up, to make the fire safe, and reached for her grandmother's Christmas gift, wrapping it tightly around her. 'I'd like to see your ship. Is she a big one? Are you sailing with the Cunard Line? It seems everyone goes to America with them.'

She grabbed Billy's arm, slamming the house door behind them before walking down the cobbled streets towards the docks. Her heart beat fast. She was with

Billy again and even though he was about to leave her, she felt as if she was walking on cloud nine as they laughed and chatted together.

'No, it's the White Star Line that goes to America. I wish I was in the saloon class, but I've only got a ticket for steerage, along with the rest of the rabble that's hoping to change their lives,' Billy said and held Amy's hand tight.

'We were in steerage when we went out to the Yukon. My mother didn't like it because everybody had to sleep in the same place – men and women and their children all had to turn a blind eye to whoever was in the bunk next to you, although you made some good friends on the voyage. Then we came back in saloon class. Now that was posh, the food was lovely, but I couldn't help but think about the steerage passengers who were bunked up below our deck.'

'Sure, well, beggars can't be choosers. I'm just glad I'm on my way. There she is, the one with the buff-coloured chimney with black around the top. Look at her red pennant with a white star in the centre, fluttering in the wind. Isn't she a picture? The *Oceanic*. I never thought I'd be sailing on her. I've seen her coming and going many a time and wished I was on her.' Billy looked out to the ship, the busy docks and then out further to the wide ocean that he was to cross the following day.

'Yes, she's a bonny ship. Have you got sea legs? Or are you going to be sick on your voyage? I was alright, but Mother was no good at sailing,' Amy said and remembered her mother being ill for most of the trip.

'I am not bothered if I am or not. I'm going to America – it's all I've ever wanted to do.' Billy grinned, and Amy gazed at the colour in his cheeks and at his black hair blowing in the wind. She might not be able to forgive him for leaving her, but she still felt her heart beat fast as she looked at him. It was a lost moment in time as both of them gazed out across the docks and knew that the next few minutes together might perhaps be their last.

'I'll miss you, Billy. I know we said only friends, but it was starting to be more.' Amy looked at him and knew he felt the same. Her eyes started to fill with tears. She didn't want her Billy to leave her.

'Aye, I know. I thought the same.' Billy held her hand tightly. 'Why don't you come with me? I took the liberty of checking this morning if there are tickets still available for a passage. Tell your father you are going with me, and ask him to wish you well.' He put his arm around her. 'I don't want to leave you. I think I might love you, Amy Postlethwaite.'

'Don't say that, Billy, please don't say that. I can't come with you, you know I can't.' Amy looked at him and knew she felt something for him, although whether it was love she wasn't sure. Billy was a bit fickle, and he had a devil-may-care attitude to life, but it was that which attracted her to him.

'Yes, you can. Meet me here at midnight, then we'll be first in line for a ticket for you. Nobody has to know that you are with me. We can say that we met on the ship, once we have landed.' Billy held her tightly and kissed her. 'Come with me – we'll make a life together.'

'Oh, Billy, I don't know. My father would never let me. I'd have to sneak away without him knowing. I have my own money, as he gave me some at Christmas, so I could withdraw some money later this afternoon for my ticket, I suppose.' Amy stared at the lad she thought she loved.

'Sure, do that – you'll not regret it. I'll always be supportive of you.' Billy kissed her again, and Amy felt herself blush as a married couple shook their heads in disgust at their display of love for one another. 'Now, go get packed, get your money and I'll meet you here at midnight. Father Thomas is expecting me. He's got various forms and letters, to make my stay in New York smoother.' Billy paused. 'You will come, won't you? If you've not shown your face by one o'clock, I'll know you've changed your mind, but please don't.' He let go of her hand and smiled. 'I love you.' He started to walk briskly down the dockside.

Amy watched him go. He'd said he loved her! He'd kissed her as she'd never been kissed before, and yet there she was doubting what to do. Did she love him enough to turn her back on her father, her grandparents and even Joshua? She'd lose all of them if she ran away with Billy. She knew it was only herself who could make the decision – the biggest decision of her life. What had she said? There was only land, sea and sky wherever you went. But sometimes there was somebody you loved there too, and that made all the difference!

The grandfather clock at the bottom of the stairs struck twelve: midnight. Amy sat on the edge of her bed, case packed and money in her purse, with a set of letters to the ones she loved next to the photograph of Joshua. If she was going, she would have to leave now, as one o'clock would soon come and then Billy would give up on her. She felt her stomach churn and her heart flutter. She'd decided to give up on her love for Billy, before he'd walked back into her life that very day, and now she was thinking of running away with him.

She picked up the photograph of Joshua, planning to put it in her case, but instead she looked at it in the lamp-light and remembered his voice and his loving words in the letters he'd been sending her. His was a love that was fixed in time – not flippant and full of lust, like Billy's love. If she went, she'd never see Josh again. Who to do right by was the question on her lips, as she looked once again at the image of Joshua and the minutes ticked by.

It was still dark as Billy looked out over the bow railings of the *Oceanic*. He was leaving Liverpool, leaving his old life and leaving Amy behind. She'd never shown her face at the ticket office. He might be broken-hearted for a few days, but there would be plenty of good Catholic girls to replace her, as Father Thomas had told him, he thought as the distant lights of Liverpool started to fade. It was her loss, and he was on his way to America – that was all that mattered. Amy Postlethwaite would soon be old news; she was only a dairy maid anyway.

20

'Lord, I wish that minister could have married us earlier than the end of March,' Gladys complained as she sat at the dinner table. 'My belly is going to be so big that I'll waddle down the aisle. I'm glad there will only be us three to see it. I feel so tired as well. I can hardly put one foot in front of the other today.'

'Oh, Gladys, there's never been anything on your bones anyway. You are not as big as you think you are. You should have seen Grace when she was carrying Amy. I swear she used to grow daily. Do you not think you should perhaps go and see the doctor and tell him you are expecting, and that you are really tired all the time?' Ethan looked at Gladys, who was struggling with her pregnancy and was starting to worry him.

'What, and spend money on what I already know! That I'm far too old to be a first-time mother and I should have had more sense. The minister was bad enough, giving us both a lecture, like we were only young 'uns.' Gladys sat back in her chair and went quiet as Amy entered the kitchen, after doing her chores in the dairy.

Amy took off her apron and mob cap and sat down at the table, reaching for the dish of mashed potato to go with the cold mutton that had been served for dinner. 'That's the dairy clean, and all done for another day. You seemed to be struggling this morning when you were milking the cows. Do you want me to milk them tomorrow morning and you can do the dairy? I don't mind changing. You are going to find it hard to bend down and sit on that stool shortly anyway,' Amy said innocently, not having been part of the earlier conversation.

'You see, even she thinks I'm looking fat!' Gladys felt her stomach glumly under her skirts.

'I didn't mean it like that. It's just that you've got to take care. Bending down and milking every morning isn't going to do you any good, and you've made it clear to all of us that you are tired all the time. You could stay in bed a little longer. And I don't mind being up and about. I like being in the shippon.'

'Amy's right. The shippon is getting to be no place for you. If a cow kicks you, you could lose the baby.' Ethan looked at Amy and winked.

'What a bloody pickle I've got myself into, and all because of you, Ethan Postlethwaite. I suppose we could swap jobs until the baby is born, and then I'll get back to my lasses. They are used to my hands on them – you'll have to be gentle. Mind Florrie, as she does kick; she tries to up-scuttle the milk pail, if she's not kept in line. And Buttercup likes an extra helping of feed or hay, else she gets restless when you are milking her,' Gladys said as she pushed her dinner away from her, hardly touched.

'I have milked them before. I know their ways. I know you treat them like spoilt children, but they'll be alright with me. I've got faster with milking, since helping you when you were feeling sick the other month. I shouldn't need you, Father, but if you could fother them, it would be one job less.' Amy ate her dinner and screwed up her nose at a mouthful of fatty mutton that had been presented at dinnertime for the last few days.

'Aye, I'll do that. Anything to make this one slow down. I was telling her to get herself to the doctor, as she looks worn out.' Ethan reached for Gladys's hand and smiled at her.

She pulled it away and glared at Ethan. 'Leave me be! I don't need a doctor. I'll be right when this baby is born. Let's hope it's a lad, and then he can inherit the dairy after my day. I never thought I'd ever say that, but it sounds good. I think I'll call him Leonard, after my grandfather.' Gladys touched her stomach gently.

'Do I have any say in this naming?' Ethan smiled, not really worried about what the baby was to be called.

'You can choose its second name, as long as it's something I like. You know, "Joshua" is growing on me. I thought that when the post delivered a letter for you this morning, Amy, it's on the mantelpiece.' Gladys smiled as she watched Amy go quickly to pick the letter up with a huge smile on her face. 'He writes at least once a week. Can you understand what he writes, because his handwriting is terrible?'

'He never did like schooling. He'd rather be with his father, looking after the sheep. I always remember on his first day at school, Josh looked at the teacher when she was trying to tell him something and he said, "What are you looking at, you blue-eyed old bugger", because his father had said it to a sheep the previous day. He didn't half get walloped.' Amy grinned and fingered the letter, wanting to read it there and then, but choosing to put it into her pocket to read in private.

'Mmm . . . Well, he obviously thinks something of you. Perhaps it's a good job Billy did go to America, else you wouldn't know which you thought more of,' Ethan joked.

'I miss Billy. I'll never hear from, or see him, again. I never really said goodbye to him properly.' Amy bowed her head, partly regretting not going to say goodbye to Billy and leaving him waiting for her to run away with him. True love just hadn't been there, when she had sat and thought about it in her bedroom the night of his departure. She hardly knew him, unlike Joshua.

'Aye, well, he's best gone. You keep writing to that Joshua of yours. I've never met him, but he must be keen on you, else he wouldn't keep writing the way he does.' Gladys smiled at Amy. Since their talk in the dairy there had hardly been a bad word between them. After all, they had something in common – and that was Ethan, whom both of them loved.

It was the last Saturday in March. Ethan stood in the yard outside and looked around him. It was his and Gladys's wedding day, for what it was. He exhaled and ran his fingers through his hair as he waited for Gladys and Amy to join him on the walk, in their Sunday best, to Pitt Street. They hadn't bothered with the tradition of not being in the same house, and not seeing one another, on the eve of their wedding. Instead it had been just another day: Amy doing the milking, Gladys seeing to the dairy, and Ethan delivering the milk. And now, in what should have been a time to take things easy before the next milking, they were to get married.

There was no excitement or frivolity in the house, as Gladys and Amy dressed and prepared themselves for the wedding day. Ethan had noticed a bunch of primroses on the table, which Amy had bought from the flower seller on the nearby market while he had been delivering milk; it was for Gladys to carry in her hands as she stood beside him in the small, austere chapel. It would be the only bit of brightness in the day, as he found himself regretting what he was about to do, while Gladys forced herself into a dress that only just fitted where it touched, and complained about how ill she felt. He himself was dressed in the suit that he had bought from the tailor's on Lord Street; it had been meant to be for him to stroll and look his best in, when he had become established in a business that gave him some time off to do that. Now he was working seven days a week and was about to become a father again. How stupid he had been, he thought, when he lifted his head as Gladys and Amy stepped out of the back door into the yard.

'By, look at you – don't you make a bonny picture.'

Ethan smiled at the woman he was about to marry, and at his daughter, with their arms linked together. Amy looked stunning in one of her new dresses bought from Lord Street, a blue one with a cream bow at the side, while Gladys was in her Sunday best, a grey high-necked dress that only just stretched across her growing belly.

'I don't know about that, Ethan. I feel like a beached whale. Look at this belly.' Gladys stared down at her stomach and tried to smile. 'You don't look so bad yourself. All dressed up – a proper dandy. I like to see you in that tweed suit.'

'I can't see owt wrong with you. Anyway it doesn't matter; another hour and you'll be Mrs Postlethwaite.' Ethan smiled and offered Gladys his arm, as Amy unlinked hers and walked to open the yard's large gate. 'Now best foot forward.' Ethan smiled at Gladys. She looked ill; her legs and ankles were swollen, and sometimes she was really short of breath. Being pregnant was definitely not agreeing with her. Perhaps once they were married she would perk up a little, he thought, as she held tightly to his arm while they walked down the busy streets, filled with shoppers, merchants' deliveries and horse-drawn carriages. Nobody gave the couple and Amy a second glance as they made their way to the square-set Methodist chapel, with a congregation that was lessening daily in mainly Catholic Liverpool.

'Well, this is your big day.' Amy smiled and passed Gladys the small bunch of primroses as they stepped into the chapel. 'I wish you both well. Perhaps I've not been the most understanding, but I want you both to be happy.' She kissed Gladys on the cheek and watched as her father smiled at her, then took Gladys's arm and walked up the aisle.

The chapel smelt of polish as Amy stood and watched the couple and hoped that whatever lay in front of them, everything would be for the better. No organist was playing and no congregation was smiling and greeting them; only the stern-looking preacher and two sidesmen to witness the marriage of her father to Gladys, as their vows were read out and the ring that Gladys had said should be reused from her first marriage was placed upon her finger. The minister gave no lecture, but shot a disgruntled look at Ethan as he bent his head and kissed his new bride. After they had signed the wedding register, he opened the chapel doors and grudgingly bestowed his best wishes on both of them, as they walked out into the bitter spring wind that blew along Pitt Street.

'Well, how does it feel to be married again, Mrs Postlethwaite?' Ethan looked down at Gladys and kissed her, once they were safely back at home.

'No different than it did when I walked in here an hour ago,' Gladys said as she sat down in her chair.

'You both looked lovely. You make a most handsome couple,' Amy said as she took off her blue bonnet and tended to the fire. 'I must admit the minister hadn't much to say.'

'That's because we are not part of his usual flock, and he's not happy that we've put the cart before the horse,' Ethan replied, looking across at Gladys. 'We happen should have had a bit of a bigger do, but I've nobody on my side. And you've said all along, lass, that your side are not happy – the ones you have told – so what was the point?'

'It's alright. As long as this baby carries your name, I'm not bothered with a fuss. What have Grace's parents had to say about your father getting married again? I presume you have told them?' Gladys quizzed Amy.

'There's nothing they can say. They've moaned about it in their letters, but it isn't their doing. They'll have to be content. And I've told them nothing changes with me and my father, and that I will still be living here, especially with you feeling ill at the moment.' Amy stopped giving her attention to the fire, and watched her father as he undid the collar from his shirt and put the circular piece of starched white material and the stud that held it in place on the table, before unbuttoning the top button on his shirt.

'They can please themselves what they think. I'm nowt to do with them. They can have their say when it comes to you, Amy, but not me. We'll be alright, Gladys, now stop your worrying. Put that kettle on, Amy. My surprise will be arriving shortly and we'll want to wet our whistle with tea, if nowt else.' Ethan stretched his legs out in front of him and closed his eyes. He could have done with an hour's sleep, but thought better of it, as there was a knock on the door and his surprise arrived, for everyone to enjoy.

Amy opened the door to reveal Percy Mounsey standing on the doorstep, with a large straw basket in his hands.

'Amy, it's good to see you.' Percy looked her up and down and smiled. 'My mother's sent me with this basket. She said your father ordered it this morning. Is it a special day or something? My mother's been baking since the moment he called. She's been in a right flap, moaning that she could have done with more notice, and to be told what it was for.' Percy peered over Amy's shoulder and tried to see what the event was that had required his mother's attention.

'Thank you, Percy.' Amy took the basket from his arm and grinned at the lad, who was nearly breaking his neck to see into the kitchen. 'You might as well know that my father has married Mrs Lund. No doubt the whole street will know shortly. This must be my father's treat for them both. We'll return the basket when we have finished with it.' She turned and tried to close the door, despite Percy standing in the way.

'Well, I suppose congratulations are in order. I'll have to tell my mother,' Percy said and peered in yet again.

'Aye, you do that, lad. And while you are telling her that, you may as well say there will be a baby arriving shortly, and then she's a double morsel of gossip.' Ethan stood behind Amy. 'Now, on your way. We've got a small celebration to enjoy between us, and you are not invited. Thank your mother for her efforts.'

Ethan closed the door and left Percy making his way back down the street as fast as he could, to tell his mother the latest gossip.

Amy unpacked the hamper, which was filled with salmon-and-cucumber sandwiches, sausage rolls, tea loaf and delicately decorated butterfly buns – a real treat for the newly-wed couple – then poured the tea and sat down at the table with her new stepmother and father.

'This is grand, Ethan – so thoughtful,' Gladys said and looked at her new husband. 'But was there any need to tell Percy everything? Old bag Mounsey will be telling everybody now.'

'Let her. We are married, and if she's nothing better to talk about, then it's her lookout. I can't abide that snivelling lad of hers. Thank the Lord, Amy, you didn't take a fancy to him.' Ethan chuckled as he ate one of the sandwiches.

'Please, Father, give me some credit. He'll never walk out with a woman; he's a mother's lad and such a gossip. No lass in her right mind would look twice at Percy.' Amy grinned as she tried a sausage roll.

'Listen to you two! What a difference six months in Liverpool has made to you both. What have I done?' Gladys sighed.

'You've got married again, Mrs Postlethwaite. Now enjoy what's left of the day.' Ethan kissed Gladys on the cheek and looked at Amy. 'Thank you for your support, Amy. It means a lot to us both, and we'll need you in the coming months.'

'It's alright, Father. As long as you are happy, that's all that matters. I'll look forward to a sister or brother. It will be strange, as I've always been the only one.' Amy looked at Gladys; she'd stolen her father from her, but she would have to learn to share him – and not just with

Gladys, when the baby arrived. Or perhaps it was time to go her own way in life.

Amy sat on her bed and read the penned letter from Joshua, who told her that there had been snow in Dentdale. That snowdrifts had buried some of his sheep behind the limestone walls, and that he and his dog had searched for them and dug them out before they suffocated or starved to death. He told her that her grandparents talked about her every day. And that Roland Harper's brother was sending milk to him from Dent on the train to Liverpool; he often thought of Amy when he saw it being placed on the train, and hoped that she was well. His letters weren't overflowing with soppy sentiments and easily written words, but they were filled with love and a knowledge of what Amy was really like and where her heart truly lay. Josh reminded her that, when they were younger, they'd soon have been rambling over the banks covered with primroses and violets, and would both have taken joy in finding the first bird's nest, with its eggs carefully laid within.

It was such things that Billy had not been able to convey. Amy was not a town girl at heart. Now that she'd got used to living in Liverpool, she realized there were only so many clothes she needed, and that the busy, dirty streets were no substitute for the wide-open spaces of the Klondike or Dentdale. She looked at the last line and kissed Josh's letter, wiping a tear away from her cheek as she held it in her hand and read it:

I'll always be here for you, Amy, no matter what the month of the year. It can snow, rain, hail or the sun may shine – I'll be standing there in my pasture, looking down on your old home and thinking of you.

My dearest wishes,

Joshua

One day she would return to him, but just not yet, as the time wasn't right. She'd return home when the baby was born and her father didn't have time for her any more. She knew that would happen, as she was from her father's past, and Gladys and her baby were his future. He'd have no time for a grown-up daughter, of that she was sure.

21

Amy rested her head on Florrie's flank and wedged the cow's tail between her head and its side. Florrie was flighty this morning and wouldn't let Amy milk her, as she paced her four feet up and down and swished her tail. To make matters worse, Gladys was standing watching, as she told Amy how to go about calming the creature, while she moaned about a customer who owed for two weeks' milk and said that Ethan was too soft to demand the money.

'Here, out of the way – she'll not do that to me,' Gladys yelled as Florrie kicked her leg out at Amy and spilled nearly all the milk that was in the bucket. 'She's an old bugger if she gets it in her head to play up as she does.' Both women looked at the troublesome beast and at the milk wasted on the shippon floor.

'No, I'll manage, don't come near her. She has to know who's boss.' Amy glared at the Jersey cross, which gave the best milk but was the most skittish animal, and bit her lip as she patted the cow on her flanks and sat back down on the stool to continue milking.

'Warm your hands – she likes warm hands on her.' Gladys stood at the back of the troublesome cow and watched, thinking she could do better.

Amy took no notice and set about her job, while the cow bellowed and looked wild-eyed and suddenly lashed out with her hind leg, kicking Gladys and knocking her back against the shippon's walls.

'Gladys, are you alright? You shouldn't have been in here, especially near Florrie. You know she's trouble some mornings.' Amy left the cow and the milk bucket and went to her stepmother's aid. 'Are you alright – did she hit you? Is the baby alright?' She grabbed Gladys's hand and held it tight, putting her arm around her waist. 'Father, come quick! Florrie's kicked Gladys!' she yelled to Ethan, who was tacking the pony out in the yard, ready for the daily delivery.

'I'm alright, I'm alright. She only caught the side of me. She's shaken me up more than anything, the old devil.' Gladys held on to Amy's hand and drew a deep breath. 'My heart's going ten to the dozen. I thought she was going to step back and pin me against the wall. She's done that before today – she knows how to pull on her collar and loosen it.' She gasped and fought for breath as Ethan rushed into the shippon.

'What the hell have you done? You shouldn't be in here, especially not near that one. Lord, you look white. Here, take my hand and let's get you home. Amy, run and get Dr Murphy from Church Street. Tell him what's happened and that I'm concerned for both Gladys and the baby.' Ethan helped Gladys out of the shippon and across the yard.

'I don't want a doctor – she didn't hurt me. I'm just shocked. Don't go for the doctor, Amy, I'm alright. A cup of tea and I'll feel myself again.' Gladys gasped and felt faint as Ethan picked her up in his arms. 'Don't go for the doctor; they cost money. I'm alright,' she insisted as she held on to Ethan.

'Will you hold your breath? You are having the doctor. You've not been right ever since you found out you were having this baby. Stop bothering about the money – we are not without any,' Ethan said sternly to Gladys, then yelled at Amy as she wondered what to do. 'Go on, Amy, go and get Dr Murphy. He'll not be on his rounds yet, it's too early. I'll stop with Gladys. The milk round can wait this morning. There are more important things than making a bit of money.' Ethan struggled across the yard and threw open the door into the house, then carried Gladys up the stairs, where he laid her on their bed.

'I'm alright, Ethan. Stop worrying,' Gladys said quietly as he helped her undress and pulled her nightdress over her head. 'I'm simply tired all the time, and old Florrie has shaken me up with her kick. She hardly touched me.'

'This is my opportunity to get the doctor to have a proper look at you, like he should have done weeks ago. You've been nothing but sick since you first found out you were carrying this baby. Well, now the doctor's on his way. So hold your noise and make yourself ready for his visit. We'll sell that bloody Florrie – she's nothing but trouble every morning. It doesn't matter if she gives good milk or not.' Ethan glanced down at Gladys looking so pale and drawn. There was definitely something wrong with her, besides Florrie kicking her.

'Don't blame the cow. I shouldn't have stood where I did. I'll be alright.' Gladys closed her eyes and languished in the warmth of the bed. She was past caring. Her heart was racing, she felt faint and she was fighting for breath. She gave up arguing with Ethan, who sat on the chair at the edge of her bed and watched as Gladys closed her eyes and waited for the doctor. She knew the doctor would tell her what she had known for some years, which was the real reason for her remaining childless until now.

Amy stood on the doorstep of the Victorian town house, waiting for the doctor to join her. The straight-talking Irish doctor had been in the process of sitting down to his breakfast when she had disturbed him, and he had not appreciated the interruption.

'Sure, what's the woman got herself pregnant for? If I've told her once, I've told her ninety times that she's not to carry a child, else it will be the end of her,' Dr Murphy said sharply as he grabbed his cloak and Gladstone bag and stepped out onto the street with Amy by his side.

'What do you mean?' Amy asked as the doctor followed her, hardly able to keep up with her fast walk. 'She's never said anything about being ill.'

'Her heart is weak, and she's not strong enough to carry a baby, let alone get it into the world. Ted had the sense not to get her that way, thank the Lord! However, it seems your father hasn't been that careful.' Dr Murphy sighed. 'And for her to be kicked by a cow, that'll have made things more complicated, unless she's not too many months pregnant. And then, with a bit of luck, she might lose the child.' He shook his head and rushed along with Amy.

'I think she's at least six months pregnant,' Amy said as they reached the dairy gates and hurried into the yard.

'Then we are going to have to pray to the good Lord above that He preserves her and the baby, but there's not a lot I can do for either, and she will know that.' Dr Murphy entered the house and left Amy worrying in the kitchen. She hadn't realized her stepmother was ill but, worse still, neither had her father. And it did not sound like good news for Gladys or the baby she was carrying.

'Sure, Gladys, now how did you get in this predicament? Or should I say why?' Dr Murphy looked at his patient as she lay in her bed and shook his head.

'I'm sorry, Doctor. You know what it's like when you have a new man in your life.' Gladys struggled for breath as she replied. 'I've always wanted a child of my own, so I took a chance.'

'Did you not know that your new wife's heart is weak? She's been told time and again not to get herself in the family way. Ted had the sense, even though it made it a loveless marriage, but it seems you have not.' Dr Murphy looked up at Ethan as he listened to Gladys's heart through his stethoscope and felt her extended stomach.

'I knew nothing of her illness, but I've been telling her to come and see you for weeks, she's been so ill.' Ethan sighed. 'What are we to do? Will she be alright – and the baby? Although I curse the day I put it there.' He stood at the end of the bed and looked at Gladys.

'I'm sorry, but your heart's failing, Gladys. There's water retention in your legs, and your heart is only just managing to do its job. You should have come to me earlier. I'd have told you to follow my instructions and stay in bed until the child was born.' Dr Murphy watched the tears running down Gladys's cheeks. He gently took Ethan's arm and urged him to join him on the landing, out of earshot of his patient.

Ethan looked at the doctor and tried to take in the words he was telling him.

'Gladys is seriously ill. Her heart is failing, her ankles and legs are full of fluid because the heart is not pumping as it should, and her lungs are struggling with the excess water. I can't hear a heartbeat from the baby, so either the cow gave it a lethal blow or Gladys has not been able to support its life. It will have to be born, either naturally or by Caesarean, and either way her heart will not withstand the trauma. I can't do anything for her except pray. I'm sorry. It will simply be a matter of time. She should have told you of her illness before you bedded her.'

'I'd no idea. I'd have controlled my urges if I had.' Ethan couldn't look at the doctor. He'd killed Gladys with his lust, which had waned since he'd got to know her better.

'Sure, well, Ted did. But in the end there was no love lost between them, and all Gladys wanted was a child. It's no surprise that she didn't say anything to you. I'll give you these pills to ease her pain, but I doubt it will be long before you are asking me to return. She's dying, and there is nothing that you and I can do.' Dr Murphy patted Ethan on his back before walking down the stairs, stopping at the bottom to turn and say, 'The good Lord be with you.' He left the house without talking to Amy, who watched as he departed, looking downhearted and upset about the state of his patient, who had not listened to his advice and was about to lose her life because of it.

'Oh, Father, why didn't Gladys tell us? I'm so sorry. I thought things were going to be fine for you both,' Amy said as she sat across from her father and watched him holding his head in his hands. 'She was so looking forward to the baby being born, even though she didn't like the size of her stomach. She'd only started knitting for it last night – look at the bootees she was making.' Amy picked up from the table the knitting Gladys had been concentrating on, and smiled at the tiny bootees that were beginning to take shape.

'She wanted the baby so badly that she risked her life for it, and now neither is going to survive. Why didn't the stupid woman tell me? I'd not have laid a finger on her,' Ethan sobbed. 'Women and I don't mix. I lost your mother because I was too busy trying to make money, and look what good that has done me. I have a comfortable bank balance, but not much else in my life, if Gladys and the baby die.'

'You've still got me. I'm still here for you,' Amy said quietly.

'Aye, and I appreciate that, but you'll not be with me forever. You have a life of your own to live, and I'm not about to hold you back.' Ethan smiled across at his daughter. 'I love you, Amy lass, but out there is someone who loves you quite as much, and he wins you over more with every letter he sends you.'

'Father, we've always been just friends.' Amy went quiet. She could hear the cows mooing loudly out in the shippon; some were still unmilked and would be in pain if they were not seen to. 'I'll go and finish the milking – you stay with Gladys. I'll put the milk into the dairy until it can be delivered. No doubt the locals will come and knock on the door for theirs, and the others will have to go elsewhere today.' She got up from her seat. 'You are alright, Father, aren't you?'

'I'm alright, lass. I'll go and sit with Gladys and try and keep her spirits up, and I'm not going to say anything about the baby to her. Dr Murphy might have got it wrong.' Ethan sighed as he started to climb the stairs. 'Tell our customers who call that I'll try and get back with the milk in the morning. Gladys will have something to say to me, if I don't.' He smiled as he climbed the stairs. He must show a happy face to the woman who knew she was dying for the sake of her baby within her.

*

Amy had been run off her feet all day. She'd served the customers who had come to the dairy, had milked the cows and made butter. She'd not even shown her face for dinner, making her father come out with a plate of bread and cheese while she churned the milk. It was near the end of the day, and the sun was just about to set as she ventured into the kitchen. It was all in darkness and the table hadn't been cleared from the morning. Upstairs she could hear her father talking to Gladys, as she lit the oil lamps and cleared the table. He'd not left his wife's side all day. He too must be tired and hungry, she thought, as she stirred the dying coals on the fire and put new life into it with the aid of kindling sticks and coals.

'Is that you, Amy?' Ethan shouted down the stairs.

'It is, Father. I'll make us all something to eat. How's Gladys?' she shouted back.

'She wants you to come up and see her. Leave what you are doing and I'll come down,' Ethan yelled back, as Amy wiped her hands and climbed the stairs, meeting her father on the landing. 'She's tired but awake, and she's insisting that she talks to you. I'll go down and leave you to it.'

Ethan hugged Amy to him. He knew that Gladys was not good; her breathing was laboured and she'd started to hallucinate, saying she could see things that weren't there.

'Alright, I'll not keep her long if she gets too tired.' Amy breathed in deeply. She didn't want to go into the patient's bedroom. She'd been there before and remembered her own mother dying, as now she sat by the side of the bed and looked at Gladys lying in her nightgown, with her greying dark hair long and loose on the pillow. The oil lamp flickered as she made herself comfortable on the chair next to Gladys and then reached for her stepmother's hand.

'Why didn't you tell us that you were so ill? My father and I would have looked after you better, if we had known,' Amy said gently.

'I didn't want your father to think I was dying and leave me. I'd lost him once before, and I didn't want to lose him again. I wanted to carry this baby so much. All I wanted was a child of my own and a good husband to love,' Gladys said in almost a whisper.

'He'd not have left you. He loves you. And he'll love the baby when it's born.' Amy held back her tears, and the truth.

'That's not going to happen, Amy, as we are both dying. You know it – I can tell by the look in your eyes. I want you to promise me that you'll do everything to help your father after I've gone. He'll need you. He might not need my dairy, but he'll need you,' Gladys whispered.

'I'll always be there for my father and you. Now you must rest, and no more talk about dying. You'll be up and milking those cows in the morning.' Amy smiled.

'I don't think so, lass. Roland Harper will buy them off you, after my day. He'll help you with other things as well. We might not have seemed to get on, but in a crisis we Dales folk stick together.' Gladys smiled wanly and closed her eyes.

'Shush now. I'll not talk of suchlike. I'll get my father

to come back up and sit with you.' Amy stood up and looked down at the woman who had always been in her father's life, but he had left it too late to marry her.

'You live a good life, Amy. And if you love that Joshua, let him know it before it's too late.' Gladys moved gently in her bed and moaned. 'Life goes too fast.'

'I will. Now sleep and stop your worrying about me.' Amy turned her back on the motionless Gladys. They'd started out as enemies, but were parting as friends. She doubted the woman would see the night out.

'She's not good, Father,' Amy said as she looked at her father, sitting crumpled in his chair. 'I told Gladys that you'd go back up to her. She seems to be giving up on life,' Amy whispered.

'She can't do that – she can't leave us. The baby and she will be fine.' Ethan shook his head and looked at Amy. He didn't want to believe the inevitable, now that he had left Gladys's side. 'I'll go up. Make her some supper, Amy, as she'll be hungry.' Ethan stood up and hung his head. 'What are we going to do? I'll not want to live here and run this dairy after her day. Why didn't she tell me she was unable to carry children? It's all my fault that she's dying in that bed, and I can't do owt about it.'

22

The day dawned bright and clear; there was not a cloud in the sky and it was a perfect morning that broke over a sleeping Liverpool. It was the first of May, winter was behind everyone, and spring put hope and joy in their hearts as they woke to another busy day, ready to go about their work.

It was not, however, a day full of joy at Lund's dairy.

Dr Murphy sat at the kitchen table and wrote out the death certificate for Gladys and her unborn baby, then sat back and looked at the distraught father and daughter. 'Mrs Emmott on Bolton Street will help you lay Gladys out, and I'll call on her and the undertakers for you on my way home.' He shook his head as he signed off the death and looked at Ethan. 'You can't blame yourself, man. If only she'd told you how ill she was. She always was a pig-headed woman – that's why Ted was strict with her. God rest both their souls. She drove him to an early grave as well, as she was always wanting something she couldn't have.'

'She should never have married him,' Ethan said quietly, then looked up at the doctor. 'We shouldn't have listened to anybody when we were younger, then things would have been different for us both.'

Amy glanced at her father. Had he forgotten her mother so easily? Had he not really loved her or wanted her as a daughter?'

'Now we all have regrets, but look at the bonny daughter you have sitting at this table – she's been supporting you all night. Gladys knew what she was doing when she married you. She shouldn't have risked her life for the sake of a child that she knew she was too old, and too ill, to carry. I dare say she saw you, remembered the good times you both had and threw the consequences of her actions out of the window. She was a complex woman, was Gladys: strong and determined, and a wee bit selfish when she wanted to be.' Dr Murphy stood up and looked at Ethan. 'What will you do with this place? Will you be keeping it on? Gladys lived for her dairy and cows; she was a better farmer than Ted – and she knew it.'

'I don't know. When I first came across her and the dairy, I thought Gladys was the woman for me, and this place was perfect to see my days out in. Now I think I've realized I was wrong on both counts.' Ethan didn't look at the doctor as he walked to the door, with Amy opening it for him.

'Well, that's your decision to make. It sounds as if the cows will need milking whether Gladys is in this world or the next, by the noise they are making. I'll away now and let you see to them. It's the living you need to tend to now, not the dead.' Dr Murphy patted Amy's shoulder as he stood and turned in the doorway. 'My condolences to you both. May God be with you.' He made his way across the yard and out of the main gate.

'Dr Murphy is right. I'll go and milk the cows and, while I'm at it, I'll put a note on the dairy's door to let everyone know we will not be delivering milk for a day or two. I'll put a kit of the milk next to the gate, and hope that folk are honest enough to pay for what they take, in a dish that I'll put beside it. I'm sure they are honest. Folk might not have a lot of money on these streets, but they are true to their word and will have sympathy for our situation.' Amy looked at her father, who said nothing in reply. 'I'll away then. Are you alright with the undertaker and the woman who's coming to lay Gladys out?' Amy asked as she tried to make him look at her.

Instead, Ethan just nodded his head and then hid it in his hands. She wasn't going to get much sense out of him this morning, so she'd go and do the work in the shippon and dairy. It would keep her mind off the death of Gladys and her unborn baby.

Once in the shippon, Amy set about her work. It was best that she kept herself busy, she thought, as she relieved the cows of their milk and took it to the dairy. She placed a kit full of the fresh milk outside the gates for their regular customers to help themselves.

Mrs Dougherty from across the street shouted to Amy as she placed a dish for payment next to it, 'Is everything alright, lass? Where's your father? Is he not delivering today?' She walked across to Amy and quickly read the notice that she had placed alongside the kit and dish. 'Aye, lass, I'm sorry. I'd seen Gladys struggling, but I didn't realize she was ill. Did she die in childbirth? The baby must have come early?'

Amy looked at the kind-hearted old woman and suddenly found herself welling up with tears. 'No, she had a weak heart, and Father and I didn't know. A cow kicked her and she took ill there and then, but the doctor said the baby wouldn't survive anyway,' she blurted out and sobbed.

'Now then, now then, come on home with me for five minutes and I'll make you a brew. Share your troubles – I've got broad shoulders.' Mrs Dougherty put her arm around the young lass and walked with her over to her terraced house, which she kept spotless. 'You'll be feeling it, no doubt, as this will be the second time that you've lost a mother. And your poor father, he'll be beside himself.' Dora Dougherty put a mug of tea in front of the sobbing Amy and ran a hand over her shoulders.

'It's my father I'm feeling for. I think he's blaming himself for Gladys's death, but she never told him she couldn't carry children.' Amy looked at Dora. She was a kindly woman, round and tubby, a real home-maker, with pots and ornaments on every shelf in her terraced house. Quite the opposite of Gladys.

'Well, he wasn't to blame then. Gladys always did keep her cards close to her chest. She never gossiped or joined in with the rest of us on the street. I always thought it was Ted who controlled her a bit too much, but when your father came along I realized it was just her way. I didn't know she had health problems, as she never said. But looking back, there were days when she'd take to her bed. I thought she was lazy, as she was no housekeeper, let's face it. She thought more of those blessed cows of hers than of her home.'

'Yes, she loved her cows. I've tidied the house up a bit since we arrived but, like you say, Gladys was no home-maker – unlike you and this lovely house.' Amy blew her nose on her hanky and looked around her. 'I feel guilty, because I really did not like her when I first met her. I didn't want her replacing my mother. I hadn't realized that Gladys had always loved my father, but he was just in love with her memory – until he knew she was carrying his child and had to marry her.' Amy sighed.

'So they knew one another years back? I hadn't realized that,' Dora said and looked with concern at her young neighbour.

'Yes, they courted one another before my father met my mother. But my father wasn't good enough for her family, so they ended their affair. And then they met again when we arrived back here, and the rest you know.' Amy sipped her tea and tried to smile at her kindly but nosy neighbour.

'Well, he will be feeling it. He should be thankful he's got you to lean on, as losing two women from his life must have hit him hard.' Dora went to the window and pulled back her lace curtains, observing the comings and goings in the street. 'The undertakers are here, along with old Mrs Emmott. They'll be seeing to Gladys, no doubt, if your father opens the door to them. They look as if they can't make him hear.'

Amy stood up and watched. 'I'd better go and let them in. He's not answering the door, and he was in a bit of a state when I left him to milk the cows.'

'Aye, go and see to them. He'll not want to face them perhaps, but he'll have to, no matter how he feels. You come back if you need a listening ear or a shoulder to cry on. I'll go and knock on a few doors and tell folk they've to come to the dairy for their milk this next day or two, and that will help you out.'

Dora watched as Amy ran across the street and opened the door for her unwelcome visitors. The poor lass seemed to be holding it all together while her father wallowed in self-pity.

'I'm sorry. My father is probably upstairs – he will not have heard you.' Amy looked at the small woman who was obviously Mrs Emmott, and at the tall man dressed in black, with a sombre face and a tall black hat on his head. 'Please do come in.' She opened the door to the deathly pair and asked them to go through to the front room until she found her father to deal with them.

She looked around the kitchen for him, then went upstairs to the bedroom where Gladys lay, where she found her father with his arms around the dead Gladys. He was stroking her long hair and speaking to her as if she was still alive, cursing the fact that he had made her pregnant.

'Father, leave her be now. The undertaker is here and Mrs Emmott; they will see to her, and the undertaker will need to speak to you.' Amy pulled on his arm and met his eyes. 'She's gone. Father, you can't bring her back. She's like my mother – she's gone to a better place, where they'll both be looked after.' She looked down at Gladys's extended belly and thought about the dead baby inside it.

'Come on now, Mr Postlethwaite, leave her to me. I'll see that she's laid out properly and looking bonny before they come with the coffin. Go downstairs with your daughter and see to the undertaker. He needs to know what to do with her body.' Mrs Emmott took one glance at the bereft man and smiled at Amy. 'Take him downstairs, dear, and help him with his decisions.'

'Father, come, leave her be. We've things to sort and I can't do them on my own.' Amy pulled on her father's arm and he followed her downstairs, knowing that he must keep himself together as he talked to the undertaker.

'You are sure you don't want to bury her back home in Garsdale? We can arrange for her body to be taken there – a lot of the Dales folk do that, not wanting their final resting place to be in the city.' The undertaker saw Ethan's face cloud over.

'No, they were never right with her at her home, so why should she go back to them now? She can be buried in the same chapel yard as her first husband. He was the only man who perhaps did right by her – he can have her back.'

'That'll be the chapel along Pitt Street. I remember burying her husband there less than a year ago.' The undertaker made a note in his book.

'Aye, and we were married there at the end of March. A lot has happened in a year. A lot that shouldn't have happened. Gladys should never have set eyes on me, else she'd still be here,' Ethan said and bowed his head.

'We don't know what's in the future for us, and sometimes it's a good job we don't,' the undertaker said. 'Funeral tea: do you want one, and how many do you think will attend?'

'No funeral tea. There will only be me and my lass at the funeral, and a few other cowkeepers perhaps. There won't be any family; they'll not show their faces, as there is no love lost between me and them.'

'Are you sure, Father? Do you not want to give Gladys a good send-off?' Amy butted in.

'No, let's just get her buried. There's no need to celebrate her life and death. The whole of it has been one big mistake, and she'd not want a fuss.'

'Very well. Then that's everything. I'll go and measure her up and then my men will bring the coffin round. Would you like her to stay with you or in my parlour?' The director rose and looked around him. 'She'd fit in this front room until the funeral day.'

'We'll keep her here. She'd not want to go anywhere else,' Ethan said, then got up and walked out into the yard, leaving Amy with the undertaker.

'Thank you. My father, I'm afraid, is taking this hard, as he's not only lost Gladys, but also the baby she was carrying.'

'I understand. We will try and make her passing as easy as possible – leave everything with us,' the funeral director said with feeling.

The next few days were hard on Amy. Her father was lost in his grief and self-pity, hardly speaking to her, while she kept the dairy going as well as she could. Milk was being wasted daily, and the cows were only just getting the attention they needed, as she tried to manage until the funeral, after which she hoped her father would come to his senses and help her. Along with running the dairy, she'd also been making all the meals and running the house, while her father sat and thought about himself.

Her patience was running thin as she put pen to paper and wrote to Joshua and her grandparents, explaining what had happened over the past days and the situation she was in. Amy poured out her heart to them, and told them she was at her wits' end with her father, but hopefully he would come round after the funeral. And then they would have to decide what was to be done, now that Gladys had died. While she wrote, Amy thought about home and the love that was waiting for her there. But she was loyal to her father; she knew he was simply lost in grief and self-pity, and she knew he loved her as much as he always had, if only he would show that to her.

The funeral day came and Gladys was taken from her beloved dairy in a hearse pulled by two black horses, to the small Methodist chapel where she had been married not long before. The neighbouring houses drew their curtains in respect, and the people they passed stood and bowed their heads, and gentlemen doffed their hats at the sight of the hearse. Ethan and Amy walked slowly behind it, along with Mrs Dougherty, Roland Harper and other cowkeepers who had dealt with Gladys over the years. None of her family had appeared. Ethan had been right; they had washed their hands of Gladys once she had married him, and knew full well that the dairy would automatically be left to Ethan after Gladys's day, so they weren't prepared to waste their time or money on a woman who had always been too headstrong for their liking.

'Are you alright, Father? You'll feel better once we have got Gladys laid to rest.' Amy held her father's hand as they both stood at the grave's edge, after blessing the coffin with a scattering of soil.

'Will I, lass? If it hadn't have been for me, she'd still have been alive. Her folks were right: I wasn't meant to be with her or with your mother, as I didn't take care of either of them.' Ethan looked at his daughter, who he knew had been a pillar of strength since the death of Gladys.

'Neither death was your fault, Father, so stop blaming yourself. My mam died from drinking bad water, and Gladys had not told you of her ailments. Now I shouldn't say this, but it's time for us both to look to the future, and for you to decide what you are going to do with the dairy. I can't run the place on my own. Besides, we are not making any money at the moment.' Amy hated talking to her father in this way, especially discussing business over Gladys's grave, but it had to be approached sometime.

'Mind what you are saying – this is not the place to discuss our affairs. It's time to grieve, show some respect,' Ethan snapped. 'There's enough vultures around this grave as it is.' He raised his head and looked across at Roland Harper. 'But you are right. I should go and have a word with Rolly Harper, as he might be able to help us out, once I've thought what to do with everything. If nothing else, these last months I have had the sense to see that I'm no cowkeeper – you are more the farmer than I am.' Ethan nodded at Roland and went to talk to him and the other Dales folk who kept cows on the back streets of Liverpool.

The cowkeeper from the Dales lifted his head, with worry on his face as he took off his tweed cap. He was a small man, wiry and tanned, and still spoke with his Dales accent. 'It's a bad do, Ethan. Gladys looked full of life when last I saw her at the cattle show before Christmas. In fact she was a different woman; there was a sparkle in her eye, and I never thought we'd be burying her a few months on. You must be feeling it. And to lose the baby and all – life can be cruel.' Roland looked at Ethan; he hardly knew the man, but he'd obviously made Gladys happy for the short time they had been together.

'Aye, it came as a blow, and I've no heart for anything at the moment. It's a good job I've my lass here, else I'd have given up on everything.' Ethan put his arm around Amy as she stood next to him. He watched Roland Harper, as he talked to the man Gladys had told him to seek help from, as she lay on her deathbed.

'I know this is not the place and the time, but do you think you'll be keeping the dairy going? I know you are not a cowman, as you made that obvious at the show, but I hear your lass here is good with the stock.' Roland smiled at Amy, then waited for Ethan to reply. He could do with buying the dairy, if Ethan had a mind to sell it to him. It was a profitable patch that Gladys supplied; and now she was gone, he wouldn't mind buying it, if it was going to be put up for sale. Rumours had been rife that the Postlethwaites were not coping since Gladys's death, so the time was right to clinch a deal.

'I don't know what I'm going to do. Me and my lass need to discuss it. As you say, she is at home looking after the cows, but I found out quickly that I wasn't cut out for suchlike. I'll let you know if I have a mind to sell it. I don't even know if the dairy is now mine. Gladys died without a will, so I presume it is mine, seeing as we'd recently wed.' Ethan sighed.

'Aye, well, you know where I am, so let me know. Send word to Chestnut Grove and I'll come round and we'll come to a deal, I'm sure. She'd some good stock, had Gladys – always gave me a run for my money at the shows.' Roland went to stand with the other cowkeepers before walking back to their homes.

Amy linked her arm through Ethan's as they both walked back over to the graveside and looked down at the coffin for one last time. 'Time to go home, Father. There's nothing more to be done here,' she said eventually.

'Aye, I suppose you are right. Gladys has gone, and there's nowt more I can do. Let's be away. I'll milk the cows tonight – you've done enough of late. Tomorrow we will get back to normal, as I've skulked about long enough. It gets you nowhere, and only brings everybody else around you down. I'll go and see a solicitor tomorrow, make sure the dairy is mine to do with as I wish, and then we'll have a talk. It's not just my home; it's yours, too,' Ethan said, and glanced back as they left the graveyard. 'Sleep well, Gladys – tha was a fair lass.'

23

'Well, it seems that as Gladys had no children, the dairy and everything else is mine.' Ethan sat down at the kitchen table with the deeds to the dairy in his hand. 'I didn't marry her for her brass. I married her because I thought I loved her, and to give the baby she was carrying a father. And now it seems all this is mine, and I still have brass in my pocket.'

'Well, that's grand. You've no financial worries – not like we used to have. When we were in the Klondike, sometimes there was hardly anything on the table, and my mother used to be nearly in tears.' Amy remembered the days when life was hard, with her mother making something out of nothing and never complaining about her lot. In her eyes, her mother had been ten times stronger than Gladys.

'Aye, I know. I asked a lot of her. I'm a selfish man, and I should change my ways. That's why I'm going to ask you what you want to do this time. I'm no cowkeeper, but you seem to be at home with it. This could be your dairy. I'd stop and do what I've been doing until the right man walks into your life. Which he will do, once they all hear that you are a woman of means. Then I'd move on, once I knew you were settled and happy.' Ethan looked across at Amy. He'd not done right by her these last few days, and she was tired and pale.

'I don't know, Father. The dairy is yours, and it shouldn't be mine. Just because I milk the cows doesn't mean I want to be doing it all my life. I only took on the job to help Gladys. I didn't think I'd be doing it for a lifetime. Besides, what would you do if you left here?'

'Don't you worry about me. I've still most of my money from the Klondike, and Gladys was not short of a bob or two. I could walk away tomorrow and, providing I'm careful, I needn't lift a finger for the rest of my life. The urge to make money and become rich has lost its flavour lately. I've learned that it's best to enjoy life while you can – brass isn't everything.' Ethan saw that his daughter was struggling with her thoughts. 'Sleep on it tonight. Have a think about whether you want to go back to Dent and your grandparents. I wouldn't be mad with you. Your heart has always been in that dale or in the Klondike. Both are wild places, and you are not a city girl, despite your liking of city clothes.'

Ethan glanced at yet another letter from Joshua on the mantelpiece, as yet unopened, waiting to be read by Amy in the privacy of her own room, out of the sight of his prying eyes. The lad was keen, he'd give him that, but it would come to nothing if Amy didn't go to him or

Joshua didn't come to her. And that would never happen. Joshua Middleton was a sheep farmer and, like his sheep, he was hefted to his land in Dentdale. If anything was to come of her love for the shepherd, he would have to let his daughter lead her own life and be happy.

'I don't know, Father. Whatever I decide, I hurt somebody.' Amy sighed.

'Do what is best for you. I'll always be right behind you, no matter what your choice is. The dairy can willingly be yours, but you'll need help running it, and I won't always be here. I'll be honest: I thought it would be the ideal thing for us when we moved in, but I soon realized I'd made a wrong decision. If it hadn't have been for Gladys, I think I would have said both of us should have moved on.' Ethan got up from his chair. 'I'll go and let those poor beasts stretch their legs for a while. Like you, they've been a bit neglected by me. Once they are back in, I'll swill down the yard and make it all tidy, just in case we ask Rolly Harper to come and see if he wants to buy it all. Gladys said he'd want some of her cows, but I think he'd probably buy the whole lot, if he's offered it at a decent price.' Ethan walked to the door. 'I'll be back in for my dinner. I don't want a lot, and my appetite has left me of late. So that'll give you time to read your letter from lover-boy.' Ethan winked. Amy never said as much, but he knew that when letters were written so frequently it was more than friendship going on between them.

Amy sat at the table and looked around her. She had never liked the house they had been living in with

Gladys. It was a typical city terraced house, and if it had been in a different area, it would almost be classed as a slum. The rooms were dark, and the smell of the cows was never far away, no matter how much she cleaned. It wasn't a home and never would be. There was no view from the windows; the wind never blew fresh; and the only birds that flew overhead were the scavenging seagulls that followed the ships out to sea. This was not her home and never would be. She'd no intention of staying here all her life. Perhaps now it was time to return to where she was born, and let her father do as he pleased.

She stood and picked up the letter from Joshua. She'd unfolded her heart to him in her last letter – the ink had actually smudged a little, as she had folded the sheet of paper. She'd been so upset with Gladys dying, and her father thinking only of himself. However, now she wished she hadn't bothered Joshua with her worries. He probably had enough of his own, but at the time of writing he had been the only person who would know exactly how she felt. Indeed, Josh had always known how she felt and had always been supportive. Amy knew that she loved him dearly, as he did her.

She sat back down and, as she opened the letter, a sprig of wild thyme fell out on the table. She picked it up and smelt the sweetness of the mountain air that still lay upon it. Bless Joshua. With the coming of the spring, he had sent her a flower they had both picked when younger, to remind her of the countryside that he knew she still loved. Amy swept away a tear that was falling down her cheek. Her world was in disarray, and for the first time in her life she was not about to follow her father. She didn't need to come to her decision overnight. The letters from Joshua had been telling her to come home for some time now, just as her heart was. She read his letter, which was filled with love for his childhood sweetheart. She'd be breaking her father's heart by leaving him, but the time had come to follow her own dreams, and now was the moment to tell him.

Amy hadn't slept all night, tossing and turning with the decision that she knew would hurt her father. She also had thoughts of Billy: where was he now, and did he have a girl on his arm? Along with her thoughts of Joshua and home, she was full of worries about the past and the future.

She'd woken early and milked the cows, and now her father was out delivering the milk and butter – back in their usual routine for the time being. They had both agreed to talk about their futures once he returned, over a cup of tea and some cheese and bread for their dinner. It was a conversation Amy was dreading, as she saw Ethan return into the yard with the pony and float. She felt her stomach churning as she led the pony into its stable and placed the empty kits in the dairy, ready to be washed out for the evening's delivery. She held her breath as she saw him enter the kitchen and take his cap off, before sitting down to unlace his boots.

'Well, folk have been right decent, given I've not been showing my face for a while. The folk who gave their condolences were unbelievable – the old lass was thought a lot of around here.' Ethan sat back and watched as Amy brewed the tea. 'I'm jiggered, though. I'll have five minutes' kip after we've eaten. What are you going to be doing? Do you want to go and have an hour around the shops – spend some of that money I gave you, to lift your spirits? It's no good moping around, as that will not change anything.' Ethan glanced across at his daughter, who looked worried to death as she replied.

'Father, you said you wanted to know what I was thinking of doing, now that we have lost Gladys.' She wanted to run and leave the room, but knew she would have to explain how she felt.

'Aye, I did. It's time we both know where we stand. To be honest, the last few months have not been that easy. I should never have bumped into Gladys – there wouldn't have been the heartache there has been, this last week or so. Happen it has made us think that life's for living, and it's certainly made me realize that you are no longer my little girl; you are your own woman and should make a life for yourself.' Ethan sipped his tea and saw Amy struggling with what she wanted to say. 'Spit it out, lass. It'll be right, whatever you say.'

'I don't want to stay here, Father. I think it's time to go back to my grandparents and Dentdale. It's where I belong – I've always belonged there.' Amy breathed in and hoped she hadn't hurt her father.

'Aye, well, your mother said this day would come, and she said we'd have to let you go. She'd be suited that you are going back to Dent and to a local lad.' Ethan smiled at his daughter.

'I'm off to my grandparents, Father,' Amy protested.

'Nay, we both know that lad, Joshua, turned your head and reminded you of the love you have always had for one another, when he came to see you at the cattle show. You've written to each other nearly every day since, and he's the one you are really returning to. I'm glad for you, Amy. You go and enjoy your life with him and plough your own furrow.' Ethan sat back and took a bite out of the cheese in front of him.

'It's no good, is it? You know me too well! It is Joshua that I want to return to. And he tells me he loves me more and more in every letter that he writes, and I feel the same way. But I don't want to leave you, Father. Could you not come back to Dent with me?' Amy walked round the table and put her arms around her father. He could be moody and retreat into himself when things weren't going right, but she loved him with all her heart.

'No, I'll not come with you, lass. You forget that I'm not Dales born and bred. I was brought up on the back streets of Burnley. If it hadn't been for the railway being built through Dentdale, I would never have heard of the place. It's your home, it's where you belong, and you return with my blessing,' Ethan replied as Amy knelt on the floor and took his hands.

'But what will you do? I can't just leave you!' She looked into her father's eyes. He seemed worn down and was showing his age.

'I've enough brass to find somewhere nice; somewhere on the Wirral, I think. It's nice out there. I'll find a little cottage with a garden, and happen a part-time job to keep my belly full and help keep the roof over my head – that is, when I'm not writing letters to you. So don't you worry about me. I can look after myself. Besides, by the time we have sold the dairy, neither of us will be short of a bob or two. I'll go and see Rolly Harper tomorrow afternoon. If he could have made us an offer for this place in the chapel yard, he would have done, I could tell that.' Ethan sat back and smiled. 'I'll make him pay a good price – it's worth it to him.'

'It doesn't seem fair that we will profit from Gladys's death.'

'It's the way of the world, lass. Just as long as nobody accuses me of marrying her for her money, knowing she was ill. I can see them saying that, back in her home in Garsdale. It's how they think, that family. Now, you go and write to your lad and your grandparents that you are about to come home. I bet there will be some celebrating when they read that letter. You are best travelling back on the train. You can sit and enjoy the view and it is a grand journey, from what I understand.' Ethan looked at his daughter and saw her start thinking about her trip home.

'That's how Joshua came to see me. He'd come down on the milk train – he'd set off at five in the morning.' Amy grinned.

'Now that shows how fond of you he is. You are making the right decision, lass. You need your happiness, too. We'll both go our own ways, but we will always be there for one another, no matter how far apart we are.

You'll always be my lass.' Ethan kissed Amy's head. 'Now, letters to be written by you, and I'm just going to have forty winks. I've not slept well of late, and everything in the dairy is tidy now and we are back on top of things.'

Ethan sat back in his chair and closed his eyes. His heart ached – his daughter was to leave him for a new life. She had always been his, and now he'd lost her to another. He only hoped that when she returned to live with her grandparents, Joshua Middleton would look after her a lot better than he had Grace. He had so many regrets in life, but having Amy as his daughter was not one of them.

Roland Harper stood in the centre of the yard and walked between the cows, which had been turned out of the shippon for him to view. He was dressed in his best housecoat, with a trilby on his head and a switch of a stick in his hand, which he kept placing across the backs of the cattle, to see how they moved and to assess their best assets.

'Aye, you've got to give it to Gladys, she knew a good cow when she saw one. There's nowt up with any of these. You've happen an odd one that's a bit lame, but that comes with standing on hard surfaces all the time. Now the big question is: what do you want for all the stock and the dairy? Am I going to have to beg, steal and borrow to buy it off you?' Roland Harper stood and waited for Ethan to give his reply.

'I don't know what it's worth. I was thinking of

asking Jim Mackereth, the auctioneer, to value it for me. He seems to be well respected by you Dales folk; he takes all the auctions and sorts deals out.' Ethan looked around him. 'I'll not sell it to anyone else. Gladys said I'd to come to you to sell the cows, and she wouldn't think I'd want to be selling the whole of it. So I'll honour her wishes and give you first refusal,' Ethan said, meeting Roland's eye.

'Well, I could make you an offer here and now, but to make sure I'm not undercutting you, get Jim: he's always fair, he'll not do either of us. What he says it's worth, I'll pay.' Roland looked around him. 'It's a good job Gladys is not alive, as she'd be playing hell about you selling her yard. But it will be in good hands, and it will leave you and your lass free to start afresh.'

'Yes, it's time we moved on. Amy's got a mind of her own, and I'm not cut out to be a cowkeeper – I never was.' Ethan sighed.

'I know that, lad. When you walked that cow around the ring at the show, I was surprised you knew its head from its tail. You are doing right; the dairy will be in good hands. I'm sure Gladys will forgive you, when she looks down and see's what's going on.' Roland slapped Ethan on the back. 'I'll be in touch. The money's waiting, when you know your price.' He walked out of the yard to the pony and trap that were waiting to take him back to his ever-expanding empire of dairies. The yard would be his. Jim Mackereth would see to that.

24

Amy and her father stood on one of the many platforms of Lime Street Station. The platform was crowded and busy with passengers travelling in all directions, and with their luggage and parcels being loaded into the goods wagon by the busy porters. The steam from the mighty engines billowed down under the glass roof, and the noise of the pistons and turning wheels filled the station as people greeted one another and said their goodbyes.

Amy looked at her father. Her emotions were divided: she loved him, but she longed to be back in the Dales where she was born and to be held in the arms of her grandparents, who needed her now more than he did. She also knew that Joshua was waiting for her, and she longed for the minute she fell into his arms, now that they had both realized their love for one another.

'Well, here we are,' Amy said, as Ethan stood outside the train carriage that she knew she was booked on. He'd sold the dairy and all the cows, and the house contents, to Roland Harper; and come the weekend, he would be homeless. 'Will you be alright? You'll find somewhere to live, won't you, and you'll send me your address?' She looked up into his eyes and saw the sadness in them.

'Aye, as soon as I buy somewhere, I'll let you know. I'm back with the old bag Mounsey from Friday, so you can write to me there. Grosvenor House will only be a stopgap. I'll not be staying long, with her and her rules.' Ethan smiled. 'You stop your worrying. I'm old enough to look after myself, and it should be me worrying about you.' He felt the tears welling up in his throat as he grabbed Amy and pulled her close, putting his arms around her and whispering, 'You take care, my lass. I'm going to miss you. I'm sorry if I've not been the father I should have been. My intentions were always there, and I have always loved you since the day you were born.'

Amy buried her face in his jacket. She'd miss her father beyond belief – she loved him so much. Even though he was stubbornly set in his ways and not that keen on work, he had always backed her and had always shown her love and kindness. 'I don't want to go, Father. I shouldn't be leaving you,' she sobbed.

'Now then, my lass, you get on this train and make yourself a new life. That Joshua Middleton is waiting for you. He'll make you happy; he's always been there waiting for you. And your grandparents will have your room ready and the baking done, and will be counting the minutes till they see you. I can just see them looking out of that porchway, following the train as it appears out of

Blea Moor tunnel and crosses the viaducts to pull into the station and bring you to them. They'll be glad to have you back in the nest.' Ethan held his daughter at arm's length and watched as tears trickled down her cheeks. 'Hey, no tears. "Klondike" awaits you, though why your grandfather took it into his head to call it that, I don't know!' Ethan smiled.

'It was for my mam, so that folk would know where she was buried at.' Amy wiped away her tears and tried to smile.

'Aye, well, it'll always be talked about – I'll give them that. Now chin up, best foot forward, as we always say, and write to me. Give me good warning if I have a wedding to attend, because I bet that is on the cards when you get back.' He held her once again and kissed her on the cheek. 'Now go on: the whistle's blowing, so go and find your seat.'

'I love you, Father,' Amy said as she opened the carriage door and climbed into the train as it started to build up steam.

'Aye, I love you, lass,' Ethan yelled back to her as he watched her, and the train, move away from the platform and out of the station. 'I love you more than you'll ever know until you've had your own bairn, and then you'll understand,' he whispered under his breath. Everything he had done with his life had been for Amy. Sometimes it had been for the better, and at other times he had badly misjudged things. Now she was her own woman, with a beau waiting for her; she was no longer his little girl.

*

Amy looked out of the train carriage. She'd never travelled on her own before and felt quite nervous. However, as the mills and terraces of Liverpool and Lancashire gave way to the open fields and farmland she sat back and relaxed. She had not seen the English countryside since they had left Dentdale, and the journey reminded her of the one made with her mother and father when they were full of hope for a new life and wealth in the goldfields of the Klondike.

She remembered how her mother had laughed, and her father had dreamed of what he was going to do with the money that he was easily going to make, once his strike proved profitable. Her father had always been full of dreams but unwilling to work for them, while her poor mother simply followed him, as she loved him so much. Where would he end up now? Amy wondered, as the train pulled up at Hellifield station and changed tracks, to continue its long journey up to Carlisle. She smiled to herself. She knew this station, as a lot of the railwaymen from Dent worked there, either in the signal box or looking after the track; they'd been friends of her father and mother, and had often called at her grandfather's farm for a cup of tea and the latest gossip. Hellifield was a railway village, built because of the line running down into Lancashire and serving the mainline from Scotland to Leeds. There were good people from all over the country drawn to live there, with the offering of work on the Lancashire and Yorkshire Railway. The railway had opened up the Dales for people when it had been built, and that should never be forgotten, Amy thought as the train passed through Long Preston and then Settle, stopping at the busy market town to take on another load of passengers.

She recalled getting off there, with the stationmaster's house and waiting rooms painted in their livery colours of maroon and cream, as were all the Midland Railway buildings in their Gothic styles. She and her mother used to visit the market on a Tuesday and go to the many shops, bringing their purchases home and eating a ha'penny of sweets as they returned. Amy's eyes filled with tears as the train pulled out of the station and made its way across the wild Ribble valley, with its white-washed farmhouses set snugly under the fellsides and its limestone walls criss-crossing the green fields. She looked down onto the bleak moorland of Ribblehead as the train passed over the mighty viaduct that spanned the bogland below her.

The man sitting opposite her quickly closed the small window against the smoke and soot as the train entered the darkness of the nearly two-mile-long Blea Moor tunnel, which had taken so many lives when it had been built. Once out of the tunnel, Amy was home, and she felt her heart beat wildly as the sun shone down and lit up the dale that she knew every inch of, from wandering with Joshua when she was young. She looked down at the sparkling River Dee running the length of the steep-sided dale, and at the farmhouses where she knew the families who lived within them. The farms were handed down from generation to generation, just like her grand-parents' farm would be. She knew now why she had to come home: this was where her roots were, where they had always been. She stood up and reached for her bag of worldly goods, and the man who had shut the window came to her aid as she struggled to pull it from the rack above her head.

'Thank you.' Amy smiled. He was handsome, but not as handsome as the man who would be waiting for her as the train pulled into Dent station, the highest mainline station in England. She stepped off the train with numerous other people. She tried to recall her family's faces as she struggled with her bag along the platform to the gates, where horse and carriages were waiting to take everybody to the village of Dent, just over two miles away down the steep hill and along the valley. There was no sign of Joshua as she quickly looked around her. She lifted up her face to the sun as the train departed. The swallows and swifts dived and screeched over her head as she gazed down the dale and smelt the fresh mountain air. She was home, regardless of Joshua not being here to meet her, she thought, as she hitched up her skirts and passed the tall white stationmaster's house, then walked out onto the road that led down to Cowgill and Dent, and to Garsdale the other way. She shrugged her shoulders and looked down the dale to summon the strength to carry the bag the quarter-mile uphill to her grandparents' house. She'd expected Joshua to be here, she thought, as she stood with her hands on her hips and took in the view.

'Amy, Amy, I'm here. I'm sorry I'm late.' Joshua came running over the railway bridge, his blond hair shining in the sun and his cheeks cherry-red as he rushed towards her. 'A bloody sheep was stuck down an old coal shaft, and it's taken me all morning to free her.' He stopped short and looked at the lass he'd written to nearly every day of late, then plucked up the courage to kiss her, as Amy stood gazing around her. He put his arms round her and kissed her on the lips, then looked into her eyes. 'I'm glad you are back, lass. I've waited so long for you to return to me.' He swallowed hard.

'I'm glad I'm back as well, Josh. I should never have left.' Amy returned his kiss and smiled. 'You don't realize what you've got until it's taken away from you. I never want to leave again – I know that now.' She reached for Josh's hand as he grabbed her bag and lifted it onto his shoulder, in readiness to walk up the hill to her grandparents' farm.

'Well, you are back now, and I'm not going to let you leave me again. Your grandparents will tell you the same. They've been making ready for you all this week. Your grandmother must be jiggered – she's cleaned and scrubbed, baked and polished so much you'd think it was the Queen visiting.' Joshua smiled and walked backwards up the hill, so as not to take his eyes off the lass he loved.

Amy stared around her, as the wind blew in her face and the sun shone down. Thyme and wild scabious were flowering in the hedgerows as they walked the last few yards to the track that led to her grandparents' home.

'Look, your grandfather has made a sign for the farm's new name. It caused a few comments when he first did it, but everything soon calmed down.' Josh opened the farm gate with a wooden sign attached, and the name 'Klondike' in poker-work upon it.

'Bless him. They must have missed my mother when she left them. I've left my father this morning and it nearly broke my heart, but I know he will look after himself and he's better off without me – he can do as he pleases,' Amy said as she walked along the stone pathway leading to the ancient stone-built farmhouse that had been the Oversbys' home for centuries.

'I thought your father always did. That was half the trouble,' Josh said and smiled.

'Yes, you're right, he did.' Amy stood at the garden gate and looked at the green-painted door of the old farmhouse. She'd been crying the last time she walked through it. She'd not wanted to leave her home, and now she felt like crying again – not with sadness, but with joy.

'Come on, they're waiting for you.' Joshua peered through the small-paned window and saw the ageing Oversbys sitting beside the fireside, kettle at the ready and table laden with a welcome-home feast.

Amy held her breath and followed Joshua into the low-ceilinged kitchen and looked around her. A million memories came flooding back: the steady ticking of the grandfather clock, the smell of her grandad's Kendal Twist as he smoked. And now here were the faces of her beloved grandmother and grandfather, who looked so much older.

'Amy, you are home! Our little lass is back with us.' Ivy held out her arms to her granddaughter.

'She's neither little nor a lass, Mother. She's a beautiful young woman – look at her.' George Oversby smiled and walked over and hugged Amy. 'No wonder this young fella was excited about your return. He never let on what a beauty you had turned into. He'll have to act quickly, if he's to keep you.' George winked at Joshua.

'Hold your noise, you silly old fool. Now, Amy, take your hat off, pull up a chair and have something to eat. We've all the time in the world to catch up,' Ivy said and saw the young couple blush. 'Josh, tuck in – there's a place for you. It will be like old times, and you always did have something to eat when you called here.'

'Oh, Grandma, it's so good to be home. I've missed everybody so much,' Amy said as she sat down and fought off the tears. 'I just wish my mother was here with me.'

'Aye, so do we, pet. It was a sad day when she took you and followed your father to that wilderness. I never slept for worrying at night.' Ivy sighed.

'Your father should never have taken her, and you, to that godforsaken place. She'd still have been with us if he hadn't. But never mind; there's nowt we can do about it now. What's he going to do with himself now that he's lost that Lund woman?' her grandfather asked and looked across at Amy.

'He doesn't know, I don't think.' Amy hung her head.

'Aye, well, I don't say this often, but he's not welcome in this house. After our day, this farm is left to you, Amy. He's not going to get his hands on this bit of gold.' George looked at Ivy and noticed her scowling. 'Aye, I know, Ivy. I'll shut up now, as it's a day to celebrate our Amy's return. Let's bow our heads and thank the Lord for what's on this table, and Amy's safe return to us.' George said grace, something Amy had not done since leaving the dale.

She looked at the ham sandwiches, cake and scones that her grandmother had made in her honour, and enjoyed every mouthful as she talked about her years away, and as Josh and her grandparents told her all the news of the dale. Her grandfather had said what he'd wanted to say, and now they could all enjoy one another's company without fear of offending.

The sun was setting by the time they had eaten their fill, and the table was cleared by Amy. Age was catching up with her grandmother, she noticed, as she washed the pots in the brown stone sink.

'Amy, I'm going to have to go home now. My father will want me back.' Josh put his arm around her waist as she dried her hands and turned to him. 'Come and walk out to the road with me,' he whispered, as he looked at the Oversbys, who were napping next to the open fire.

'Yes, I'll come and say goodnight to you.' Amy smiled and put her drying towel down. 'It's a lovely sunset. I missed these when I was in Liverpool. There were only back-to-backs as far as the eye could see.' She grabbed her shawl and smiled at her grandparents.

Josh looked at them both and smiled, too. 'They are content, now you are back home. They have worried about you since the moment you left – just like me,' he said softly and kissed Amy, thinking that both grandparents were asleep.

'Nobody needs to worry any more. I'm not going anywhere ever again, and this is my home now.' She ran her hand down Josh's shirt and looked into his eyes. 'You said a lot of things in your letters, Josh. Did you mean them?'

'I meant every word, especially the ones asking you to be my wife. We were meant for one another, and I don't want you to leave my side ever again.' Josh held her tightly and hugged Amy, then took her hand to lead her out of the farmhouse and walk along the pathway to the road.

There they stood in the sunset, looking across the dale, planning their future and dreaming their dreams, while unbeknownst to them, Ivy and George had heard every word said in the kitchen.

'Thank the Lord for that,' George muttered. 'She's travelled halfway around the world with that father of hers, but at last she's had the sense to know that her heart and soul will always be in this dale.'

'Aye, and she's got a good lad in Joshua Middleton. He's a canny farmer, and he'll be just right for taking over "Klondike" after our day.'

They both got up from their chairs, looked down the farm's path and watched the couple embracing in the dying sunset.

'By, that's a grand sight. We've got Amy back at last – though not for long, once there is a ring on her finger. But that's life, and she's chosen the right lad, unlike her mother, God rest her soul,' George said and looked at Ivy.

'If she is as happy as we've been, after thirty-seven years wed, I couldn't wish more for her. You are an old, soft lump, George Oversby, but I love you. And I wish you happiness, our darling Amy.' Ivy smiled and then gave a loving peck to George's cheek.

'Now don't be getting excited – we can't have that, at our age,' George sniggered. 'My old woman, you are a good 'un. As you say, let's hope they will be as happy and content as us two. If they are, we couldn't wish for more.'

Klondikers' supply list

While doing some research on the gold rush and the Klondike, I came across this list of supplies that anyone seeking their fortune in the Klondike had to have, before being allowed into the Yukon by the Canadian government. The list consisted of suggested equipment and supplies sufficient to support a prospector for one year, as generated by the Northern Pacific Railroad Company in 1897. The total weight was approximately one ton and the estimated cost amounted to $140.

It is quite a list – I wouldn't want to pay for it, or carry it on the journey out into the snowy wastes.

- 150 pounds of bacon
- 400 pounds of flour
- 25 pounds of rolled oats
- 125 pounds of beans
- 10 pounds of tea
- 10 pounds of coffee

- 25 pounds of sugar
- 25 pounds of dried potatoes
- 25 pounds of dried onions
- 15 pounds of salt
- 1 pound of pepper
- 75 pounds of dried fruit
- 8 pounds of baking powder
- 8 pounds of soda
- ½ pound of evaporated vinegar
- 12 ounces of compressed soup
- 1 can of mustard
- 1 tin of matches
- stove
- gold pan for each man
- buckets
- knife, fork, spoon, cup and plate
- frying pan
- coffee and teapot
- 2 picks, 1 shovel, whipsaw, pack strap, 2 axes
- 6 eight-inch files and two taper files
- draw-knife
- brace and bits
- jack plane and hammer
- 200 feet of rope
- 8 pounds of pitch
- 5 pounds of nails
- tent and canvas for wrapping
- 2 oil blankets
- 5 yards of mosquito netting
- 3 suits of underwear

- 1 heavy mackinaw coat
- 2 pairs of woollen trousers
- 1 rubber-lined coat
- 12 heavy woollen socks
- 6 heavy woollen mittens
- 2 heavy overshirts
- 2 pairs of rubber boots
- 2 pairs of shoes
- 4 pairs of blankets
- 4 towels
- 2 pairs of overalls
- 1 suit of oil clothing
- several changes of summer clothing
- a small assortment of medicines

The Liverpool Cowkeepers

Dalespeople from Yorkshire and Westmorland arrived in Liverpool as the city was expanding. They came from upland farming areas, where the land was scarce and families large. By 1881 there were around 470 cowkeepers in Liverpool, serving the city from their terraced farms. They were known as 'cowkeepers', not 'dairymen', because milk was sometimes brought from their families into the city by train, although in summer especially the milk was invariably sour and not fit for consumption. This milk was known as 'railway milk'. As the years went by, farmers from Cheshire, Lancashire, Shropshire and Wales arrived in the city, but not as many as those from the northern Dales, who tended to socialize in their own groups and have their own dialect.

Many milk houses sprang up on street corners, serving the public fresh milk each day. The cows never saw a proper blade of grass, being fed on hay, oilcake, brewers' grains, turnips and mangolds. It is known that one cowkeeper regularly grazed his animals on Everton football ground – those cows were the lucky ones. Cows were not bought at auction; instead, cattle dealers supplied the milk houses with their cows, or the family back in the Dales fulfilled their needs. Some milk houses also supplied butter, cheese, eggs and, on occasion, fresh baking.

The Great Liverpool Show was held for three days in December at the Old Haymarket. It was the highlight of the cowkeepers' year, and a winning cow was held in high esteem.

Most cowkeepers retired back to the Dales sometimes, leaving their family behind to carry on the business. Cowkeeping in the city was still being practised up to the 1940s, but the outbreak of the Second World War and the heavy bombing of Liverpool brought it to an end.

Glossary of cowkeeping terms

Boskin – stall where the cows were tethered

Fodder – dried food for the cattle, such as hay

Fothering – feeding the cattle with fodder

Shippon – barn where the cows were kept for milking

The Mistress of Windfell Manor

DIANE ALLEN

Charlotte Booth loves her father and the home they share, which is set high up in the limestone escarpments of Crummockdale. But when a new businessman in the form of Joseph Dawson enters their lives, both Charlotte and her father decide he's the man for her and, within six months, Charlotte marries the dashing mill owner from Accrington.

Then a young mill worker is found dead in the swollen River Ribble. With Joseph's business nearly bankrupt, it becomes apparent that all is not as it seems and Joseph is not the man he pretends to be. Heavily pregnant, penniless and heartbroken, Charlotte is forced to face the reality that life may never be the same again . . .

OUT NOW

The Windfell Family Secrets

DIANE ALLEN

Twenty-one years have passed since Charlotte Booth fought to keep her home at Windfell Manor, following her traumatic first marriage. Now, happily married to her childhood sweetheart, she seeks only the best for their children, Isabelle and Danny. But history has a habit of repeating itself when Danny's head is turned by a local girl of ill repute.

Meanwhile, the beautiful and secretive Isabelle shares all the undesirable traits of her biological father. And when she announces that she is to marry John Sidgwick, the owner of High Mill in Skipton, her mother quickly warns her against him. An ex-drinking mate of her late father who faces bankruptcy, Charlotte fears his interest in Isabelle is far from honourable. What she doesn't realize is how far he's willing to go to protect his future . . .

OUT NOW

Daughter of the Dales

DIANE ALLEN

The death of Charlotte Atkinson, the family matriarch, at Windfell Manor casts a long shadow over her husband Archie and their two children, Isabelle and Danny. With big shoes to fill, Isabelle takes over the running of Atkinson's department store but her pride – and heart – is tested when her husband James brings scandal upon the family and the Atkinsons' reputation.

Danny's wife Harriet is still struggling to deal with the deaths of their first two children – deaths she blames Isabelle for. But Danny himself is grappling with his own demons when a stranger brings to light a long-forgotten secret from his past.

Meanwhile, Danny and Harriet's daughter Rosie has fallen under the spell of a local stable boy, Ethan. But will he stand by her or will he cause her heartache? And can Isabelle restore the Atkinsons' reputation and her friendship with Harriet, to unite the family once more?

OUT NOW

The Miner's Wife

DIANE ALLEN

Nineteen-year-old Meg Oversby often dreams of a more exciting life than the dull existence she faces at her family's farm deep in the Yorkshire Dales. Growing up, she's always sensed her father's disappointment at not having a son to help with the farm work.

So when Meg dances all night at the local market hall with Sam Alderson, a lead miner from Swaledale, a new light enters her life. Sam and his brother Jack show Meg a side to life she didn't know existed. But when her parents find out, she's forbidden from ever seeing them again.

Although where there is love, there is often a way. When Meg's uncle offers her the chance to help run the small village shop, she leaps at the opportunity, seeing it as a way to escape the oppressive family farm and see more of her beloved Sam. But as love blossoms, a darker truth emerges and Meg realizes that Sam may not be the man she thought he was . . .

OUT NOW